UNCLEAN PAYBACK

JERRY HAYES

To Emily

CHAPTER 1

"**D**amn," John muttered. "Somebody left a pile of shit in the toilet." He thought: *Evidently, they wiped their sorry ass by the looks of all the toilet paper, and couldn't even flush it.* He cursed again. The stinking pile had been there since his crew left at 9:00 and it was almost 11:30 pm. The smell was intolerable. He pushed the flush handle and the dark, colored pile gurgled and began to rise. "Oh shit!"

John buried his nose in his elbow and ran to the storage room for the plunger.

Moments later he returned to the foul smelling job with a plunger, and a big yellow machine. The crap had spilled onto the floor, and was clogging the drain. He put on his mask and gloves to sweep up the pieces too big for the drain, and flushed it.

Next, the restroom needed more air than its ceiling vents could provide, so he wheeled his Kaivac machine to where it would hold the restroom door open. John unwound the hose and flicked the chemical injection switch, spraying everything with a powerful, concentrated disinfectant cleaner. The chemical was designed to destroy bacteria, clean, and leave the restroom with a fresh odor. He sprayed extra solution on the stinking toilet. Once the solution was sprayed on all the surfaces and the floor, John pulled the front end of the nozzle, turning the gun into a power-washer, blasting germs and bacteria off all the surfaces and onto the floor.

The machine was the best investment he ever made. It was called the Kaivac No Touch Cleaning System, involving a unique cleaning method that combines pressure washing, chemical injection and wet vacuuming in a single platform. Once he finished power-washing, he blew dry all the surfaces, eliminating the use of hand towels and rags. Everything that did not go down the drain he sucked up with the wet vacuum hose, leaving the restroom thoroughly cleaned, and odor-free, without having to scrub or touch any of the contaminated surfaces.

John Colby gave his work a nod of approval. He wondered: *Who the hell is so low to leave a stinking pile of shit in the toilet…no concern whatsoever for the next person. Pervert! Hope he catches crabs in his asshole and every time the bastard feels the urge to crap, his ass'll start itching and taking a crap will become a most agonizing event.*

He laughed at the image, then thought about the weird things people do in public restrooms. Today it was crap left in the toilet. The next time it could be dried blood stains down the underside of a commode in the ladies' restroom or a bloody sanitary napkin left on the floor, even worse, thrown in the toilet with the rest of the waste. After twenty years in the janitorial industry, he had seen it all.

A few months back, the state of North Carolina paid Roto-Rooter thousands of dollars to use their camera system to find out why the commodes were overflowing and running out into the hallways. The camera located the culprit in the pipes beneath the concrete hallway.

Someone had flushed a bunch of sanitary napkins. The State spent thousands more dollars tearing up the floor to get at the stopped-up pipes.

Sinks get their share of abuse too. Besides washing hands and brushing teeth, people wash their dishes, pots and pans in sinks. They soak their dying plants in the sink, and pour their coffee grounds in sinks. Once John saw a maintenance man cleaning his paint brushes and other tools in the sink. Nobody cares what happens in restrooms until it's their time to use it to transfer bodily waste.

Restrooms and floors were how John Colby built his janitorial business. Raised in a Christian home in Goldsboro, North Carolina, he borrowed from the Bible verse: *Love covers a multitude of sins*, and made it the slogan he cleaned by: A clean restroom covers a multitude of other cleaning faults. People would put up with an un-vacuumed floor or dusty partition, but not a dirty restroom. He would love to have his buildings spotless, but in a market where low-bid rules and good help is hard to find, he decided early in his career to invest in the best equipment and keep his restrooms and floors looking good.

John Colby was six feet tall and weighed 200 pounds. His wrinkle-free, dark brown skin and bald head made him look as though he wasn't a day over forty. He was fifty-five years old and had large gazing eyes that unnerved some people. He had a habit of looking too intently at someone when having a conversation, when in fact his mind would be on other things. Only his girlfriend knew of his attention deficit disorder.

John Colby despised America. He was born American and served in the Vietnam War. He was discharged with honors. And in spite of the odds against him, he started a business that contributed thousands of dollars to the economy every year. For fifteen years he averaged a half-million dollars a year and not once would a bank loan him the money he needed to pay down his debt and expand.

He was angry and seethed inside. He constantly faced racism in the world of small business and deemed it to be the sole reason he was deep in debt and why the Internal Revenue Service was breathing down his neck. Each time he applied for a loan, the bank would reject it, citing his company's high level of debt as the reason. And each time John would plead with the bank to look at the good income he was making. He tried to convince them to see that all he needed was a sizable loan to pay off the IRS, pay down his other debt and expand. Every time the bank would agree he was making good money, but would tell him to pay down some of the debt and come back.

Meanwhile, his outstanding work got him more business. There were times he refused work because he did not have the cash flow needed to service the account.

The money was not there to grow his company properly, and so his debt and IRS liability kept rising. What made him so mad was that he knew a white man with the same business and level of income would have had no problem getting a loan regardless of his debt.

John Colby believed the racism and discrimination leveled at him also played out in national politics. He thought the constipated-looking senator from Kentucky should be horse-whipped by the taxpayers and run out of town. This elected official believed it was his duty to do everything in his power to make sure President Obama failed. John figured that meant even if Obama came up with a great idea or law that would benefit the American citizen, this bigot would still vote against it. The sad thing was that John knew hundreds of the senator's peers were just like him.

Filled with disdain, he thought: *And those damn banks, the same bastards who are always telling me no, got so fucking greedy they took the country to the brink of a Depression in the housing scandal. And who bails 'em out? The American taxpayer and guys like me. Who's going to bail me out?*

He held his government in great contempt for preaching democracy at home and abroad. In a democracy the common people are considered the primary source of political power. Nothing could be further from the truth in America. It was not true when the Constitution was written, and it was not true today.

Everybody knows it's the rich and powerful corporations and bankers who control the country. He grunted to himself...*Too big to fail, too small to survive.*

John often worked in his buildings after everyone had left; there were hardly any interruptions, except for the few people who had no life. His two major contracts, the New Education Building and the Dobbs Building, were located in downtown Raleigh, the capital city.

Tonight he worked the Dobbs Building, a six-floor, long rectangular building, with two restrooms at both ends. The specifications listed the square footage at 180,000 square feet. The North Carolina Insurance Commission occupied most of the building, and they fell in love with John because of his excellent cleaning, and the fact that whenever there was a problem, John could be found and would solve the issue right away.

He finished his last restroom on the north end of the building on the sixth floor. At both ends of the building there was a door that led to an open area where people use to smoke, before smoking was banned in all state buildings. There was another door that led to the stairway.

Before putting his equipment away, John opened the door and paused, looking across Salisbury Street to the state parking deck. His mind turned to his girlfriend and the ounce of weed under his truck seat, causing a horny thrill to surge through his body.

He turned to leave but thought he saw someone. *Looks like Sam Boswell, what the hell is he doing out this late, and coming out of my building?*

Sam Boswell was a state building inspector whose job was to check contractors' buildings to insure they were cleaning to certain specifications.

John yelled, hoping to scare the go-fer acting inspector. "Yo, Sam Boswell, what you doing out this late?"

It worked. Sam jumped and stuttered, "Joh… John, that you? Just closing a few loose ends. I see you working late yourself."

"Yeah Sam, doing the same, closing a few loose ends. *I'd like to close your dumb ass in the dumpster along with the rest of the trash.*

He did not reply to Sam's wish of a good night, and wondered what he was up to, making a mental note to talk to his night supervisor.

John Colby lived on two acres of land in Wendell, a quiet farming town fifteen miles east of Raleigh. Named after Oliver Wendell Holmes, the city recently began advertising its charm in the media with one minute sound bites to attract some of the thousands of people moving into the Raleigh area. He found out on Google that Oliver Wendell Holmes had little to do with the beginning of the town. A few guys needed a name for the little town they were starting and one of them suggested they name the town after his favorite poet's middle name.

John packed his pipe with the strong smelling weed he'd bought from Big Ed. He took in a long pull from the pipe and felt guilty. He could lose all his government accounts if he were caught. He promised himself he would stop. Each time he bought a bag would be the last time; until his pipe was empty.

He took another pull off the pipe and coughed hard; tears filled his eyes and rolled down his face. *Shit Big Ed right, this some sho' nuff choker!* The little demon in his head laughed again, repeating the same words John had heard a hundred times. John answered, *I'm not hooked.* He promised this would be the last time.

He put his pipe in the ashtray to pay attention to the road. After you cross Raleigh Boulevard on Poole Road, the population is low-income, heavily black and Hispanic. Residents who lived in this part of town didn't care about life; they would cross the street when you were close enough to run them down. Most of them did not have valid licenses but drove recklessly. It was past midnight and the last thing John needed was an accident.

⋏

John Colby was born and raised in Goldsboro, a small town fifty miles east of Raleigh. Goldsboro would be another nameless town on a map, were it not for Seymour Johnson Air Force Base, home of the 4th Fighter Wing. With the assignment of the 337th "Falcons" in 1982, it became one of the Air Force's largest operational tactical fighter units.

There were not enough prostitutes or girls in Goldsboro for the airmen and the local guys, and what John remembered most about the base were the fights they had with the airmen over girls.

His parents raised their five boys and two girls in the fear and admonition of the Lord. Their favorite Bible verse must have been: *Train up a child in the way he should go and when he is old he will not depart.* For the Colby family that meant church every Sunday, at Pentecostal Holy Church, and attending some of the revival meetings when they were held. His mother also made sure the family gathered in the living room to pray once a week.

John never lost his faith in God, he just lost all the desire to be involved in church activities. By the time he graduated high school, he was weary of the hollering ministers who were more into money, and removing the drawers of the shouting sisters, than into the gospel message.

All the black kids during the '50s and '60s went to black-only schools. Everything was segregated. Even department stores, like Woolworth on Center Street, were racist, defined by separate drinking fountains. The only reason white-owned businesses let blacks in the door was to get their money, the only thing not segregated.

John's mother worked as a housekeeper for a rich family who lived in the whites-only neighborhood. After school he watched the pretty Buick pull up in front of his house. His mother would be in the back seat; she wasn't good enough to sit up front. "Yes ma'am, I'll see you tomorrow," he'd hear his mother say. The strained look on his mother's face told him she hated her second-class status.

When she saw John looking, the stress would leave and she would be happy to be home. He despised the smiling white lady who made his mother sit in the back seat.

One day when the white mailman delivered the mail, John was in the yard with the family's dog. When he was leaving John said to the mixed German Shepherd, *Sic him, Bucky.* The dog growled but did not attack.

The next day his mother beat him until her arms became too tired to continue. She screamed at him, "Do you know what kind of trouble you could have got us in. You lucky I'm beating you and not your father!" After that, he hated the old wrinkled mailman even more.

Every child in the Colby family had specific chores. His two sisters kept the house clean; his two brothers did things like cutting the grass and chopping wood, but it was John who cleaned the bathroom. When he finished, the sink, commode and bath tub would be sparkling. Even the cheap linoleum on the floor would be shining. He would pour a little pine oil in the toilet and open the small bathroom window to let the breeze blow the smell throughout the house. His parents and siblings marveled at his work. His profession started at an early age.

⅄

He pulled onto his concrete driveway. The moon played peek-a-boo in the clouded sky. June was drawing to a close and the weather was hot and dry. John hoped it would rain, to restore his thirsty garden. He left the weed under the truck seat so his girlfriend Ashley would not know. Grinning, he thought, *she probably already knows, but has given up fussing with me.*

⅄

The note on the kitchen table read: *I've been horny all day, hurry to bed.* He peeped in on Sonja, Ashley's eleven-year-old daughter who was fast asleep.

White women were not on John's list of women to fall in love with. He saw himself with an Afro-American, Spanish or Asian woman; someone of color. He cringed at the thought of growing old with a white woman who would wrinkle up, get pale and look like a ghost, especially at night, or early in the morning with no makeup on. The face of the wrinkled old white mailman still haunted him.

All that changed when he saw Ashley Whitfield. She was a few inches shorter than John's six feet. She had shoulder length blond hair and wore it in different styles. One day she might have a braided up-do, or loose pony tail; the next time she might have it in a classic bun or French twist. Her eyes were a mesmerizing green and when she smiled her deep dimples on each cheek made you wonder how someone could be so beautiful.

She was a massage therapist and John had gone to her for a two-hour session. He fell in love with her before ever going on a date. If she was not married he had to have her. She was divorced and had custody of her daughter Sonja who was seven years old at the time they met. That was four years ago.

Ashley worked on him once a month and he begged her for a date each time, and each time she told him it was against her policy to date clients. After seven sessions he asked her if he were not a client, would she go out with him. She said she might.

So John stopped going. Two months went by. Ashley called him. "Mr. Colby, I have not seen you, are you all right?"

John heard the smile in her voice. "Where would you like to go on our first date?" Once they had fallen in love she admitted that each time he asked for a date, she wanted to say yes, but was playing hard to get. Nevertheless, John did get her, and now every inch of her beautiful body belonged to him.

He entered the bedroom and Ashley turned and sat up, letting the sheet fall from her naked breasts. Like Pavlov's dog, John salivated.

"What took you so long, lover boy? I've been thinking about that big thang inside of me all day."

Pavlov's dog dribbled, never removing his socks, falling into Ashley's outstretched arms. They kissed over and over, touching, caressing and squeezing each other. She moaned upon his entrance and wrapped herself around him.

For almost an hour they passionately loved on one another, changing positions twice. As la-la land approached, they cried out, gripping each other with all their might.

Slowly returning to normal, their bodies tingled and twitched in spasmodic delight. John was spent. Ashley rolled on top of him.

"Did you eat dinner?"

John thought, and Ashley said, "Never mind, that means no. Take a shower; I'll make you a sandwich and soup."

Since Ashley saw her clients in Cameron Village, where John's post office box was, she often picked his mail up and brought it home. On his way to the shower he saw the certified envelope from the Internal Revenue Service. The red, capital letters stated the same words he had seen before: Notice of Intent to Levy.

Bastards! Shit! Not again! Hell, I'll never get out of debt.

CHAPTER 2

John rummaged through his file cabinet in the computer room looking for his last mail from the IRS. He had tossed and turned all night, sleeping no more than two hours. Ashley was still calling *zzz's* from Georgia, or somewhere. She was out. On Tuesdays she didn't see clients until 1:00 pm, and worked until 7:00. John did very little on Tuesday. His main thing was to look after Sonja, which he loved. He took her to school, picked her up, and they did a lot of things in between, like going to eat, or out to Pullen Park. On Tuesdays and some Fridays Sonja spent the night with her father. John chuckled, *Won't be long fo' she be poking out those pretty lips with Oh Mom, do I have to go?*

John came across an old newspaper and smirked at the headlines: *Obama Proposes Expansion of Small Business Loans.* The $36 billion was to come from some of the big banks who had paid back their TARP (toxic asset relief program) funds. He smirked, *More bullshit from Washington. You assholes want to help small business folks; stop giving the funds to banks that will use the money for what they want to. They always say there were no qualified borrowers, and then pay themselves big bonuses.*

That is what ticked John off, and was the real reason he could never get from under the thumb of the IRS. And it was probably the reason so many new businesses failed within the first five years. Most businesses that cannot get adequate financing for payroll, equipment, and new contracts, and they use the quarterly taxes they should be depositing with the bank. Once you get behind good old Uncle Sam becomes the Mafia, charging not only high interest, but tacking on penalties and other fees. John thought about how hard it was to match an employee's social security deductions, stay current in federal and state taxes, pay for business insurance policies, and vehicle insurance. *At the end of the day is this shit worth it? Seems like I'm just bank-rolling a doomed economy. Guess that's why so many businesses fail; it ain't worth it.*

His mind would not focus on the disinteresting article; he had to pay the suckers. He remembered the first time his bank account was levied. The year was 1995; he had pulled into the drive through window at his bank to get $200. The teller said: "I'm sorry Mr. Colby, a lien has been put on this account."

"A what?" John remembered replying. The teller had seen John's bewilderment, and asked him to come inside.

The IRS had sent threatening letters before, but John never thought they would really shut him down over a few thousand dollars. He was wrong. Unless he paid the $2,000 in back taxes, Colby Cleaning Service would no longer exist.

There was no one he could turn to. He had maxed all his credit cards and could no longer borrow from high-interest finance companies. Yet as fate would have it, he and the previous contract administrator had become good friends and he was meeting her for lunch. He had meant to call and cancel their date; the last thing he wanted was food. The call was never made.

⋏

Sarah Jenkins ate her soup. She had short black hair that was beginning to grey, and warm sky-blue eyes. Ever since her husband died ten years ago, she stayed in shape working out at the gym.

She watched John play with his shrimp. "What is wrong with you, John Colby? It's been five minutes since the waitress left, by now you should have put away three shrimp."

He mustered a smile and wondered if he should tell the contract administrator he may soon be out of business. What would the talk be like at Facility Management, and bid proposal meetings? He would be shamed, ridiculed, and have to file for bankruptcy. He struggled to say something but put a shrimp in his mouth.

Sarah smiled, "Do you need money?"

John almost choked on the shrimp, his eyes wide in disbelief. "How did you know?"

"You remind me so much of Oliver. When he was worried about a money problem, he would pick at his food and look all sad."

⨀

During their many talks, Sarah often mentioned Oliver Jenkins, the only man she ever loved. They were both teachers, but Oliver became bored with high school, and started a restaurant and catering service. At times, Sarah's eyes would water recalling the good times she had with OJ, as she affectionately called him.

Business was good and after five years Sarah retired from teaching to join her husband. Then tragic news that Oliver had prostate cancer halted everything. When it took his life she sold the business and took the job as contract administrator with the State of North Carolina. She was getting close to retiring and had never told John the things she imagined him doing to her in bed. She had thought: *After I retire, there will be no conflict of interest if John brings a few of those payments to my place.* She wrote him a check for $3,000.

John almost cried, "Sarah, I don't know what to say, you know I'll pay you back."

Sarah giggled at her nasty thoughts and told John to eat his food and stop worrying.

⨀

"Whatcha thinking 'bout Colby?"

John grinned, as Sonja jumped in his outstretched hands. "Hey baby girl, want some cereal? Ashley bought bananas."

He carried her into the kitchen and started fixing the cereal. Sonja was eleven years old and did not like cereals much until John came into their lives and would eat cereals with bananas, strawberries or canned peaches.

"Your father is coming to pick you up today, right?"

The force of air from Sonja's curled bottom lip made the top of her blonde hair fly back. She resembled her mother so much, John often called her little Ashley.

He laughed and shook his head. No one could sigh better than Sonja.

"He said he would be here after lunch; do I have to go, Colby? It's always boring on Tuesdays. We just sit around and watch movies."

"Stop complaining, young lady," Ashley interrupted.

John was sitting at the table when Ashley came up behind him and bit him on the ear. "Your father is paying good support for you and has a right to see you. Keep him happy."

Sonja sighed deeper than before, blowing out more hot air.

John laughed and changed the subject. "What are you doing up, thought you were going in late."

"I was, but a first-time client called and begged if I could see him at eleven."

Ashley poured her coffee, and became serious. "It looks like I may need to work harder if we are about to have one of those IRS fiascos you told me about. Sarah Jenkins is not around now. Is this notice bad news, honey?"

His thoughts returned to his friend Sarah who was living in Boone, a mountain city in western North Carolina. After she retired, she stayed in Raleigh for a few years, and John would take payments on the loan to her apartment. He remembered her words: *John that day I loaned you the money I wanted you. I wanted you for raw sex; I had not been with a man in years.*

All of John's blood had rushed to one area. Their raw sex was wild and passionate. Standing out in John's mind was how loud Sarah screamed, and how tight she held him upon climax. The relationship changed somewhat after that. Their friendship grew stronger. When Sarah retired, John was not seeing anyone, so once a week they would get together.

The two of them talked infrequently now, but when they did it was laughter and a few moans about the good old days. What they had had was good for that time, and both cherished it.

John frowned his answer to Ashley's question: "Anything is bad from those…."

"Don't say it, Colby," Sonja chewed through the last mouthful of her cereal.

John and Ashley chuckled. He said: "It's not too bad if you can loan me fifteen hundred." He averted her eyes, looking into his empty coffee cup.

"What am I going to do with you, John Colby? She looked towards his averted eyes and thought of how much she loved him. *If you only knew. I've already given you myself, so you can have anything I have.*

"Colby, Colby, Colby," Sonja grinned, waging her finger back and forth in a *no, no* sign.

When Ashley told Sonja they were going to live with John, Sonja asked what she should call John and Ashley said to ask him. John said it didn't matter, so Sonja chose Colby. When asked why, she said there were too many Johns.

Ashley didn't let up. "Why don't you sell me your business and you work for me?" She stood up as one does when a light goes off in the brain. "We'll name it A & S Janitorial Company, for Ashley and Sonja. Or, honey, listen to this. I'll just pay the entire tax bill and take ownership of the business. John…"

John laughed. "Naw, now, that ain't fair, I have equipment costs more than the tax bill." He knew Ashley was making fun of him, but did not care. She was the most beautiful person on earth. Her breasts were round, full, and set high on her chest. She could hardly wear any top without showing some cleavage. John looked at her behind and thought of how soft and good it felt last night. He said to himself, *Sisters y'all known for your prowess in the ass department, but Ashley be right in da wit y'all. I waited long enough, I'm proposing.*

Ashley realized John was lusting on her. "John…."

The phone rang. Ashley walked to pick it up, shaking her head at him. "Hello…hey Frederick." She listened for a minute, and then said, "Hold on."

"Honey, can you keep Sonja with you all day and drop her off at Fred's house this evening about seven?"

Frederick Parsons hated to hear his former wife call a black man *honey.* His teeth clenched so hard the muscle on his jaw rolled back and forth. *Why did she have to move in with a nigger?* What angered him even more was that his daughter spent more time with Ashley's black lover than with him. That was going to change. He was going to file for sole custody. Sonja would be upset and lonely for her Mom in the beginning, but she would get over it. He would convince the court that he could provide a better life for Sonja, and that the present environment in which she was being raised was not wholesome.

Ashley smiled at Sonja who was pouting. The child's father might not be as exciting as John to be around, but she knew Sonja loved him. He gave her anything she wanted.

"He'll have her there, Fred. Okay, bye." Ashley hung up and when she turned her silky robe fell open revealing a velvety lush thigh.

John stared and kept on staring until Sonja started giggling.

Ashley blushed, "What are you staring so hard at, John Colby?"

He looked as awestruck as he could. "How could a man let the most beautiful woman on earth get away from him?" He got up and held out his arms to Ashley.

Sonja said, "Hey what about me?"

They both held out their arms for Sonja and all squeezed each other with love in one of those cherished moments. John decided that after he dropped Sonja to her father, he would look for the right moment to ask Ashley to marry him. If he waited until the Internal Revenue was paid along with the rest of his bills, it might be three years down the road. He did not want to wait that long.

⚔

Otis Wooten was half drunk. During a bitter argument and fight with his wife Greta, he discovered that she had an affair and that Pauline was not his real daughter. After the fight he left and had not been back in a month. He thought she would have changed the locks and so was surprised an old basement key still worked. He made his way upstairs. The house was quiet; he would take a shower, grab his belongings and never come back. When he reached the top of the stairs, Pauline's door was ajar, and he peeped in.

Pauline thought she heard something, but turned over and went back to sleep. She was half naked. The thin, white blouse she had on was too small and revealed most of her full, young breasts. Otis was not too drunk to see that the small panties she wore had become a thong.

The half-naked young flesh of his thirteen-year-old stepdaughter aroused him in a way he had not felt in years. He moved towards the bed and lowered his frame. When he stroked her soft brown thigh, he grew harder. *Damn, I thought I was impotent.*

Pauline moaned and suddenly turned, pulling down her blouse. She screamed. "Daddy, oh, you're not my daddy! What are you doing? You're drunk, get out of here!"

The booze, hatred and lust overwhelmed Otis and he heard nothing except the command of his raging flesh. *That bitch used me all these years. She ain't your daughter, serve 'em right, sorry as niggas, take her, man, fuck her.* He heard himself say, "Don't be so mean, girl. I was just admiring how much you look like your mother and nothing like your dear ol' dad. Umm, you do kinda favor a nigga I know name James Winton." His fingers dug harder into her soft meat. "Now is that so bad, sweetie?"

The ugly scowl on her stepfather's face was terrifying, his breath reeked of liquor and unwashed teeth. Pauline screamed as loud as she could. She hoped their nosy neighbor was nearby.

Otis slapped her and ripped off her flimsy blouse. Pauline's young breasts swayed and jiggled from the rough treatment. She was about to scream again but he covered her mouth. His wide receiver hands were so big, his fingers stretched from the top of her nose to the bottom of her chin.

Pauline could not breathe; she swallowed a thought. *This sorry ass man tried to choke my mama to death, now he's going to smother me to death and rape me.* She bit so hard into one of his fingers that blood spurted out.

"Ahaaha, shit!" Otis howled in pain.

Pauline felt his grip loosen, and tried to spring free. He came across her face with a vicious back-hand to the jaw and she blacked out.

Even in his drunken state Otis knew that what he was about to do was not right, but he had no control. *Git even man, poke her; it'll serve her two-timing mother right, especially if you plant a baby there. Damn, s'pose Greta walk her sorry ass in that door...hell knock her out and fuck her too! They been playing me for a fool.*

He trembled with excitement and removed his stinking clothes. After spreading her legs open he reached for his stiff membrane, only to have vast amounts of semen squirt into the air. "Oh shit, naw!" He pumped the rest of his old sperm onto Pauline's thigh and the sheets.

Otis sobered up quickly. The same problem still existed. When he tried to have sex with Greta, they would both be horny as hell; but as soon as he inserted himself he would ejaculate, driving Greta insane.

The room began to spin and Otis forgot why he came home. He hurriedly put on his clothes and ran out the same way he came in; through the basement door. He almost knocked over Mrs. Williams, who was out walking her dog.

Damn, of all the people I got to run into, the nosiest person in the neighborhood. Otis begged Mrs. Williams' pardon and kept going.

Mrs. Williams knew some of her neighbor's problem and wondered where he was going in such a hurry. She had not seen him for a while and smelled alcohol. Greta's car was not in the driveway, and school was out for the summer, so she knew Pauline was at home. She went home and called the police.

Pauline suffered a fractured jaw and would be okay. The doctor determined Otis had a premature ejaculation, but there was no entry.

An all points bulletin was put out for Otis. His family did not know where he was and pleaded with him on local news shows to turn himself in. A year passed, then two. Otis was never seen again…except by one person.

⋏

Twenty years later the memory of her drunken stepfather crawling over her gave Pauline Wooten a dull headache.

She was endowed with an hourglass figure, had black skin and an attractive face. At age thirty-three her biological clock was ticking. She told her mother that if she had not found Mr. Right by age thirty-five, she would go to a clinic and use a sperm donor. They both laughed when her mom asked what if she got the sperm of a sorry ass rascal like Otis Wooten?

Pauline Wooten had no time for a sorry man, especially a sorry black man, and made sure she would never have to depend on anyone but herself.

She graduated among the top classmates at North Carolina Central University in Durham, North Carolina. She majored in business with an emphasis on administration.

After college she worked a few years for a local bank but decided that promotion was too slow. When she searched the employment section of the North Carolina website, she saw the position for Contract Administrator. The payment package with benefits started at $40,000.

Her mother's law firm, the bank, and the university gave her outstanding references and she got the job after two interviews.

Her cell phone rang. "Hello."

"Hey boss, where you at? Got somn' for you on Colby Cleaning Service."

It was one o'clock and her inspector Sam Boswell was checking in. He worked for the state twelve years in housekeeping and became supervisor of a work crew. When the state of North Carolina began cleaning their properties with private janitorial contractors, they needed some watch dogs, so Sam applied for the inspector position.

"Good, Sam, I just finished lunch, wait for me there."

Facility Management was a five minute walk from the Administration Building. The weather was hot, the air muggy. Pauline had on tight brown pants and a beige, short sleeved blouse that hugged her body in the right places. She took the cross walk at Lane Street behind the Albemarle Building.

Landscapers worked nearby and peeped over their dark shades while smiling dirty thoughts at Pauline. She smiled and waved at their supervisor. *Lust all you want low-lifers, you'll never get in these drawers.* She liked men lusting for her. It was the only thrill she was getting lately. Her last attempt at love, like all the rest, was a disaster. Her mother told her it was because the black men she dated were intimidated by her success, and that she should try dating white men, or Asians. A lot of black men, her mother said, could not deal with a successful black woman.

Pauline walked into the side door of Facility Management from the parking lot. She went to Sam's cubicle and nodded for him to follow her.

Her office was simple, adorned with cheap furniture consisting of desk, old sofa and two chairs. She had gotten a raise recently, and after ten years on the job, she could not wait for the new red oak furniture to be delivered that signified the importance she was worthy of.

"What you got on that bastard, Sam?"

Sam Boswell followed her to her office. He could not believe how fine his boss was and that she was not dating anybody. He flipped through his notepad. "Your boy ain't stripped the 6th floor yet. A couple of people on the 4th floor complained that candies and food items were missing. And last night, can you believe this; I saw a propane tank in the storage room near the loading dock."

Pauline looked pleased. "What about the blinds? Have they been dusted or washed? He was written up for those two months ago."

"Well, ah boss, nobody is doing anything on the blinds. If we go after him on blinds, we got to go after every…"

"Sam, the question was has he done anything on the blinds," Pauline said, frowning.

Damn, wonder why she hates Colby Cleaning Service so bad? "Okay, no, nothing's been done on the blinds."

Sam's boss thought for a moment, turned to her computer and punched a few keys, waited, then smiled. She hit more keys and waited. Ever since the last contractor's meeting she had been steaming. John Colby more than once made reference to how the contracts were administered under Sarah Jenkins. The woman had been retired almost a decade and he still kept mentioning her as if things were better then. She was tired of that shit. If she canceled one of his big contracts, maybe he would learn to keep his big mouth shut, and start calling her Miss Wooten like everybody else. She looked at the screen one last time, and then turned to Sam, who had been watching her in silence.

"I'm going to cancel the Dobbs contract." The words sounded good to her. She looked at Sam, whose only response was a look of shock. "You heard me right. All I need for you to do is keep watching him while I put this together."

Sam looked at his notes and flipped a few more pages. "Pauline, I hate to say it, but except for those few things, the overall appearance of the building is good. In fact Colby's buildings look a lot better than the other contractors'."

Pauline looked at Sam with fire in her sharp brown eyes. "How can you say that? This man is not only ignoring our request, he is endangering the lives of state workers after being warned about storing propane tanks in these buildings; and can you believe it, he has been canceled for the same thing before."

Sam decided that it was time to get his ass out of there. He no longer cared what she did. All he wanted was her furniture to be delivered. That would be the time he moved into her office and she would get the bigger, re-carpeted office down the hallway. "Okay boss, I can see you know something I don't." He got up to leave.

"I do, Sam." She winked and turned back to her computer. "Oh yeah, don't forget you are taking the contractors on that bid tour at three o'clock."

Sam nodded and was gone. The Albemarle Building was up for bid and the housekeeping inspectors were responsible for taking the contractors on a tour to familiarize them with the property. He was happy to do the tour; it would keep him busy until Pauline left for the day at five. Then he and the rest of the inspectors would sit around, shoot the bull, take an hour lunch, and just before going home at ten o'clock, fill out inspection sheets for buildings they never inspected.

⅄

The talk around the room-length conference table was the same: *Who got the Archdale building; they bid what? They bid two grand lower than the previous contract just to get in; the State ain't shit.* Shop talk, who got what and for how much. Janitorial contractors had gathered for the proposal conference for the Albemarle Building, one of the state's largest buildings.

In order to bid, attendance at the conference was mandatory and all the familiar faces were there. John noticed there were more Chinese and Korean companies attending the conferences. Some local contractors felt threatened, but John was not worried. He loved what he did and was good at it. He loved competition and had been toying with a new way to bid contracts. If it worked, the Albemarle would be his for eleven grand a month.

Shop talk may have abounded, but it was the pretty little white girl sitting beside John that drew all the attention. Everyone could feel the love the odd pair had for each other. John was embarrassed to have Sonja with him at such an important contract meeting, but forgot about the meeting when Ashley asked him if he could keep Sonja. It seemed John's memory was getting worse and he wondered if it was because of long term marijuana use. He thought, *I desperately need this account and here I am about to forget it.* He made a mental note, and wrote on his notepad not to forget his appointment with the loan officer at his bank in the morning.

Max Cleland was the only one at the meeting who had a sour face, and he looked resentful. He hated Colby Cleaning Service ever since John outbid him on a big contract by $1,000, nailing down a three-year contract for $9,000 a month.

They gave each other the *I don't care for your ass* nod. John laughed inside: *Cracker ain't gon' never get over losing to a black man.*

Pauline Wooten entered and everyone became quiet. She greeted a few contractors and nodded to John. "Is that your daughter, Mr. Colby?"

John laughed, "Yes, this is my darling Sonja."

Sonja giggled.

Pauline became serious. It was exactly 3:00 pm and Sam Boswell closed the door; late arrivals could not bid.

"This is the proposal conference for the Albemarle Building. My name is Pauline Wooten. I'm the contract administrator. Mr. Washington from the purchasing office could not be here." She nodded to Sam. "This is Samuel Boswell; he'll be taking you on a tour of the building. You've had a chance to look over the contract, are there any questions?"

A contractor John had never seen asked: "Are there day people required in this contract?"

Everyone, especially Pauline frowned and gave him the dummy look. Daytime housekeepers, usually one male and one female, were always required in buildings over 100,000 square feet, to service restrooms, and do other daytime cleaning duties.

"It is clearly stated in the contract, page seven, that two day people are required, one female, one male. Please read the contract." She rolled her eyes away from him. "Next question."

"Are we responsible for cleaning the area around the underground parking lot where the elevators run?"

Be patient, Pauline told herself. "Yes, on page eighteen of the contract there is a clause that clearly describes what is to be done in this area." It was frustrating; she had to say it at every meeting. "People, people, these proposal conferences are not to answer questions clearly stated in the contract. Read your contracts."

Everyone wanted to know the answer to the next question: the price of the contract. John and his buddy Earl Horn started about the same time in state government. Earl named his business: Horn Janitorial Service, and had a big horn under his name on the truck that read: *We Blow the Competition Away.* He asked, "What is the price of the current contract?"

Pauline looked down at some papers. "One hundred and forty thousand dollars a year. Let me warn you, do not bid low just to get this contract." She cut a hard look at Earl who had bid so low on a previous contract that Facility Management requested a work plan to see how he would clean the building at such a low price.

There were a few more questions; then Pauline said, "After the tour, you will return here for final questions and answers. Anyone who does not sign in and out on the sheet that Mr. Boswell has will not be allowed to bid."

Everyone filed out of the room. There were ten companies present. It would have been more if the contract were smaller. Large buildings required more equipment and insurance than many smaller companies could afford.

The Albemarle Building was eleven stories tall, and rose above many of the other government buildings in the area. The floors were small and one person working four hours a night could clean two floors on the evening shift. Despite his problems with the IRS, John needed another account to pay down some debt. If his new formula worked the Albemarle would be his. It would complete his triangle of three of the largest state properties within five minutes' walking distance of each other.

When they reached the sixth floor during the tour Max Cleland came up behind John and began the inquiry John expected. "Hey John, what you doing with this pretty little lady?" He reached down and patted Sonja's head.

John laughed inside; Max Cleland was only being nosy. "This is Sonja Whitfield, my girlfriend's daughter."

"Hmm, I see. I been watching how close she is to you; do we hear wedding bells in the distance?"

John laughed out loud this time. "Yeah Max, those bells are ringing mighty loud these days." He thought of his proposal to Ashley and forgot about Max.

Max Cleland acted as if he was happy for John and suddenly drifted to another part of the crowd walking the tour. Max thought, *Nigger loves white women, why can't they be happy with their own kind?* He spotted Earl, John's talkative buddy. "Hey Earl, your boy said he was getting married soon. Must have a pretty gal judging by that cute little girl."

Earl Horn and John periodically treated one another for lunch to shoot the bull. They had talked about Max many times and knew he cared nothing for blacks and other minorities. "Well, you heard something I ain't. Tell you what though Max, if he let that fine honey get away from him, he's crazy as hell. Have you seen her?"

Max shook his head. "No, don't believe I've had the pleasure."

"Well it'll definitely be a pleasure when you lay your eyes on her. Don't mean any harm Max, but for a white woman, she's fine from head to toe, all in the right places." Earl wanted Max to feel even more resentful.

Max decided he wanted to meet her. "Is that why John is hiding her; scared somebody might steal her away?"

"He ain't hiding her," Earl said, "She's a massage therapist. Got her own business in Cameron Village."

"Oh, I guess that's a good reason, she stays busy too." Max changed the subject to contracts and the weather. He had what he wanted from Earl. He could not think of a better way to meet John's girlfriend, than lying naked on a table for her to rub him down. He would Google massage in Cameron Village to locate her.

The contractors gathered back at Facility Management for final questions and sign out. The only interesting question came from a new Chinese company. He wanted to know why the building was so dirty.

Pauline Wooten gave a lame response that put the blame at the foot of an inspector who got too cozy with the cleaning company in the last year of the contract; something she would never allow again. In reality, it was her fault.

The present company in the building was Danita Jones Janitorial Service, owned by a black woman. Pauline wanted to see her make it in state business, but she was constantly getting bad inspection reports and people in the building were always calling Work Control with complaints. Pauline was relieved the contract would soon be over.

⚓

It was almost four o'clock. Ashley Whitfield sipped her herb tea. The day was going well. She had already made $480. By the day's end at seven o'clock she would make $700; not bad for a college drop-out. Taking the massage training course five years ago was the best thing she had ever done. She was averaging $500 a day, $10,000 a month. With that kind of money she leased an attractive office in busy Cameron Village. Her clientele was increasing and she began thinking about hiring a part-time therapist.

And to think, her arrogant, two-timing husband Frederick Parsons said she would fall on her face without him and come running back when reality set in. Well, she shut his mouth. And unlike Fred, who got his wealth and success passed to him when his father died and left a string of profitable retail furniture stores, Ashley started with nothing, tested the waters to see what she liked, and decided to become a massage therapist. She liked that the education and training was relatively short with the potential for big income if she was good at it. She was good, and clients constantly brought her new business. When she divorced Fred, she dropped his name. Ashley Parsons just didn't sound right and the name had too many bad memories.

She was the daughter of military parents. Her father retired as a First Sergeant Major in the Army. Her mother was a nurse and usually found work where ever the Army sent them. Even when they were in foreign countries like Germany or Japan she easily found work at an Army hospital. But her mother grew weary of all the moving, uprooting, and the goodbyes to friends, and begged her husband to retire.

Both parents had their roots in North Carolina so they settled in Cary, an affluent town west of Raleigh. One and a half years after Ashley's father retired, he had a massive heart attack while fishing. Ashley's mom was heartbroken and blamed herself for his death. She said his heart ached too much for the life she forced him to leave.

Her husband's death was not the only pain Clara Whitfield bore. When he died, their only child was nowhere in the search for a career. She had dropped out of college while pursuing a registered nursing degree, trying to follow in her mother's footsteps. When that did not work out, her mother suggested she date her friend's son whose father had left him a string of profitable furniture stores.

Frederick Parsons was twelve years older than Ashley. He had been married once, but it ended in divorce when his wife could not bear him a child. Fred always said Marla was sweet, but sterile. He wasted thousands of dollars trying all the available methods to get her pregnant. When he suggested they use his sperm to impregnate the egg of a donor, Marla recoiled and said they were coming out with newer and better technologies every day. The marriage grew cold. Fred was a deacon at his Methodist church, but began having affairs. He finally persuaded Marla to give him a divorce.

When Fred laid eyes on Ashley, he had the same reaction every man had upon seeing her for the first time. His eyes widened at how beautiful she was. His throat went dry at the sight of her well proportioned body and he wanted her. *I could bring a good looking son out of that fine body,* he had thought.

Ashley was not deeply in love with Fred. He was a little too arrogant due to his success in the furniture business; and he used the *I* and *me* pronouns too much, instead of the *we* and *us*. Ashley's mom said that giving him an heir to his business would change all that. They got married after six months and Ashley did start to love her husband. She looked past his faults; everybody had them.

She loved the devotion Fred heaped on her. Gifts, dinner dates, flowers, he was there to satisfy her every whim, especially during her pregnancy. The disappointment came when they had an ultrasound done and it was a girl. He was still there for her but Ashley could tell he was not going to be happy until she gave him a son.

Once Sonja was born, barely a year had passed when Fred started saying that soon it would be time to rev up the old eggs and get on with the birth of a namesake for the business. Sometimes Fred could be so callous Ashley wanted to smash his head with a frying pan.

Clara Whitfield was furious with his insensitivity. Ashley had cried to her mom that she felt how Princess Diana must have; that Prince Charles married her for procreation; and like Charles who loved another woman, Frederick Parsons did not really love her unless she could give him a son.

Ashley's mother and mother-in-law each took their child's side and began drifting apart. Tired of all the division and stress, Ashley stopped taking birth control pills and got pregnant. When everyone learned it was a boy, about faces in behavior occurred. Fred became his loving, doting self again. The two mothers in law got back together and joked how silly they were to get involved in something they had nothing to do with.

In her seventh month Ashley went to Crabtree Valley Mall. That day was the beginning of the end of her marriage. She had left Sonja with a baby sitter. When she came to the top of an escalator for the ride down, she took her eye off the first step, twisted her ankle and fell hard to the floor, rolling down the moving escalator. She was rushed to the hospital and had a miscarriage.

Devastated, Fred blamed Ashley and never forgave her. He ignored her and they rarely had any worthwhile time together. Ashley decided this was not the life she wanted and told Fred. He told her he still wanted the best for Sonja and that he was the one to provide it. A bad argument ensued and Fred told her that if she left him he would leave the door open because she would come running back. After going back to her mother for a while she filed for divorce and Fred did not contest it.

Ashley smiled to herself, *Well, Mr. High and Mighty, it's been five years and I haven't been back and I don't intend to come back.* She had wanted that son as much as Fred, maybe even more. As young as Sonja was, she's understood that

Mommy was going to give her a little brother, and they were both thrilled. Tears began to fill her eyes. *It was an accident, Fred, a damn tragic accident.*

The telephone rang. "Hello, Body Needs Therapy."

"Hello, my name is Max Cleland and I'm dealing with some muscle tension, and thought a massage might be good to loosen me up a little."

"I can assure you it will, Mr. Cleland. Have you ever had a massage before?" Ashley always asked that question because many times she could detect from the answer if the person on the line might be a pervert looking for a sexual thrill.

Max liked the sound of her friendly voice. "Yes, but it has been quite a while; how much are your rates?"

Ashley sensed he might be all right. "For one hour it is $60, then after that it is a dollar per minute up to two hours, so that a two-hour massage would be $120."

"Sounds good, can I make an appointment for two hours?" He wondered why he was getting sexually aroused.

"Sure can, when would you like to come in?"

"As soon as possible, these tight hamstrings are killing me."

Ashley looked at her appointment book and saw an opening for next Tuesday. "Would Tuesday of next week at one-thirty be okay?"

"That would be great," Max replied, with what he thought was a little too much excitement in his voice.

"Okay Mr. Cleland, I look forward to seeing you at one-thirty on Tuesday."

They said goodbye and Ashley glanced at her appointment book and smiled. Tuesday was shaping up to be very profitable. Still she was worried about John, and loaning him $1,500. It was not the money, she knew he would pay her back; he was so sweet about sharing everything he had. If she ever needed money for something he was happy to give it and would not allow her to pay him back.

It bothered her that he was so carefree about financial responsibilities; always procrastinating and putting his business in jeopardy. She was also worried that John was addicted to smoking marijuana. For the four years they had been together he kept promising her he would stop. He told her it was a habit he developed in Vietnam, that it was nothing to worry about, and that some people liked a glass of wine to unwind, he preferred a pipe full of weed. Ashley did not worry at first. The only noticeable affect she saw was that he seemed to be hornier when he smoked; something she definitely did not mind. But now that he was involved with a contract administrator who seemed out to get him, she worried that getting caught could cost him his business. She had to find a way to make him quit.

She thought about how much she loved John. When he used to come to her for a massage, she would hide how eager she was to see him, and play hard to get by refusing to go out with him. She told him she did not date clients, and she did not; it was her rule. Then he stopped coming to see her for massage and did not call. She had never been out with a black man and wondered what a relationship would be like. She heard that most black men when compared to other races had the larger penis. She chuckled to herself when she thought about the time she got a little too curious while working on John's stomach. Her hand went a little lower than usual and he started growing. She saw that he was embarrassed from the idle conversation so he had to take his mind off what her hand was causing. A wave of shame had come over her.

When her favorite client stopped coming and did not call, she decided to call him. She laughed when he said he had found another therapist and would she now go out with him. She did, and it was the most memorable night she ever had; not because of where they went, but because of what he did to her.

They dined at Olive Garden on Capital Boulevard and talked about everything: how John started his business; where he was raised; his failed marriage in Philadelphia. Ashley wondered why she felt a sense of relief to hear he had no children. She told him the same things about herself: her military upbringing; the death of her father; her marriage to Frederick Parsons; and her wonderful little daughter, Sonja. After dinner and a bottle of wine, John asked if she would like to go to a movie, or do something else. She asked him if he would like to go to her apartment for coffee instead.

As beautiful as she was, Ashley Whitfield at thirty-two did not have much experience when it came to sex. She had done some heavy petting once in

Japan when she was a teenager. The boy whose parents were military people too, was obviously a novice and never tried to go any further. When she married Fred at twenty-five she was still a virgin.

Her sexual relationship with Fred always made her feel there was something more. When she watched a movie where a couple was making love, the woman would moan in delight, and end up screaming for joy. Fred would begin his lovemaking affairs by sucking her nipples and going down on her. Then he would break off his heavy petting and insert himself. He humped and rolled his hips for a while and soon he would be the one screaming. She would feel really hot at what his mouth was doing, but she never reached the orgasmic scream. Her body would ache for something that never came. After the marriage went downhill she didn't see having an orgasm as a priority.

Ashley was attracted to John because he was kind and understanding; yet she knew that she did not invite him to her apartment that night just for coffee. Many times she fantasized about sex with him; what he would do to her; how she would respond; what she would feel. She wondered if she would scream like the women she saw in the movies. John was sitting on the sofa as Ashley returned from the kitchen with coffee. When John told her how much he wanted her, she came over to him, sat on his lap and gave him a long passionate kiss, sending her tongue as far as it would go into his mouth. He started growing and Ashley was sure she was sitting atop a torpedo. John undressed her on the sofa and carried her to the bedroom. When Ashley saw his long, thick black penis, she got scared at the thought of it going into her. But John was slow and delicate in everything he did to her; sucking her hard nipples; while his fingers probed the moist valley. Wet and hot as could be, Ashley moaned in pain and pleasure when John finally entered that most sacred of places. She was tight and he took his time going to the bottom.

Ashley had multiple orgasms. She screamed like the women in the movies. They made love in different positions, and she could not believe how good he was making her feel; it seemed she could not get enough. While John sat in a chair drained, Ashley got on top of the torpedo, crying and moaning so much, she thought she would die from pleasure. She was glad she had left Sonja with her grandmother.

Ashley shook herself from the memory; it was her favorite. Her last client would be in soon, and the love of her life would be picking her up after dropping Sonja off to her father. *Good ol' Fred.* Fred's mother confided to Ashley's mom that Fred had called her a nigger-lover.

ᛌ

Frederick Parsons was waiting on the front porch, when John dropped Sonja off. He saw Sonja hug and kiss John as if he were her father. His face turned red and he seethed with jealousy. *Damn sorry fucker. Better enjoy it now, because I'm getting custody of my child, then you can bang her stupid mama to death and have your own child.*

CHAPTER 3

The sun was shining brightly at 10:00 am. And the dew point was nudging upwards indicating a muggy day lay ahead.

John wore a light blue suit, white shirt, no tie. He entered Branch Bank angry, but made sure he didn't show it. Banks represented all that was evil in society. To John Colby banks were ruthlessly powerful, ultra greedy, and arrogant. They take in millions of deposits from people and then overcharge the depositors for transacting business in their banks. They don't make loans like they should, but invest the deposits as they choose; usually enriching themselves and their buddies. John concluded, *The incredible thing about banks is they don't create or manufacture anything worthwhile to mankind. They just take, and take, and take.*

He smiled at the receptionist who told him to have a seat and that Mr. Dornan would be with him shortly.

John felt bad about hiding most of his debt load from Ashley. If he could just get this loan and the Albemarle Building contract, he would not have to tell her. He knew Ashley loved him, but was afraid she would start having second thoughts about making Colby her last name.

Mr. Dornan appeared and introduced himself. He was of medium height and had a large head. He had grey hair and arrogant eyes. John surmised, *Oh wow, a brother, maybe he'll understand and make me a loan.*

After they were seated, Dornan became serious. "Mr. Colby I've looked at your loan request of $40,000. It says you want to pay off some bills and have cash flow to expand. Is that right?"

John cut to the chase. "That's correct. We've been in business over fifteen years and we're making good money. I made the mistake of growing too fast, without proper financing, and got in trouble when the bank would not make me a loan. I had to use quarterly taxes at times to meet payroll. At other times I used credit cards, or borrowed small amounts from high interest loan companies to keep things going."

Paul Dornan looked like a reasonable person. While he had his attention, John decided to earnestly appeal for the money he needed. He continued. "Mr. Dornan, please, don't just see the debt, but look closely at the money Colby Cleaning Service has been making over the years and what the company is making now. I've done that without a major loan. Just think what I can do if you make this loan."

Dornan gave an unconcerned half-smile to John's speech. He cleared his throat. "I see where you're coming from. Your company has indeed made some good money over the years. But, frankly Mr. Colby, the bank feels that you have too much debt. We can't just focus on your income and your potential and make you a loan. Your debt is a huge liability. The…"

"That's what I've been trying forever to get the bank to see. The money I'm paying to all my creditors and the IRS could be coming to you as one payment. My debt load greatly decreases and I could use the extra income to expand, buy equipment. It's all good for the economy."

Behind Paul Dornan's cold eyes was an impatient black man. He was a conservative Republican who believed blacks should manage their financial affairs better. From what he saw in John's loan request, John was a person who did not know how to manage his company's income. Too many of his payments to creditors were late, resulting in unnecessary fees. He owed the Internal Revenue Service $20,000; and just recently Dornan learned the IRS placed a lien on John's bank account. Just before the bank opened that day, Dornan's boss told him to reject the loan.

Dornan replied. "We might consider a $15,000 equipment loan."

John thought, *Maybe I can get the cash and don't buy any equipment.* He asked. "How does that work?"

"Well, the bank would pay for all your equipment up to $15,000. Say you wanted to buy a floor scrubber; you would let us know the distributor you were dealing with, and we would issue a check to them for the total amount."

John was pissed. The bank had made up its mind before he entered the door. He stood slowly and growled. "No, I don't need any fucking equipment."

Startled, Dornan stood quickly and said, "Mr. Colby, there is no need for lan…"

"I'll tell you what there is no need for; uppity Negroes like yourself. And since you represent the banking industry, you can all kiss my black ass."

John paused and looked Dornan in the eye for a response. There was none.

⅄

Cynthia Newsome put her make up on. She was getting ready for her part-time cleaning job with Colby Cleaning Service. She was thirty years old and her life was going nowhere. She was on welfare: she got food stamps and housing assistance for herself and her eleven-year-old daughter, Tasha. She was in the process of getting additional assistance for taking care of her fourteen-year-old niece.

Before her sister passed away from HIV, she made Cynthia promise to take the girl in. The part-time job was perfect for making the extra cash she needed. She gave herself one last look in the full length mirror on her bathroom door. *Girl, you sho' nuff fine, look at them big tits. And when a man look at this ass,* she twirled like a ballerina and stopped with her back side in view, *all he can see is his self on top of it.* She laughed, and then frowned, *all but that fine ass boss of mine.*

She wondered what she had to do to get John Colby under the sheets. She was showing him everything. She wore a see through halter t-shirt, on top of a see through bra, all too small. Her white shorts were high on her bronze-colored thighs.

She knew her boss had a white girlfriend, but that didn't matter. Once he had a piece of her, and she got pregnant with his baby, he would drop his white girlfriend like a hot potato. John Colby was a good man and after she gave him a son, they would have one more child. They would be a happy family and work in the business.

Her fantasy drove her and she was determined to make it come true. It was her one avenue of escape from a dead end life.

She heard the blast of a car horn.

It was Clarence Farmer picking her up. He worked for John Colby, too. When he learned Cynthia lived only a few blocks from him, he suggested he pick her up for five dollars a week. Cynthia was tired of catching the bus which cost her nine dollars a week so she readily agreed.

Clarence Farmer's head was shaped like an egg that harbored sneaky eyes. He had a habit of licking his tongue in and out like a snake. He was ready to get to work, so he could see what else he would steal. There was a shipment of brand new laptops in boxes in one of the sections on his floor. The large room had been vacant but obviously the Department of Insurance was going to use it for something. He did not care. All he saw was the $300 he knew he could get for one of them. He wanted to steal more than one, but was afraid of getting caught and losing his job.

He made $240 every two weeks with Colby Cleaning Service, and earned another $300 detailing cars and helping a friend who had a small landscaping company. With that, and what he could steal he was able to afford a room at a rooming house on Newbern Avenue and keep his 1993 Escort running.

On the way out the door Cynthia hollered an instruction to her two dependents. They paid her no mind. The two of them were glued to reruns of "Sister, Sister."

While waiting for Cynthia, Clarence rolled a blunt, a thick stick of marijuana in cigar paper. He choked on the strong weed, and at the sight of what Cynthia had on. "Damn girl, you might as well be naked." His red eyes bulged with lust even though he had seen her sassy dressing many times before.

Cynthia laughed, "Shut your ol' ass up and drive. And where did you get that potent-ass weed, whew!" She rolled down the window and shook her head when he offered her a hit. She smoked but not too often. The stuff gave her a craving for food, and the last thing she needed was to gain weight. She had stopped John Colby in the hallway one day, and after walking away she could feel his eyes roaming her butt making her panties moistened. She knew if she smoked weed regularly she would be as fat as a horse, and her chances with John Colby would be over.

She heard herself repeat *Big Ed*, and remembered her question as to where he got the strong weed. She laughed again as Clarence sucked and choked on the weed. They cruised past Bojangles on Newbern and Tarboro Road. She wondered why a man in his late fifties would still be smoking weed, and drinking wine. Cynthia could never recall seeing Clarence sober. It was a state of existence that did not interfere with what he had to do.

Clarence pulled his dirty, blue Escort into the back of the Dobbs Building. The entrance was also to the loading dock of the Archdale Building that had fourteen floors, making it the tallest state-owned building in the complex.

The only way to access government properties after five o'clock was with an entry badge or key. Only John and his supervisor Lenny Williams had entry badges. Capitol Police asked John to hold off issuing badges to his personnel while they were investigating a rash of thefts. After 9/11, even vendors and other delivery people wanting to enter the building had to press a button on the concrete wall near the loading dock door so the security guard on the 3rd floor could see them on a camera and hit a button that unlocked the door for entry.

Lenny Williams, supervisor for Colby Cleaning Service, was waiting with the loading dock gate up. A wave of shame cursed through his muscular body at the sight of Cynthia. When she walked passed him, she giggled and gave him a wink.

Lenny was a deacon at his church, and had just taught a Sunday school class on the sins of the flesh. He strained to keep from looking after her, but the muscle in his neck charged with that direction almost popped; so he turned to watch her active buns. When he turned back to nod at Clarence, who knew he was in the church, they looked at each other and laughed.

"Lenny, man, I told her she might as well be naked."

They shook their heads in disbelief. Cynthia and Clarence were always the last ones to show up, and Lenny hit the close button on the gate. He lusted after Cynthia Newsome. *God, please forgive me, and help me with these un-godly feelings. The woman is hot and I'm guilty of lusting after her. Lord, my wife don't want no more sex, what's a man supposed to do?*

He and his wife Ruth were in their thirties and still had no children. One evening when Lenny was trying to warm her up for sex, she sighed and told him she was no longer interested in it; that she wanted to just spend the rest of her life living for the Lord and doing church work. She understood that he had needs and would be willing to open herself up to him once or twice a month.

She kept her word, relegating hot-bloodied Lenny to two boring sexual interludes a month. There were times she made excuses and he would only get it once. After about six months she began showing more displeasure. She started telling him to hurry up or she would gasp in frustration for him taking so long.

Ruth tried to show Lenny that they could have a good marriage without sex. Neither one believed in divorce so Lenny tried it. Besides, he had thought to himself that it was getting difficult getting on top of her. It was no better than using his hand in the shower. She would not listen to Lenny who told her to see a doctor. She was tired of sex.

Lenny's cell phone rang. "Hello, yeah John, everybody is here. Yeah, his ass was here snooping around, looking in janitorial closets. You know every time we see Sam Boswell, your girl gitting ready to come out with a bad report or somn'. Okay, I'll see you when you get here."

⚓

Sometimes when Ashley worked later than five o'clock, John would pick her up on his way to the Dobbs Building. She sat so close to him with her arm around his neck, he could hardly think. He decided to wait until Sonja was with them before he would ask Ashley to marry him.

"I thought about our first date today," she said with a chuckle.

"You mean the first time I came to you for a massage?" He knew what she meant.

"No, that night at my apartment. The first time you did it to me." She bit his ear.

John hit his brake, then kept going, missing his right turn from Peace Street onto Salisbury. "Oh, shit."

They laughed. It was not funny to the Jamaican cab driver who blew his horn, went around John and looked as though his middle finger was going into the air. As he passed, Ashley flashed a smile at him, and he just shook his head.

When they reached the Dobbs Building, they walked to the Salisbury Street entrance where the badge reader was located. The love birds held hands even for that short walk. Two black ladies leaving the Dobbs gave them disapproving looks. John was accustomed to the different looks their togetherness garnered. White men looked at them with disdain and jealousy; white women ignored them; black men gave them the *Go ahead brother, I wish it was me* look. The worst look came from black women who gave them the evil *You can't find no sister good enough for your black ass* look.

John went to the main storage room near the loading dock. Ashley was used to the building and knew John would be a while checking out things, so she went to the big conference room on the third floor to munch on the snacks she bought from the vending machines on the first floor.

She wondered if John knew how much she loved him, and how proud she was of him. Unlike her cold ex-husband who was born with a silver spoon in his mouth, John started with nothing. The odds, especially his color. were against him to succeed. She was amazed at some of the things he did in order to stay in business. He borrowed from friends; he pawner jewelry to pay his employees; he fought off the IRS by getting high-interest loans. The sad thing, she thought getting off the elevator, was that after all these years his business was making good money but he was still struggling financially, and banks would not loan him enough money to pay off debts and expand.

Clarence Farmer was removing a bag of trash from his barrel on the third floor when Ashley stepped into view. Speechless, he nodded a half smile to her. Ashley smiled back and proceeded to the conference room feeling the dirty eyes of the sneaky looking black man roam her backside.

What a lucky ass nigga Colby is. Own his business, drive good vehicles and fucking a pretty ass white woman. Some guys got all the luck. Clarence shook his head, and then remembered he had more important things to do. He needed that $300 for the laptop he was going to steal. He could buy an ounce of weed from Big Ed with money left over for gas and food.

He saw John's girlfriend go to the south end of the building, the area where the laptop was. He decided to clean the two restrooms on the north end, hoping she would be gone when he finished.

Clarence always propped the ladies' restroom door open, ever since a fat lady in a nearby office who always worked late burst in while he was cleaning one evening, lifting her skirt. Her face growled, and he ran out. When he returned the restroom was reeking of body odor and crap. He figured that was her way of telling him to kiss her ass.

He began cleaning by spraying a deodorizer cleaning solution on his toilet bowl cleaner and swishing it around the toilet and seats. The ladies' restroom on the north end was smaller than the one on the south end. There were two stalls used by twenty ladies at least four times a day; on the south end there were five stalls in the ladies' restroom frequented by far more women. When Clarence first started he did not care how many used the restrooms, he would spray and wipe all the surfaces with glass cleaner. If the crappy stains and spills did not come up, too bad. He learned right away that Colby Cleaning Service would not tolerate that.

He shook the excess water from the bowl cleaner onto the floor and began cleaning the sinks. John would scream if he saw him using the toilet bowl cleaner on the sinks. All he did was run water on the cotton-ball toilet cleaner and rinsed the faucets. The commodes were almost dry and Clarence began wiping them down. He would do the same thing for the sinks; wiping everything to a germy shine with a thin brown hand towel. With the mop that he had rung out while in the janitor's closet, he began spreading the water from the toilet bowl that he shook on the floor earlier.

Nobody would know that under the shine on the faucets were thousands of germs and bacteria from the toilet. Nobody would know that the rag he used in the restroom would be used in an office area; and nobody would know about the dirty mop used to spread water from the commode over the floor. He had learned the secret of covering up millions of germs and bacteria, spreading them wherever he went. To the untrained eye his germ-laden restroom looked okay.

His mind returned to the laptop. On Monday he told Lenny he saw a long-haired white guy in his twenties on his floor; that the guy looked suspicious and disappeared when he saw him. On Tuesday he asked Lenny if he reported it and Lenny said he did. Now it was Friday, and nobody would know Clarence stole the laptop; hopefully the police would be looking for a long-haired white guy.

While John was taking the propane tank to the truck, Lenny was stumbling at words taking his sexual needs to Cynthia. Lenny was tall and had muscles everywhere. His biceps bulged and everybody marveled at his rock hard abs. He worked out at Shaw University where he managed the housekeeping staff. His muscular frame was encased in smooth black skin.

He didn't know what to say to Cynthia. When he was strong in the Word, and getting his needs met at home, he gave Cynthia a Bible tract. The look in his eye then was one of judgment. Now he was trying to show some interest; get her to consider going out with him. He felt so guilty dealing with the two voices in his head: *Lenny you a deacon in the church. Lenny you need some pussy.*

He was wondering which direction to look for Cynthia when she came out of an office. Cynthia saw him staring at her and gave him a seductive smile. She flirted with every man but had noticed a different look in Lenny. He used to check her out and they would chat about nothing. Lately she could feel his lust. *Shame on you, deacon Lenny, you ain't wanting to get in my pants, are you?* She chuckled.

"What-chew you laughing at?" Lenny asked with an embarrassing look.

She walked to where he was standing, near the storage room. Her breasts jiggled and Lenny's knees shook.

Lenny thought, *What am I doing here? She'd probably start laughing if I asked her for a date.* He managed to say, "I'll have to get rags for you next week, John forgot to drop them off."

Cynthia burst into a laugh. "Lenny, sweetie, you gave me the rags yesterday. Now, are you going to tell me what you really want?"

He gave up. If he was going to have sex, he ought to be divorced. He could not cheat on his wife even if she was frigid. "Oh, I forgot. That's what you do to a man; make him forget things he already did."

While they were talking Cynthia had been tying her bag of trash while it was still in the barrel. When she tried to pull it out of the barrel it was too heavy.

"Let me help you with that," Lenny said.

She moved aside, and while Lenny was gripping the heavy bag, she pressed part of her breasts into his arm, and whispered in his ear, "Thank you, deacon Lenny; my what muscular arms you have, you must love working out."

Lenny cried out, "Lord help me please! This lady making me weak, mighty, mighty, weak."

They laughed so hard, they did not hear the bell signaling the arrival of the elevator.

"I've been waiting to hear something funny all day," said John smiling.

"Boss, you gon' have to talk with Miss Newsome, she's de-energizing me and Clarence. It's hard for us to do our work." Lenny was laughing harder inside. He could not believe the cry that escaped his lips. It was a true prayer. Cynthia made him feel lightheaded.

Cynthia gave John that *I want you* look. She asked him, "How about you Mr. Colby, do I de-energize you?"

"Hell yeah, I started not to hire you the day I first laid eyes on you. My energy started to leave and I wondered how I would clean a building with no energy."

Cynthia blushed at what they were saying. "You two are so full of it, I got work to do." She grabbed her empty barrel and was off to the next suite of offices, smiling at the four eyes she knew were glued to her ass. She turned and said, "John will you be here much longer? I need to talk to you."

John felt uneasy when an employee said they needed to talk. It usually meant they needed time off, or wanted him to lie on some social service form so they could receive more benefits. "Yeah, I'll be here. I'll stop by right after me and Lenny do a few things."

"See you later, Lenny." She winked at him and disappeared behind the closed door.

"I believe she has the hots for you," John said smiling as they caught the elevator to the first floor.

"Well she might have winked at me, but I seen the look in her eye when you came on the scene."

John laughed, "Well if that is the case it's too bad, I got all I can handle on the third floor."

Lenny said he would take care of her. He was sick and tired of that dead-ass woman in his bedroom.

Meanwhile, Clarence had the laptop wrapped in three black trash bags at the bottom of his barrel. He thought John's girlfriend would never leave. He had told Cynthia that he wanted to get off as soon as possible, but with the boss here that would now be impossible. It did not matter, he had what he wanted and when he took his trash to the dumpster he would put the laptop in the trunk of his car.

Ashley became bored waiting for John and decided to walk around; maybe she would bump into him. She stopped on the 4th floor in front of the ladies' restroom to read the bulletin board. She heard a vacuum cleaner in one of the offices and thought about John again, how proud she was that her man could provide jobs, and how that money helped feed families, or paid the rent.

The hallway was quiet again, and a nearby office door opened. Cynthia was backing out the door and did not see Ashley.

"Hi," Ashley said.

Cynthia dropped the vacuum cleaner and almost turned over the barrel. "Damn girl, you gon' give me a heart attack! You scared the shit outta me!"

Ashley rushed over to pick up the vacuum cleaner. "I'm so sorry; here, let me help you. My name is Ashley. I was looking for John. Have you seen him?"

"I saw him a few minutes ago. He's coming back to talk to me later." She smiled at Ashley. "Are you taking care of that fine black man?"

I know you want him, brown sugar, but he's all mine, every inch. She chuckled at Cynthia's boldness. "Yes, I'm taking care of him real good, giving him every-thing he needs. You know what I mean?"

41

Each woman had a sarcastic laugh for different reasons. Ashley could see through Cynthia's inquiry, and knew Cynthia would love to have her man. In Cynthia's mind, she did not care if Ashley took care of John, she was going to realize her fantasy.

Cynthia said, "Yeah, I know exactly what you mean. If you see John tell him I'm finished."

Cynthia thought: *At least she ain't snooty acting like some white women are when they land a fine brother. Don't matter though, I'm gon' take John from her.*

No sooner had the elevator doors closed, carrying Ashley to the first floor, that another one arrived and John walked off.

"John, is that you?" hollered Cynthia, walking down the shiny tiled hallway.

"Yeah Cynthia, what's up?"

Cynthia walked right up to John, and before he knew it she had her arms around his neck, pushing her tongue into his shocked mouth. He did not push back quick enough, so she dropped her left hand to his butt and pulled him even closer, grinding on something she thought grew bigger.

John pulled her arm from around his neck, and caught his breath, stepped back and said, "Is this what you had to talk about? Cynthia, my girlfriend is somewhere in the building, probably looking for me now."

"She's probably waiting for you on the first floor."

"What?"

"She was just here looking for you." She pushed herself onto him again and said, "I'm not finished with you boss. I got some mo' talking to do."

John just shook his head and started to the restroom to wash her off. "Lenny is the one you should be doing this to."

"Sorry, I don't mess with married men."

"Have a good weekend, Cynthia." *I got to tell Lenny to hurry up and minister to that woman.*

CHAPTER 4

The letter read:

Dear Mr. Colby: This letter is to inform you that Facility Management is recommending cancellation of the Dobbs Building for improper storage of propane tanks.

This is the second time your company will be canceled for the same reason.

Your company's disregard for leaving propane tanks not properly stored endangers the lives of state workers and cannot be tolerated. Therefore, I'm recommending that your company be disbarred from doing business with the State of North Carolina.

Attached are reports on accidents directly related to improper storage of propane tanks.

The cancellation of this contract is to take place thirty days from the date of this notice.

Pauline Wooten
Contract Administrator

Pauline could not believe how stupid John Colby was to get caught leaving propane tanks in a building a second time. She had discussed what she was going to do with Chuck Davis, the Building Manager, and Ronald Height, the Director of Facility Management. The two of them agreed that Colby

Cleaning Service did some of the best work the state had seen, but he could not go on endangering the lives of state employees.

While Pauline Wooten wondered about John's carelessness, Ronald Height sat at his desk and chuckled at the circus going on around him. His imperious personality matched his hulking physique. He use to play fullback for the Wolfpack at North Carolina State University, and had a thick neck and broad shoulders.

He was retiring in six months at the end of the year and could care less what happened to a bunch of inept black folk. He remembered the good old days when most of his staff was white, and most of the companies that did business with the state were white. He enjoyed coming to work. Then came the 1980s and the Civil Rights push by local, state and federal government to hire more minorities.

Around 1985 the state of North Carolina realized that minority contractors were not taking advantage of the many janitorial contracts that were up for bid. The new purchasing officer, a black man, told the state why this was happening and came up with the solution.

In each contract there is a page titled "Performance Guarantee." Bidders had to choose between two choices on how they would post bond to cover any financial loss the state might incur if the contractor defaults on its obligations. One choice was that the amount of the performance bond shall equal one-third of the bidder's cleaning cost and was to remain in force for the duration of the contract. The other choice was that within fifteen days after notification of an award, the bidder was to submit a cashier's check in the amount of six percent of the annual price of the contract.

The purchasing officer knew minority companies did not have the capital to choose either one of these options and so came up with a third choice. The bidder was to agree to invoice the state ten percent less than the amount of the monthly invoice for the first three months of the contract. For the remaining nine months of the first year, the bidder was to invoice the state five percent less than the amount of the monthly invoice. All janitorial contracts were for three years and if the bidder did not default, the bond money would be refunded at the end of the contract.

This third choice opened the door for minority contractors to do business with the state of North Carolina. Black-owned companies could now bid and be awarded a contract without posting a bond.

Once contractors got their foot in the door, and knew the price being paid to clean a building, they lowered their price by $2,000 to $5,000. This created a bidding war and another problem for the state. Many of the new companies did not have enough experience or proper equipment to perform to the specifications of the contract. The cleanliness of the buildings went down, and complaints from state employees escalated.

Facility Management was feeling the heat, but their hands were tied. The Department of Administration wrote the specifications of the contract and awarded the contract, usually to the lowest bidder. Ronald Height constantly bickered with DOA over this problem. His department would make a recommendation for a company they knew could do the job, and DOA usually chose another company. They told Ron it was their duty to save the taxpayer money, and had to award the bid to the company with the lowest price. Ron countered that the state had an obligation to its employees to provide a clean working environment. Even when Facility Management issued a cancellation notice to a minority company for poor service, DOA would drag their feet, trying to give the company time to correct the problems.

Ron told his white friends the color of the department was changing too. It was being invaded by minorities who sympathized with their brothers and sisters who were trying to build their businesses with state contracts. He was tired of all the bureaucratic bullshit and was taking early retirement at the end of the year.

⏃

Pauline put a copy of the letter in John's box. She enclosed another certified copy to be sent to his post office box. She sipped her coffee, delighting in the visions in her head. He could not deny he was caught red handed; he would lose $90,000 a year; his white girlfriend and that spoiled brat would walk out on him; and the proud John Colby who keeps mentioning the way things use to be would fear and respect her like the rest of the contractors doing business with the state of North Carolina.

She wondered why so many brothers were getting white women, then chuckled; what was forbidden back in the day had vanished. White women had always wanted to see what a brother was like in bed, and brothers always wanted to show them.

Her thoughts turned to her own loveless life, and then to Tony Bizaro. He told her a fine upstanding black woman ought to have a fine upstanding Italian and would she do him the pleasure of going out with him. They laughed, talked over the phone and had lunch a few times, but never a date.

Tony worked at the Department of Administration as the assistant purchasing agent for a number of commodities and services, including janitorial. He was 5'11", with a muscular build and had dark wavy hair. A lot of people said he favored Tom Selleck.

Pauline had to admit he was fine, and that if she did go out with a white man he would have to look good. *No low-life crackers for me,* she thought. She had not told her mother a white guy was chasing her; there would be too many questions.

Pauline Wooten did not have much experience in the love department. After the horrible attempt by her stepfather to rape her, she had problems with men when the relationship turned to sex. There was the hot and heavy foreplay; she would be horny as ever but when her date started to undress her, she protested and said it was that time of the month. Only a few times, when she thought she had found Mr. Right, had she gone all the way. And then it was the guy doing all the moaning. She learned to play with her clitoris when she was a little girl, and that was all the pleasure she was getting lately. She heard white men knew how to go down on a woman, and suddenly she saw her legs wrapped around Tony's head while screaming for joy.

"Morning Pauline, how you doing today?"

Chuck Davis, the building manager, saw Pauline's door open and peeked in. He still was not happy about barring Colby Cleaning Service from doing business with the state of North Carolina. John's buildings had the best looking floors in the entire complex. In light of all the cleaning complaints he was getting about other contractors, he hated to lose a good company.

Pauline stopped her dirty thinking. "Hey Chuck, come on in and take the load off."

Chuck was forty-five years old. He had been with the state for twenty years. When he started in the early 1970s, housekeeping was done by state employees. He advanced quickly to supervisor. However, it was costing millions of dollars in salaries, benefits and vacations, so they put most of their buildings up for bid.

Since Facility Management would regulate contracts, Chuck was promoted to head inspector. His selection over Pauline for the position of Building Manager caused enmity between them, but they acted as if it did not matter.

Their boss, Ronald Height, chose Chuck because of his experience and knowledge of state buildings. Pauline had a degree in business management and her administrative skills were much better than Chuck's. Ronald Height chose Chuck because he would be a good ass-kisser.

Chuck dropped his short, wide frame in one of the chairs facing Pauline. "Have you given the letter to Colby Cleaning Service yet?"

"I put one in his box and will send a certified copy to his post office box."

Chuck shrugged, "Well it's too late now, but I still wish we did not have to go so far as disbarring John from doing business with us."

Pauline was not in the mood to hear a sob story for John Colby. Chuck may have had more experience in housekeeping, but he definitely did not know how to handle people. She tried to be patient.

She smiled and thought she saw her reflection on the bald spot dividing Chuck's hair. "Come on, Chuck, the disbarring is not so bad. It's more of a statement about the severity of the careless storage of propane tanks. John will appeal that decision and more than likely will win, and just lose the Dobbs Building. If it'll make you feel better, remember he's providing service to the New Education Building, our largest contract."

Chuck leaned back considering what she said. "Yeah, I guess you right. I hadn't thought of that." Smiling, he changed the subject. "You know Ron is retiring at the end of the year; are you going to apply for his position?"

Pauline wanted the position so bad she could taste it. It would add $20,000 a year to her salary. Local television stations would call for interviews of the first black woman to be named Director of Facility Management. She craved the power that came with the position. Thinking about it gave her goose bumps, but her answer to Chuck was nonchalant.

"I did give it some thought, but being black, and a woman does not help my chances."

When Chuck Davis laughed it was loud and throaty. "Girlfriend, being black period, ain't gon' help neither one of us." He lowered his voice, "I heard that redneck boss of ours is thinking about bringing in one of his white buddies from the Department of Transportation.

Look at this fat-ass bald-headed rascal. Mad now after having his nose up Ron's ass all these years may not pay off like he thought. She knew Ron would recommend neither one of them, but that would not keep her from applying. "Well, we will see; looks like we are always applying for the same promotion."

Chuck got up to leave. He wondered why Pauline seemed disinterested in the job. His friends at the personnel department said she showed great interest in the job. The woman loved power and the position would be the ultimate. She would make his life more difficult if she got it, since he beat her out for Building Manager. Like Pauline, he acted as if he could care less. He glanced down the hallway to make sure no one was listening. "These sorry ass crackers would love nothing better than to see one of us fail in such an important position."

"Yeah, guess you right on that one, Chuck." *If they pick your dumb ass they will definitely see a failure.* "Close the door for me, Chuck."

"Check you later," he said.

I'm surrounded by dummies. Pauline shook her head in disgust and advanced the thought. There was Sam Boswell, her go-fer inspector. *I could shit on his head, and his nose would never lose its position up my ass.*

She laughed at him. *And how does Chuck Davis' wife put up with him? Everybody and his mama knows he's banging the big-butt secretary in the New Education Building.*

She wondered about black men; if there were any good ones left. *Okay, okay, of course there are some very good black men out there. Just because I had a jackass stepfather, and seemed to be surrounded by misfits, don't mean they ain't out there.* She subscribed to *Essence* and *Ebony* magazines, and read all the articles on good black men, and what black women had to do to hold on to them.

Her mind returned to Tony's head between her legs. She dialed his number.

"Purchasing, Tony Bizaro, may I help you?"

"Hey Tony, Pauline. What you up to?"

He lied. "I was just thinking about you and what does it take to get a date with you."

Pauline knew what he wanted, and she knew what she needed; there was no need to waste words. "I'm working late today, wanna pick me up about six for dinner?"

Tony smiled. He thought about Pauline ever since he made her blush with a comment about how rare it was to see someone with a beautiful face and a terrific body. It was time for a new piece of ass. He was tired of banging the few single women there at DOA, and making the rounds at clubs was getting old. When he saw Pauline at a meeting he wanted her. Tony wondered if she was looking for a long term relationship, or just good sex. *Maybe she wants both.* He tinged his melodic voice with excitement. "Where would you like to go?"

"Olive Garden on Capital Boulevard would be nice."

"I love the food there, see you at six, and thanks so much for calling me, Pauline."

Pauline loved the way he said her name. "See ya then, Tony."

What will we do after dinner? Will he ask me to go to his place? If he takes me home, do I ask him to come in? Of course silly, you can't go to la-la land on the doorstep. The telephone rang.

It was Greta Wooten, her mother. "Hey Mom, what's going on; you never call me this early on a Monday morning."

"Too much stuff on my mind, did not sleep well last night, had a bad headache, but I'll be fine. How's my baby?"

"I'm doing good, lots of stuff going on here." She wondered if she should tell her mother about Tony.

"Stuff like what, work problems, love life? Have you got so much going on that you forgot about our shopping date this evening?"

A trip to the mall or a trip to Ecstasy Island? "Gee Mom, I completely forgot. I'm sorry, but we'll have to do that another time. I have a date tonight."

"A date," Greta repeated herself. "A date?"

Pauline loved her mother deeply, and knew she was teasing her about her no-life status. "Yeah Mom, a date, like going out with a man."

"Well, I'd rather see you involved in a relationship that might lead to marriage than us going to the mall."

"Mom, it's a first date, not a proposal meeting." Pauline got upset and defensive when her mother talked about marriage. She knew her biological clock was ticking, but she was not about to rush into a marriage and end up with a husband who might be a child molester.

"Okay baby, calm down. Is he cute? Where did you meet him? How long have you known him? You ain't been dating behind my back, have you?"

Pauline sighed, "Mom you are the nosiest lady I know. No, I have not been dating behind your back. I've known Tony for a few months. He's a purchasing agent over at DOA."

"When do I meet him?"

"You're impossible, Greta Wooten, I've never dated the man, and you want to know when you will meet him."

"Well, is that so bad?" Greta thought: *Maybe I am being ridiculous and too pushy about marriage. That damn sorry ass Otis, trying to rape her.* She knew that was the reason for her daughter's failed relationships. Deep down, Pauline was afraid of men, afraid of sex. She cursed Otis again, but said to Pauline, "What does he look like, is he cute?"

"He's fine as can be; a little taller than me, dark wavy hair, the darkest blue eyes you ever did see, he...."

"Hold on baby girl, you describing a white man," Greta interjected with a laugh.

Pauline laughed too, "Yeah Mom, a lot of people say he looks like Tom Selleck."

Pauline and her mother had joked many times about her failed relationships and that maybe she should try a white man.

Greta said, "Call me tomorrow and let me know if you like him any better after tonight."

"I will, Mom, now let's talk about you. The only time you can't sleep is when something is bothering you. Here you are getting in my business, but there's something you are not telling me."

Her mother exhaled a weary sigh. "I was going to tell you after we went shopping. "I've been feeling this lump in my right breast, it's…"

Pauline became hysterical, "Mom, Grandma and Aunt Sarah died from breast cancer, you…how long have you felt the lump? And why are you just telling…I'm canceling my date with Tony!"

Greta wished she had waited to tell her daughter. Breast cancer ran in her family. The ugly disease had claimed her mother, and put a sister and aunt into an early grave. She felt the lump a month ago and was terrified. She knew it was cancer, but had waited to schedule an appointment.

She lied, "I just felt it the other day, and I'm scheduled to see the doctor this Thursday. Now I'm ordering you to keep that date with Tony." *Maybe the Lord will let me live to see you marry.*

Pauline calmed down. "Well, you said, I've been feeling this lump, like it's ongoing, so the first thing came in my mind was that you knew about the lump for some time. Why the hell is life like this? Things will be going fine and you feel like you are on top of the world. Then the bottom drops out. Shit! Life just ain't fair!" She was about to cry.

⋀

Contractors' mailboxes were outside the door of Pauline's office and John thought he heard her voice. He could tell by the envelope that trouble lay inside. *Probably some shit from the bonehead on the other side of that door.*

He went to his truck, let down the windows and read the notice of cancellation for the Dobbs Building. He yelled *Bitch!* so loud, two ladies walking the nearby sidewalk gasped and looked at him with disdain. He trembled at the thought of losing $7,500 a month.

Every time something goes wrong for me, a nigga gon' been in it, over it or under it. How the hell can I ask Ashley to marry me if my business is going down the tubes? I can't afford to lose the Dobbs.

Colby Cleaning Service was the first company with the state to use high powered propane buffers. The weight of the machine, and the propane driven motor, tripled the revolutions of the buffing pad, burnishing the shine into the floor. The director of Facility Management told John the state had never seen high-gloss floors like that.

He wondered if his attention disorder was getting worse or whether or not he was doing too many things. That was one of the problems small businesses faced when they could not get adequate financing; the owner winds up working twelve-hour days. He was paying the Internal Revenue Service $2,000 a month, and could not afford to hire a full-time supervisor.

He cursed himself for being careless and forgetful, but that was no reason his contract should be canceled. He had a thought. *That's it.* He knew how he would respond to the cancellation.

⚔

Pauline dried her tears.

Her mother tried to sound funny, "Now you just hush, I ain't dead yet. You are going out with Tony, and enjoy yourself; then come over and tell me all about him, you hear me!"

"Okay Mom, guess you're right. I'll take the rest of the week off and stay with you through the weekend."

That made Greta happy. She had a lot of things to tell her daughter. "Now that's my baby girl. Call me in the morning. Love ya, sweetie."

"Love you too, Mom, bye, bye."

⚔

Tony Bizaro was taking a leak in the men's restroom. Pauline dominated his thoughts ever since she called him. He was going to set her on fire, while enjoying a hot piece of black pussy. There was no soap in the dispenser; he frowned and rinsed his hands.

The door flew open and Charles Simms, Tony's boss rushed to the urinal, unzipping his trousers. "Hey Tony, you ever seen that Flomax commercial where the guy is always missing the big moment, cause he got to rush to a restroom to take a leak? That's me in the flesh. Whew that was close... aahhaahaa!"

The Department of Administration Building was long, stretching from Salisbury Street to McDowell Street. The two men worked on the end closest to Salisbury Street. Flomax was for men like Charles Simms who had an enlarged prostate gland and had to be careful about waiting too long to relieve themselves.

The door opened again. It was the daytime housekeeper. Tony told him the soap was out. He and Charles stood over by the urinals while he tended to the soap dispenser.

Tony said, "Guess who called me for a date?" And without waiting for an answer, he grinned, "Pauline Wooten."

The ears attached to the head of the sleazy looking housekeeper went up like radar. His boyfriend was the main cook downstairs, who had borrowed money from Pauline a number of times so they could smoke weed and bang each other silly.

Tony continued, "She asked me for a date. I'm taking her to Olive Garden at six. That hundred-dollar bet still on?"

"Hell yes it is," Charles said eagerly. "She wouldn't even go out with me; and the guy she did go out with got nowhere; and you gon' get her drawers off on the first date. I'd like all twenties, T. B."

Tony laughed and said he'd take a hundred-dollar bill. They left the restroom while the housekeeper was making sure the restroom had toilet tissue. He could not wait to tell Ralph that Pauline's ass was only worth a hundred-dollar bet to the cracker that thought he was God's gift to women.

The head of the State Bureau of Investigation fired their crime lab director because he did not know what his department did, and struggled to explain procedures. He was paid $98,481 a year for having no clue. Now, his boss, the director of the SBI, had been forced out for the same reason: unqualified.

The shoddy work of investigators and lab people botched hundreds of cases resulting in innocent men going to prison for murders they did not commit. Now the state had to re-examine 230 cases where evidence may have been withheld or tampered with.

Making the headlines earlier was the renowned North Carolina State Highway Patrol. Officers were caught having sex in the back seat of their cars. One report was of a trooper making out with a woman who was married to the trooper who sat in the front seat. There were reports of drunk driving by officers, and recently a top commander was forced to retire after he was caught sending nasty e-mails to a secretary.

The governor told the press there must be accountability. No one paid her any mind. She had problems of her own, such as explaining travel expenses.

The governor had two employees who could care less about the problems of the state. They were waiting for their food at the Olive Garden in north Raleigh. One was a ravenous-looking, dark haired Italian; the other, a worried, depressed looking black woman.

"You look sad, Pauline; what has happened since you talked to me?" Tony Bizaro sipped Chianti Classico, the house special at Olive Garden. He had ordered steak with roasted vegetables and a baked potato. Pauline ordered soup and salad.

He looked deep into her brown eyes and was attracted. Sure she was hot and as fine as can be, and what man would not want to lay her. But there was something else.

Pauline's eyes filled with tears and she told Tony everything; how cancer ran in her family; who it had claimed; and that now her mother probably had it. She told him about being abused by her stepfather. Tears were rolling down her face, and Tony came around to her seat.

He put his arms around her and Pauline apologized. It was a long moment.

Pauline began to relax and eat her soup. She needed someone to unload on, and now watched Tony devour his steak like a wild man. "I can see my problems didn't affect your appetite," she said with a smile.

Tony grunted and washed his food down with a long drink of iced tea. "Oh girl, I was so hungry. When you called, I decided to work and skip lunch. The last time I ate was early this morning and that was just a bowl of oatmeal." He stopped eating for a second and gazed at Pauline again with his probing eyes. "Don't worry, Pauline, everything will be all right."

Pauline was warm inside. She liked the way Tony held her a few minutes ago. Her nasty thoughts returned; she smiled, and told herself to wait. She had an emotional release, now she needed a physical release. They spent the rest of their time at Olive Garden trading tales about work related issues, and going deeper into each other's background.

She had left her car at work and when they were ready to leave the restaurant she asked if he would like to go to her apartment. Pauline lived at the Falls of Duraleigh, in north Raleigh. The landscaping was beautiful, and the apartment complex included an outdoor, covered saltwater pool, a state-of-the-art fitness center, and tennis and volleyball courts.

They spent another hour sipping wine, laughing and talking. They were enjoying each other's company. When Tony came out of the bathroom, Pauline was sitting on the couch with her back to him. She rolled her head from side to side as one does when relieving tight neck muscles.

He put his hand around her neck and gently massaged it. His hands felt so good to Pauline; she sighed. Tony squeezed and plied the muscles at the base of Pauline's neck smiling at her enjoyment. From listening to her background; abusive stepfather, raised by her mother; never been in love; he thought: *All she needs is a good man. Hell, at thirty-five, all I need is a good woman. Me and Pauline?* He had to admit to himself that with all the girls he made out with, he was just as lonely as Pauline. And, his background was similar to hers. His father abused his mother and walked out on them when he was twelve years old. Both he and Pauline and loved movies, eating out and tennis.

He lowered himself to one knee and dropped his hand to the top of Pauline's breasts. When she did not resist, he put both his hands on her breasts, sucked her ear lobe and whispered, "Don't you think we need to get more comfortable?"

Tony's voice traveled at lightning speed to Pauline's toes. She decided at work when he made his move as she knew he would, that she would not resist. She was going to let him have his way with her, and gave him an affirmative nod.

Once inside the spacious bedroom, Tony undressed Pauline so fast her head spinned. He was kissing her everywhere, and she wondered why she was so horny and there was no fear like it had been with black men. Why did she stop them, but wanted Tony to keep exploring her?

Tony's mouth went from her hard black nipples, down her stomach to the moist v-spot. The erotic visions she had earlier were now a reality and she hollered, wrapping her legs around his head. Before he was finished she lost count of the orgasmic contractions rippling through her entire being.

Soon after they made love, she was fast asleep. Tony listened to Pauline's deep breathing, and looked at her smooth dark skin. The two, soft round melons with the long nipples rose and fell with each breath, making him want her again. Something about Pauline was different, and now he knew what it was. After the date, and the bedroom scene with the other women, he was ready to leave; on to his next conquest. Now, he wanted to stay. He identified with the loneliness he saw in her eyes and wanted more of her, not just for sex, but to enjoy her company, play tennis or go swimming. Tony did not know if he was falling in love, but this would not be the last time he was with her. He would give his boss five twenties and tell him he won the bet.

Chapter 5

It was close to 1:30 when Max Cleland would arrive for his appointment. Ashley Whitfield hated to work on clients when she was angry. Sonja came home from her father wondering if he were going to take her away from Ashley and John. She said her father asked how she would like to come and live with him; and that he would buy her anything she wanted. Ashley cursed Fred Parsons. *The nerve of that bastard to blame me for the miscarriage and starts running around with other women. Now all of a sudden he wants our daughter to come live with him.*

She heard the door to the waiting room open, and shook herself. She would deal with Fred later. She thought of life without Sonja or John. *No way, no way!*

She wore a white sleeveless shirt, and purple pants made of soft suede. Her blonde hair was brushed back and ended in a braided circle. She looked at Max Cleland, smiled and stretched out her hand. "Hello Mr. Cleland, I'm Ashley Whitfield. It's a pleasure to meet you."

Damn, she is beautiful. "Pleasure to meet you too, Ashley. You don't mind a first-name basis, do you?"

"I prefer that, have a seat." There was a file cabinet in the corner and she retrieved a clip board. "You said you had a massage before, but since this is your first time here, if you'll take a minute and fill out this brief form, I'll make sure the room is ready and we can get started."

Max still could not believe how beautiful she was and looked so soft and sweet. He wondered why she would be with a nigger like Colby. The one-page form requested name, address, phone number, and what kind of work you did. It had a health section with a box to check yes or no on things like *Do you smoke, have headaches, diabetes,* etc. There was another page with the sketch of a human drawing asking the client to draw a line in the area that bothered them the most. He thought, *Wonder if I draw a line on my dick, will she massage that.* He grinned and drew lines in the groin area, hamstrings, low back, and buttocks. He put some lines in the upper body area so she would not think he was a freak in for a thrill, which he was.

Ashley had gone into the massage room to turn on some soft music and dim the lights; it helped clients to relax. Max Cleland looked a little sneaky, like he was up to some kind of mischievous deed, so she kept the lights brighter than usual.

She checked his chart, and just as she thought, he had a lot of lines implying he wanted work near his pride and joy. "Okay, Max, the room is ready." She smiled and held the door open. The massage room was spacious with the table in the middle and two chairs along the wall. In one corner was her stereo system, and near that was a rack on the wall for clients to hang their clothes. "You can hang your clothes on that rack Max, and call me when you're ready." She was about to close the door. "Oh, and let's start with you face down."

"Should I take all my clothes off, or leave my shorts on?"

"Whatever level of comfort suits you Max." Ashley closed the door, sure that he would be under the sheet buck naked. On his chart he wrote he was a contractor, and she wondered what kind of contractor he was.

The soft sound of the flute played, and Ashley stood at the front of the table and began manipulating the muscles on both sides of his neck. She pulled the sheet back some and proceeded to his trapezius and deltoid, muscles that run along the top of the shoulders and into the center of his back. She noticed how tight they were and applied extra pressure.

Max was an ex-marine and was surprised at the strength in Ashley's hands. He sighed in delight as her hands seemed to withdraw the stress from his body. He thought about his daughter, the one responsible for his tight muscles. Doris was a junior at the University of North Carolina at Chapel

Hill, majoring in law, and her parents were so proud of their only child whose grades were so good she made the Dean's list.

She came home for the weekend one day and told her devoted Southern Baptist parents that she was in love. Max, along with his wife, beamed at the good news, both of them seeing wedding bells and grandchildren in the near future. He had said, "When do we get to meet the young fella?" Then Doris floored them with, "Mom, Dad, I'm gay."

Max and his wife were raised to believe that good works were the key to entering heaven and they worked hard in the church. He worked in the local branch of the Southern Baptist organization, and she in the Women on Mission group at their church. He knew he had sins but God would look past his sins and see the roofs he help put on poor people's houses, or the food he helped prepare for hurricane victims. God would look past his wife's sin of malicious gossip, and spending too much money on bingo and see the care packages she help send to foreign countries and to America's armed forces overseas. But how, they wondered would He look past their daughter being a homosexual, a sin the Bible said God hates.

Max forced himself to stop thinking of Doris or the massage would do him no good. He was proud of his physique, and worked out regularly. Sometime he got turned on just looking at himself in the mirror after taking a shower. He read that the average size of a man's penis was five to six inches in length, and two to three inches in circumference. With a whopping six inch phallus he considered himself hung heavy and wondered how shocked John's girlfriend would be when she saw his size.

Ashley was ready to work on Max's thighs. She made sure only one of his thighs were exposed. Her hands carefully moved up his ham string to the inside of his thigh. Max spread his legs, hoping her hands would go further to his growing member.

Ashley placed her clients in certain categories. There was the stressed out group who were tight around the neck and shoulders. Next was the sports group, people who were athletic and wanted specific muscles and ligaments worked. The third group was the fibromyalgia group, people who ached everywhere.

Max was in the fourth group, exclusively for males. Men in this category suffer a heavy dose of narcissism and fantasize they are so hot, deliberately have an erection imagining that the therapist is as perverted as they are and gets horny by what they see.

He said, "Ashley, if you don't mind, can you go a little higher. Think I must have pulled a groin muscle in the gym yesterday."

"You're such a big man, Max, that's a hard area to get to from the backside. Let's wait till we turn you over." She rolled her eyes to the ceiling. He reminded her of Sonja's father, so full of himself.

The sound of John Colby's pretty girlfriend saying he was a big man sent his fantasies into high gear. She was relaxed with him and no doubt needed all the clients she could get. He asked himself the same question. *Why in the world would she be shacking up with a nigger like Colby.* One of the deacons in Max's church was assistant vice-president at the bank where John did business, and told him John was up to his neck in debt and owed a lot of back taxes to the IRS.

Ashley took as much time as she could on Max's backside. He was getting a two-hour massage and there were forty-five minutes to go. Just so long as he didn't get stupid with his request, she would leave him in the fourth category and hopefully he would never return. She inhaled deeply and said, "Okay, Max, it's time to turn over."

She held the sheet above her head while he positioned himself on the table. Then she pulled the sheet up to his hairy chest. Their eyes met and she smiled at the useless lust on his face. She went to the foot of the table and pull the sheet back from Max's right thigh, making sure his other thigh and privates were securely wrapped under the sheet. She began working on his toes. *My what big feet you have; matches your big head.* She wanted to laugh, but instead moved up his leg.

The adductor longus and the gracilis were muscles that led into the groin. When Ashley began working there, she could see movement under the sheet that signaled an erection was on the way.

Max decided it was time to show her how big of a man he really was. He suddenly grabbed her hand and tried to move it closer to his erect penis. "You said you would work the groin area once I turned over."

Ashley was taken by surprise and yanked her hand back. She tried to be professional but Max was getting on her nerves. "Mr. Cleland, perhaps you need to go to the advertisements in the Independence newspaper and search adult entertainment. This is as high as I go up your thigh."

Max was frustrated. "You're not afraid of that are you?" His eyes looked down to his fully erect penis.

"Why should I be?'

"Maybe it's a little intimidating to you."

Max Cleland, damn! Thought his name was familiar. He's the guy John outbid on some big contracts. Probably wants some perverted thrill by John's white girlfriend. She stepped back from the table and with a derisive laugh, said, "No, Max, is that all you have? My man is twice bigger than that little thing."

Max's face turned red, full of rage and embarrassment. He snatched off the sheet and got up from the table. "I don't need this bullshit. All I wanted was a little higher action."

Ashley knew her words would deflate his ego. "Mr. Cleland, the charge for today is $120."

Max was suddenly ashamed of his nakedness and covered his withered jewels with his t-shirt. "What! You expect me to pay you?"

"Yes I do," Ashley said with a disgusted look. "I don't think you want your wife and other janitorial contractors to know how indecently you acted on my table, now would you?"

How did she know? Max turned his bare ass to her and grunted.

John finished typing his response to the cancellation notice, and laughed at the buffoons staffing Facility Management. A redneck and bigoted director, and a bunch of black folk sitting on their ass stabbing each other in the back. And the biggest dummy of all was Pauline Wooten. Colby Cleaning Service was among the top three best companies; a fact she ought to appreciate since it meant that Facility Management would have problem-free buildings.

He thought. *What in the world does this woman have against me? Why is she always looking for a way to make me lose business?* He hit the print button on his computer and frowned. *That's it! The wench been despising me since day one when I doted on Sarah Jenkins, and kept mentioning her at contractors' meetings and how well things went under her.*

He wished for the previous contract administrator many a day. In those days if your building looked good and there were no complaints, you had no problems. Since Pauline Wooten took over, the appearance of your building did not matter. If she did not like you, your building looked bad.

His letter read:

To Facility Management: The Dobbs building cancellation notice should be rescinded immediately. The storage tanks in question were empty, and it was only over night that they were in the building.

After doing some buffing, my supervisor called me to tell me he could not finish because he ran out of propane. That was the night your inspector saw the tanks and rushed back to tell Ms. Wooten.

This rush to judgment continues to show her meanness towards our company, and she should be reprimanded.

Yours In Disgust,

John Colby

⋏

His cell phone rang. "Hey baby, what's up?"

"I just threw one of your contractor associates out of here."

"Who in the world was that?"

"A sorry bigot named Max Cleland. Funny thing is I did not know who he was until he got nasty. Then I remember you talking about a white guy who hated you for outbidding him on some important accounts, and I remembered his name."

"Nasty?" John's anger against sorry ass niggas turned to sorry ass crackers. "He had to know you were my girlfriend. He was up to no good before he walked in the door. Bastard!"

Ashley giggled at what happened and let loose a long sigh over John's jealousy and quick temper. "Well, for some reason he thought he had a lot of size, and wanted me to go higher on his thigh than I was willing. When I didn't he smirked and asked was I intimidated looking down at his thing."

"Why that nasty rascal. What did you tell him?"

"I said my man has a whole lot more than that little thing. He got mad as hell, and called me a nigger-lover on the way out the door. Too…"

John cut her off. "You wait till I see that big punk, I'm gon' break his nose!"

"Sweetie, don't worry about him. He's not worth it and he won't be back." Ashley decided to change the subject. Her man was a mild-mannered guy until you messed with her or Sonja. She had a flashback of John's fist flying repeatedly off a black guy who had bumped into her at the mall, knocked her down and then looked at her as if it was her fault. Security had to pull John off of him.

"What are you doing at home?" she asked. Thought you'd be downtown all day until Sonja got out of summer school."

John told her about the cancellation notice, and read his response letter.

"Do you think they will rescind the cancellation?" she worried.

"Of course they will. The tanks were empty, and they were there only overnight."

"Are you coming back downtown today?"

"I was thinking about it. Why?"

She wanted John to have more time to cool off. "Well, it's almost two-thirty; why don't you wait for Sonja and let's eat out. My last appointment is an hour massage starting at five. You guys could pick me up about six-thirty."

Wow! I can ask her to be mine forever! "That'll be great. See you then, Ash. I love you so much!"

"I love you too baby. Bye."

And he did love Ashley, with all his being. She was so thoughtful, sweet, and would do anything for him. He hated to ask her to marry him with the debt of his business so large. But if he could secure the Albemarle Building he would be able to pay down his debt in no time. Then for the last year of the contract he would be able to save the profit of $7,000 a month. He longed to be debt free. The economy was still bad, and the numbers of homeless people were increasing at an alarming rate. He had to do something to get out of his debt before America went down the tubes.

John believed in God and the message of the Bible that Jesus would come back and establish His kingdom. He hardly ever went to church, but from his own reading, and watching preachers on television discuss the prophecies about the end of the age, it had to be true.

As far as he was concerned, America would not be a player on the world stage in the not too distant future. The country ticked God off when they made it illegal to pray in school; removed the Ten Commandments from the courts; and told God, He was wrong on the gay issue; that it's okay.

He remembered what Brazilian President Luiz Da Silva said a year ago about the financial crisis; that it was caused by white people with blue eyes who went around the world acting as if they knew everything, only to find out they know nothing.

And now "stupid white men," as author Michael Moore called them, had driven America into a $14 trillion hole and it was all Obama's fault. John read somewhere that the debt was larger than the economies of China, United Kingdom and Australia, combined. *Yet this arrogant ass country still roams the earth telling people how to live, what to do and what not to do.*

He read how enemies around the world could bring America to its knees with an electromagnetic pulse attack, and that it was inexpensive to do. Any rogue nation like North Korea or terrorist group like Al Qaeda could easily pull it off. The article stated that Iran's shahab three nuclear missiles were designed to fit in the hull of a cargo ship that would sail into international waters close to America and aim them high over a major city like New York. Once detonated, the electromagnetic pulse would fall at the speed of light and knock out electrical power, computers, circuit boards controlling most automobiles and trucks, banking systems, communications and food and water supplies. *We'd be in deep shit. But arrogance so thick in Washington, they figure nobody would dare attack white America. 9/11 should've changed that.*

The article concluded that should an EMP attack occur, life in America would revert to that of the 1800s.

He thought of another reason God would let America suffer and become a powerless nation. It had to do with sowing and reaping. The time was coming for America to receive its just rewards for the horrendous sins and crimes against nature committed against the Indians and black slaves.

The ancestors of white America were filled with such evil and contempt they beat and terrorized their black slaves into submission. Their inhumane treatment to black people was brutal, cruel, and the worst known to mankind. Nothing made John angrier than the thought of white people taking the word *terror* to a new degree, forcing his ancestors to provide free labor while themselves becoming wealthy. *White folk beat us, raped our women to provide more slaves, tortured us if we tried to escape, and committed every other unpardonable sin against humanity to demean us into to becoming another farm animal. I got to Google if there's ever been an official apology from the U.S. Government for its crimes against nature during their enslavement of a people...my people.*

He cringed at the thought of a white slave-owner going out to the shack where his black slave woman lived and making the woman's husband go out while he screwed her. *They treated my people so bad, that respectable white folk would rather forget that perverted part of their history.*

Sonja would not be home for another hour so John went to the deck, filled his pipe with weed, and continued his thoughts. He could understand different races discriminating against each other over theological issues; but for white people to discriminate against a people based on the color of their skin was unfathomable. John coughed hard on the weed. *Hell they don't even like the color of their own skin, that's why they lay in the sun rotating like a hen on a rotisserie, and why tanning booths have popped up all over the country. What a moral dilemma. On the one hand because of the color of their skin, they subjugate a race; while on the other hand they hate their own color.*

Some people wanted to remove the word *nigga* from the English language, but not John. The name connected him to his ancestors and their bitter, tortuous struggle to survive the machinations of their psychotic masters. It connected him to the screams of slaves being whipped with the lash; to the fear and agony of slave women being raped and abused by their sadistic masters. It connected him to the sound of the dogs bearing down on a terrified, runaway slave. And it connected him to the shackled slaves who survived the miserable inhumane conditions of the long voyage to the Americas. And most of all John felt the pain of the thousands of black Africans who willfully died of hunger or who jumped overboard to their deaths rather than endure the insanity.

The word *nigga* connected John to the suffering and pain his ancestors endured. He felt the word should never be used by white people since it was their ancestors who caused the suffering. On the other hand the word was also a term of endearment to John and many people he knew. He felt it was his right to use the word any way he wanted to. One thing sure in his mind was that the word should never be banned just because blacks and whites want to forget that period.

John headed for the shower...*that's what's wrong with white folk, they want to highlight everybody's else problems while forgetting their own shitty past. Instead of analyzing black folk and all the social ills of our race, and Hispanics, crackers ought to analyze what is in their own demented brains that makes them think they are superior to blacks and other races, and while you're figuring that shit out, look into what evil lay in your forefathers' minds that they had to be so inhumane and cruel...definitely a severe psychosis that exist in clandestine form to this very day. Examine that shit!*

He walked into the shower cursing, and hating bigotry with all his strength.

Chapter 6

"**Y**ou mean to tell me you been banging the pastor?! Didn't want me to touch you...wai, wait till I get my hands on you, hussy." Lenny balled his fist and moved towards his trembling wife, who had just confessed that she had been sleeping with the pastor and wanted a divorce. He had a flashback of himself trembling in relief and disgust after jacking off in the shower because his wife did not want to have sex with him.

Ruth Williams cried for her life. "Lenny, please, I wanted to tell you but Earl said to wait until we were sure..."

"Aaaah...." He screamed and leaped for his wife who slid across the king-sized bed and yelled for help as she barreled out the door.

He rolled his agile frame over the bed to go after his lying, two-timing wife. *Lord I'm no longer a deacon, I'm sending her black ass back to you!*

His cell rang. "What the...hello!" he hollered.

"Damn, Lenny is that you? You all right? This is Cynthia."

Lenny came to a halt. "Yeah? Cynthia..." He looked at his watch; it was after five o'clock. He should have been at the Dobbs Building waiting on the employees. "You're interrupting a murder." He told her the story.

Cynthia said, "It's after five and Clarence has not shown up. You need to get the hell out of there before you go to jail, and come pick me up."

"Okay, I'm on the way."

The lull in the attack gave Ruth a chance to dial 911. They lived in the Worthdale subdivision, an old, but well-kept neighborhood in southeast

Raleigh. When Lenny made the left turn on to Poole Road he saw a police car with flashing lights. He knew where it was headed, and frowned, *Don't worry guys, her sorry ass is still alive.* He was sure Ruth would not press charges, she would not want to draw attention to her affair with the pastor.

⚐

When the waitress at Red Lobster left, John looked at Ashley and Sonja who sat opposite him in the booth. For dessert they ordered a scoop of strawberry ice cream. There was such passion and love in John's eyes, Ashley said, "What?"

John toyed with the many ways he could ask Ashley to be his wife. He would do the beg scene and get on one knee; or just slide the little black box across the table. When Ashley said *What?* he swallowed, lost his words, but heard the ever-present voice in his head say, *Just ask her, dummy, naw, beg her.*

Sonja giggled as if she knew what was coming.

John swallowed again, "Ashley I love, love you so much, I love both of you. Please marry me. Please." He finally slid the black box across the table.

Tears rolled down Ashley's cheeks as she stood up and reached for John.

They embraced and kissed each other passionately.

"Hey, what about me?" Sonja inquired, still giggling.

They laughed, extended their arms and picked Sonja up. For a moment, time stood still. Other diners had been watching the love scene. One couple at a nearby table started a slow clap, and others joined in. The three came back to reality, smiled and sat down.

Now it was Ashley who looked intently at John. "John Colby, I've been with your black…"

"Mom!" Sonja said.

They laughed. "I was not going to say the "a" word my dear. Might as well now though. What took your black ass four years to say those words? You know the answer would have been yes at any time."

"Fear." John let that sank in, toying with his melted ice cream. "I was so afraid marriage might ruin the beautiful relationship we have. I mean, you hear so many couples say we had a great live-in relationship until we got married."

Sonja chimed in, "I won't let you two break up. Besides Colby, you can help Mom give me a sister or brother."

They raised their eyes in wonder and just stared at Sonja. John shook his head at the things that came out of Sonja's pretty little mouth; then thought: *Be mighty nice to get started on that baby tonight.* He shot Ashley one of his horny looks.

She smiled, reached across the table and clasped John's calloused hands. "I need you so much, baby. Let's go home."

"Ooh, yuck," said Sonja. "Yeah, let's go, I got some homework."

As they were leaving, John saw a white man looking at Ashley's well-defined bottom. He dropped his hand just above her rotating buns and whispered, "We got some homework, too."

⅄

Lenny finished taking the load of trash to the dumpster, and went back to the third floor. Someone had to fill in for Clarence. Cynthia was helping him, and almost done with the vacuuming. All he had to do was mop the restrooms. He cursed Clarence and wondered where he was. Then he realized it might be God's will that he was out. If not, Cynthia would not have called him, and he would be in jail for doing something stupid.

He kept asking himself how he could have been so dumb. And how could that crooked, rat of a pastor work with him in deacon meetings and prayer meeting while banging his wife. *Shoot, I bet they were in bed the few times we went for counseling.* He remembered Pastor Earl telling them that sex was not everything, and that they would work through their problem with patience and much prayer.

The problem with their marriage was their backgrounds. Everybody told them that in the beginning and that they better think twice before tying the knot. Lenny barely made it out of high school, while Ruth graduated from Shaw University. That was where Lenny met Ruth, and where he work during the day. He had been there for years and was supervisor of housekeeping.

Ruth Jackson was an only child. Her father was a Baptist minister who graduated from Shaw and warned Ruth that Lenny was a good man, but not right for her. Ruth adored her father; he gave her anything she wanted. She convinced him that Lenny would one day own his own company and that she was in love with him. He reluctantly gave his approval but felt Lenny would always be a person of low degree.

Nevertheless, Lenny and Ruth felt their love for each other would overcome all the odds so they married.

It was not long before they both realized it was a mistake. Lenny did not like that Ruth always had to work late and he would be stuck with cooking or grocery shopping. She did not like the fact that she made almost $10,000 more than Lenny as an English professor at the university. She wanted more income from Lenny and talked him into getting a part-time job. Ruth was ambitious and wanted a new house in north Raleigh or Cary. All her coworkers lived in well-to-do neighborhoods. Lenny did not want to get in more debt and saw nothing wrong with the nice house they had in Worthdale.

Lenny felt he was not getting enough sex, and was irritated that Ruth kept putting off getting pregnant. Ruth had no interest in raising a family with a man she knew was not right for her. She cried to her father how she wished she had listened to him. He suggested she consider divorce on irreconcilable differences.

When Pastor Willie Earl Johnson came to Grove Baptist Church, Ruth lost interest in her husband of low degree. Pastor Johnson was charming, as fine as can be, a great speaker, had money, and was available. He lost his wife in an automobile accident, and had stopped preaching. He told the pastoral search committee during an interview that the Lord ordered him off his sabbatical; that not being married would be a plus because he would be able to fully give himself to the work of the church.

Ruth could feel his desire for her, the way he shook her hand or hugged her, and what his eyes said to her. They arranged to meet, and the tumultuous affair began. There was no way Ruth could handle Pastor Earl and horny Lenny, so she chose Earl and lied to her husband that she was losing interest in sex.

Pastor Earl told Ruth that at some point she would have to tell Lenny she wanted a divorce. He told her not to mention their affair, but it slipped out when she and Lenny were arguing. He had sneered and said she would never find a man to set her on fire like he use to before she became frigid. She told him she already had and Lenny lost it.

Lenny had the restroom door propped open, and was backing out, swinging the mop back and forth. He heard Cynthia say, "You 'bout through, Deacon Williams?"

He turned and looked at Cynthia for a long moment. "Why you looking at me like that? Lenny; don't you try nothing up in here." Her words grinned at him.

Lenny smiled and held out both hands beckoning her. "Come here," he said tenderly. When she took his hands, he pulled her into him and gave her a warm, tight hug. He let every muscle, every nerve, the fiber of his being feel what he had been fantasizing, and for a moment lost himself.

Cynthia was touched by the way he called her, and how he was holding her. She felt him aching for her.

Before he got too carried away, Lenny gently released her, and said: "You know I been with that snooty wench for so long, my nose started going in the wrong direction. So many times I looked at you and acted as though I was better just 'cause I was in the church. At the same time I was wondering what it would be like to have you under the sheets."

"Lord have mercy, Lenny, you know I know that. A woman can tell."

"I ain't finished," he said. "The Lord used you tonight to save my life, and I want a chance to make it up to you. It's going to take a few days for me to sort things out, but when I do, I want to get to know you better." He shrugged his broad shoulders and laughed. "Oh heck, why don't I just say it. I want to be your man."

Cynthia shook her head and smiled. Lenny was making her feel warm and gooey. She knew he was a good man and would be faithful to her, something she longed for but never had. She thought of John Colby and her plans to woo him away from that white woman and have his baby. *Am I being real? Do I chase a fantasy, or give this man standing here, aching for me, a chance?* She thought of her tongue probing John's mouth and how good it felt. But his white girlfriend was as pretty as she could be and deep down, she knew they were inseparable.

She told Lenny, "Let's put up this stuff, I'm through vacuuming. Clarence is doing a sorry ass job. I had to vacuum everything. Do you think it's safe for you to go back home?"

"Definitely not. I saw the cops on the way to the house when I was leaving. After I drop you off, I'll grab the first motel I see and stay there until I can sort things out."

"After what you been through; already worked a full- time and part-time job! What you need is a place you can just go to sleep. You're coming home with me." She saw his eyes light up. "Stop your dirty thinking, deacon. My couch in the living room doubles as a bed."

They walked out of the Dobbs Building talking about what John needed to know about Clarence's cleaning.

⋏

Clarence Farmer had consumed too much wine and had fallen asleep. The same nightmarish dream occurred over and over. They were fishing, having a drinking good time. His cousin looks away and Clarence quickly raises a hammer and crushes his skull. Blood squirts into Clarence's face. His cousin turns his head and starts laughing. Clarence bashes his skull again and again, but his cousin keeps laughing louder and louder with each blow.

Clarence swung at the air and fell off the bed screaming, "Die, mother-fucker, die, you son of a bitch...what the hell?"

The alarm clock was ringing. It was set for four o'clock but it was 10:30 pm. *Damn, I missed work, got to think of a good lie to tell Lenny...hell, I'll call 'em in the morning.* He lit a Kool cigarette and took a long drag, holding the poison smoke in and smacked his lips. His dream made him remember what really happened.

It was the Spring of 1993. Clarence had a cousin named Otis Wooten, whose promising football career in the National Football League ended when he busted his knee in training camp. After that Otis began to drink and would sometime hang out with Clarence, to avoid going home when he was too drunk.

After trying to rape Pauline, Otis did not know what to do or where to go. He knew he had to go on the lam, so withdrew his $8,000 from an account his wife did not know about. Then he went to take a shower at the rooming house where Clarence lived.

⋏

"You did what? You mean to say you tried to rape your own stepdaughter?" Clarence could not believe what he was hearing.

"That ain't all," said Otis, hurriedly tying his shoes. "I slugged her ass and knocked her out."

"Otis, you crazy as hell! You got to get the fuck outta here, you'll have cops all over this place looking for you!"

"Don't you think I know that, fool? I got caught up in a fit of rage, knowing that bitch married me just cause she thought I'd make her rich. And, had me fooled all these years that Pauline was my daughter; and when the little bitch chomped her teeth down on my finger, I lost it."

"Where you gon' go?" ask Clarence wishing he would move a little faster.

"Well that ol' raggedy Chevy downstairs will make it to D.C. I'll go on the lam there and wait till things die down. I'll keep in touch." He finished packing his meager belongings and pulled a fat wad of twenties from his pocket.

Clarence's eyes bulged as Otis counted out $300 and handed it to him. "Damn, man, wha's this for?"

"Just a little somn' for me hanging out here, and if the cops come through, tell them I left in a hurry and mentioned going to Florida. I got your cell number, I'll call you."

They shook hands, and Otis was gone.

⅄

Four months went by with no leads on where Otis Wooten was. When Otis did call Clarence, he suggested Clarence go by Greta's house to look for work and see if he could get any news. Greta vaguely remembered Clarence but saw a chance to find Otis, so he started cutting her grass, edging the walkway and pulling weeds from her flower beds. He had been working for her for two months when Greta decided to make her move.

"You do good work Clarence, why don't you start your own business?" She may have been denied the fabulous life style the NFL would have provided, but she could still use the $150,000 she'd get for a dead Otis Wooten. The cops were not going to spend a lot of time and money looking for Otis, but Greta ached for revenge. When she saw Pauline's swollen face and heard what Otis did to her, she swore she would make him pay.

"Takes money to start your own business, money I ain't got." *Where she coming from, she ain't hardly interested in my financial welfare.*

"Would twenty-five grand help?" Greta was bold and asked the question with a half-smile and half scowl on her face.

Clarence was sleazy and wicked enough to know what she was hinting. They talked more, and finally Clarence said he knew where Otis was and would do it. Twenty-five grand would make all his dreams come true.

Greta laid down the conditions for payment. He was to pull the gold chain with cross from Otis's neck. His grandmother gave it to him and he never removed it. And, he was to take a picture of the dead body. "I want to see that Negro dead," she had said.

Clarence had spent many days and nights thinking about how he would kill Otis. When his plans were formulated, he called Otis and said it seemed like Greta and the cops had lost interest in finding him, and that he could come back and lay low at his place.

The two men loved to fish so Clarence rented a boat for them to go fishing and camp out overnight on Jordan Lake. They bought two bottles of Jack Daniel's black label whiskey to celebrate their reunion. Otis passed out from drinking. Clarence took a gulp of Jack Daniel's, pulled the sharp, steel butcher knife from his bag and plunged it into Otis' chest. Otis sat up straight, a look of horror and pain in his eyes, then he grunted and fell back. Clarence took another drink, and reached for the Polaroid camera Greta gave him and took two pictures of Otis with his eyes still opened. He snatched the gold chain from Otis' neck. Greta did not say what to do with his body, so Clarence dragged Otis to the boat and tied two heavy cinderblocks around his waist to keep him at the bottom of the lake. He then powered the canoe out to the middle of the lake and dumped Otis' body.

The next day he went to collect his money and Greta was satisfied with the proof, even though the picture of Otis made her want to puke. She was furious that he did not leave the body where it could be discovered. It never occurred to her that he would dump the body in the deepest part of Lake

Jordan. How was she going to collect on his insurance policy? Nevertheless, she felt relieved he was gone and paid Clarence.

"I hope we won't be seeing each other again," she said to Clarence.

He assured her he was going to Greenville, North Carolina, where he was raised and start his landscaping business.

Clarence finished his cigarette and thought, *Damn, that was 'bout twenty years ago, and I still ain't got shit.* In just six months all his money was gone; spent on drugs, alcohol and women. He lit another cigarette and complimented himself for at least buying a new car. The 1993 Ford Focus was still running, even though repairs were needed.

Hell, ain't no need to cry over spilt milk, I sho' enjoyed all that pussy, specially them white gals. Tomorrow is payday, I need to go see big Ed.

CHAPTER 7

New York becomes the most populated state in America to pass laws permitting gays to marry. Nation of Islam minister Louis Farrakhan calls President Obama a murderer and assassin. Flooding continues throughout the Midwest while the worst fires in Arizona continue to eat up thousands of acres. Democrats and Republicans fight over a $14.3 trillion federal debt ceiling. Sarah Palin is on her way to Iowa for a showing of a new documentary about herself.

Whoa, is this the same woman who just four years ago during the '08 campaign could not tell Katie Couric what magazines she read? John scrolled the news headlines on Google and AOL. Bristol Palin gets drunk by Levi, loses her virginity and gets pregnant, then writes a tell-all book, and starts making the rounds on FOX, ABC and other talk shows promoting it. No matter what one thought of the Palins, you had to give them an "A" for being masters of the opportunistic moment. Hardly anyone outside of Alaska knew who the Palins were before Senator John McCain picked Sarah Palin to run as vice-president.

John Colby recalled the events leading to his opportunistic moment. In high school he was quiet, a loner who had few friends. When he graduated most of his classmates went off to college or entered a trade school. He had no idea what he wanted to do, so he went to Brooklyn, New York, with two of his buddies. His mother was worried about him because he was the youngest one in the family and lacked motivation. He had been living in a fantasy where he never grew up. Before he left, she put her arms around him and prayed God would protect him. She told him to never forget that he had a home.

While in New York he worked for a printing firm, packing orders and making deliveries all over Manhattan. The printing shop's restroom was deplorable. The urinals had long, yellow urine stains, and the commodes had black rings. The smell of urine and built up germs over the years was disgusting and unhealthy.

One day when activities in the shop were slow, he spent four hours cleaning the male and female restroom. He even got a ladder and cleaned the filthy light lens cover. When he finished, the restrooms were sparkling and had a clean smell. The boss and other employees were flabbergasted. He was rewarded with a dollar-an-hour increase.

He loved the praise and admiration coming from his co-workers. However, it was all for naught. His mother called and said he had been drafted into the Army. His boss pleaded with him to come back after his two-year stint.

He promised he would, knowing it was a lie.

When John finished his basic training at Fort Benning, Georgia, he was shipped to Ft. Eustis, Virginia, and took an eight-week course to be a parts supply specialist in the transportation department.

He was now ready to serve and as the war was drawing to a close he was shipped to Vietnam. When he got there, his division did not need a parts supply specialist so he was trained to drive a tractor and trailer delivering supplies from Qui Nhon Valley to Anke and Pleiku in the mountains. Potent marijuana was plentiful and he smoked every chance he got. What impressed the quiet, country boy from Goldsboro was the poverty and lack of food for the Vietnamese people. On the long convoys to the mountains hundreds of men, women, and children lined the village streets, raising their hands begging for food. If you threw a case of C-rations from the truck, they would run for it like chickens and fight for it as though it was gold.

His two years in the Army was a blur, and when it ended he wasn't any closer at knowing what he wanted to do than when he was drafted.

His siblings had all moved to Philadelphia, with the exception of a sister who married a career soldier in the Army.

The post office was a haven for veterans so he got a job at the 30th and Market Street station in Philadelphia. He had no life, so the graveyard shift of 10:00 pm to 6:00 am was perfect. He stayed at the post office for ten years making good money and yet he was not happy with what he was doing. The post office routine had become monotonous, and unfulfilling. His fantasies had always been about successful people who owned things, so one day he would have to own a business.

As the '70s drew to a close, the Colby family was shocked into the hard, cold realities of life. Alex, one of his brothers, was gay. He invited the wrong people into his apartment. According to police, a vicious fight occurred and Alex was stabbed twice in the neck and bled to death.

Six months later a sense of urgency came over John to settle down and get married. He was tired of being alone. His oldest brother Marvin was a minister and John had always hoped to find a Christian woman like his mother, so he started going to Marvin's church, Mt. Pisgah Holy Church in north Philly. He began dating a girl name Sophia Brunson for three months. They got married.

It was the worst decision he ever made. They argued and fought all the time. He could not believe how sweet she acted in church, and how loving she was on dates. She was so holy she wouldn't have sex with John until they got married. Her father was a henpecked man and she wanted John to be the same. She wanted to be the boss, telling him what he should do and what he could not do. One day they were at the top of the stairs arguing and John was so mad, he picked her up suddenly and swung her in the air as if he was going to throw her to the bottom of the stairway. Sophia screamed and John put her down, and stormed out of the house.

When he came back that evening, he went to the front door and realized his house keys were inside. He rang the doorbell but Sophia would not let him in. It was good he kept a spare key under a mat at the back door. They lived in the middle of a row-home complex, so he had to go around the block and down a long alley way to get to the back of his house.

The police arrived and asked him what he was doing. John gave them a nasty look and told them he was going inside his house. Sophia then opened the door and asked the police to come in and speak to her mother on the telephone. They sensed a bad argument was going on and pleasantly asked John to wait outside for a moment.

A metamorphosis took place in the policemen in just a few moments on the telephone with Sophia's mother. They came out completely belligerent. One of them angrily twisted his grip on his club as if itching to use it on John's head. John knew if he argued they would be happy to beat him up. They demanded he leave.

He went into the first bar he saw on Cheltenham Avenue, a few blocks from his house and ordered a double shot of brandy on the rocks. His brothers and sisters always teased him about fantasizing too much. He now realized how right they were. But how could you go wrong marrying a good Christian church girl? That was the reason he started going to church again. He cursed Sophia and all of her hypocrite family and ordered another drink.

All of a sudden he heard his mother's words: *Never forget that you have a home.* He stopped paying the mortgage and let the house go into foreclosure. He packed his bags and headed to Interstate 95 south towards Goldsboro.

After being home a few months he filed for divorce citing irreconcilable differences. He wanted to say that Sophia was a bitch.

John remembered how glad he was to be back home with his mother who was now seventy-five years old. His father died from complications of diabetes and high blood pressure nine months after his brother Alex was murdered. John was also happy that a good, widowed friend of his mother had come to live with her.

John saved $10,000 while he was at the post office, and decided to move to Raleigh, the capital city of North Carolina. After living in New York and Philadelphia, Goldsboro was just too small and quiet. Before he left his mother prayed for him again and told him that soon he would have more than he could handle. He asked her what she meant; she laughed and said God did not tell her that part.

He recalled reading somewhere that most people hate their jobs, and that people who made their living doing what they love enjoyed life more. John loved to clean and learned how to use a buffer in the Army. He did not know anything about the janitorial industry but figured the best way to learn was go work for a cleaning company.

He found a one-bedroom apartment near North Carolina State University, and opened the telephone book to janitorial companies and began making calls. He would introduce himself, lie about his experience and ask if they had any openings. On the seventh call, Triangle Cleaning Service said they had an opening for a night supervisor. He applied and was hired. His duties were to maintain the floors in the Cameron Brown building on Six Forks Road, which had seven floors. All the floors except the basement and lobby were carpeted. The entrance to the lobby was marble and the rest were tile. Also part of his job was to supervise the seven other housekeepers and make sure they had supplies. He inspected their floors twice a week.

Two of the black male housekeepers resented John because they were passed over for the job. When he inspected their floor, their cleaning was not good, so he had a meeting with them. John was blunt and to the point, looking hard into their mean eyes. He told them he knew of their resentment to him because they were passed over for the job; and that it was a shame that there were some blacks who have the *Yes sir boss* attitude when a white person is in charge; and *Kiss my black ass* when a black person is in charge. He remembered saying, "I'm sure you know what category I put you in; some call it the Uncle Tom syndrome. My responsibility is to the clients in this building and to the people who pay us. It's Tuesday; by Thursday if your floors are not up to par, I will have to get rid of you. It would be nice if we could work together, but it's your call."

The two men who were older than John still looked mean and walked away poking their lips further into the air. When Thursday came, their floor looked better than John had expected.

A year passed, and then John's opportunistic moment occurred. The owner of Triangle Cleaning Service was so impressed with John's work and his management of the account that he asked John if he would like to become area manager. He would have multiple buildings to attend to, and be authorized to hire supervisors, perform inspections, meet with clients, order supplies and collect timecards in each building. His salary would go from $19,000 to $22,000 a year.

John accepted the challenge and loved the idea of going to work in nice clothes. This was the opportunity that helped him to learn how to run a janitorial company. He worked for Triangle Cleaning Service for one more year, and then decided it was time to see what he could do on his own. He bid on a small, 30,000-square-foot property belonging to the State of North Carolina and was awarded the contract. Since that time, he had been so successful bidding on state properties that he did not have time to look for commercial accounts. He remembered again his mother's words: God said you will soon have more than you can handle.

John leaned back from the computer, removed his reading glasses and thought about what he should do for the day. Ashley took Sonja to her mother's house in Cary where they would be for most of the weekend, making wedding plans. Clara Whitfield was excited for Ashley. She had never seen her daughter so happy. At first she was concerned about John's age. When she met him in 2006 he was fifty years old, even though he didn't look a day over thirty-five. Ashley was only thirty at the time but told her mother not to worry; she preferred older men.

John's cell phone rang. "Hello." It was Lenny. He told John about what happened with his wife and that he was staying with Cynthia until he could sort things out. John smiled. "You got yourself a lot of woman, just what you need."

Lenny chuckled, and then told him about Clarence, that he missed work and did not call; and that he was doing a sorry job on his floor.

"Did he call you this morning?" John asked.

"Yeah, said his alarm clock didn't go off and he overslept. He swore he was telling the truth and that he would definitely be in tonight."

"I should fire that sorry rascal, but we'll give him one more chance. I'll be in tonight and talk to him."

⋏

Frederick Parsons was talking on the phone to his lawyer. "Harold, I've been waiting to hear from you. Have you got the papers ready?"

Harold Diggs was the Parsons' family lawyer for the last thirty years. He cautioned Fred that sole custody of a child meant he wanted exclusive legal and physical custody rights over Sonja; and that the court rarely grants sole custody unless a parent may be deemed unfit because of drug or alcohol abuse, has a history of violence or mental instability, or that the child would be in a dangerous environment or situation.

"Yeah, Fred the papers are ready, I just need for you to stop by and sign them. Again, as your lawyer and friend of the family, this lawsuit will not be easy. The court frowns upon parties that attempt to utilize child custody arrangements as a means of retaliation, or because of vindictive feelings towards the other parent."

Frederick Parsons became irritable. "Vindictive, retaliation! Harold, you just handle the paperwork, I know some people down at the Wake County Courthouse. I'm getting my daughter back because I can provide a better life for her. It's Friday, and I'm tied up. I'll see you Monday morning."

Listen to this asshole, more pompous than his father was. Probably jealous and mad he let that fine ass babe get away from him. And what really gets him is she moved in with a black man. What a dunce. "Okay, Fred, see you then."

꙳

John spent the rest of the day working in the yard. First he gathered vegetables from his garden. He always planted more tomatoes, cucumbers, okra and eggplant than the three of them could ever eat. Each year he took buckets of vegetables to the homeless shelter on Hargett Street in Raleigh. His mother had told him that he was like his grandfather who loved to see things grow. After the vegetables, he checked the oil on his riding mower and began cutting the grass. He loved caring for his two-acre lot. What he hated were the biting flies that took great pleasure in worrying the hell out of him. He wondered why the ornery pests had to buzz all around your head and into your face before biting you. What John could not cut with the lawnmower, he got with the weed-eater. Ashley's flower garden was overtaken with weeds so he spent time pulling them up.

He wondered why the tabulations for the Albemarle Building had not been posted on the Internet. On the date the bids were due, they would be publicly opened, and a day or two later, the prices that companies bid would be posted on the Internet. He would log on again before he went downtown to see if they had been posted.

Like the rest of the states across the country, North Carolina was dealing with a budget deficit. The total budget deficit of all the states was $125 billion. The State of North Carolina's budget deficit was $3.7 billion. Many people in John's buildings were being laid off. Social programs for the poor were being cut, or closed down, and everybody was worried.

The bidding process had stopped because the purchasing department had enough problems trying to find money to keep its current contracts in force. An exception had been made for the Albemarle Building because it was so dirty and had too many complaints. John figured that most of the contractors would be bidding $12,000 and higher, so to make sure he got it, his bid was $11,000.

He finished the yard and put up his tools and equipment. During the time in the yard a battle had been going on in his mind. The one that took place every time he thought about some weed, and whether or not to go see Big Ed. He would have tonight and all day Saturday to himself and lied again that this time would be the end. The same fear and guilt feelings came over him; he could lose his business. But each time he went to buy some weed it was a breeze. He would go in, joke with Big Ed for a minute and was gone.

This time would be no different; at least that's what he told himself.

It was close to four o'clock so John took a shower and got dressed. He logged on to the North Carolina website and typed in the bid number. Sure enough it was as he thought it would be. He was the low bid at $11,000. *Yes! Wait till I call Ashley. Just what we need.*

John usually went to get his weed at night under the cover of darkness. He was excited about the contract and decided to go before he went to work. Besides, it was Friday and traffic around Big Ed's house would be too busy on a Friday night. Instead of taking his truck he drove his BMW.

Big Ed lived in an old red brick house on Tarboro Road not far from Bojangles on Newbern Ave. Also on the same corner was the Department of Motor Vehicles which had a big parking lot. An unmarked police car sat on the lot with a few other vehicles. The two officers were watching Big

Ed's house. The neighbors had been complaining to police that they thought drugs were being sold. The officers had seen a few people come and go but decided to do nothing. Then John pulled up in his BMW. They called for backup and told them to wait for their signal before they bust in on Big Ed.

"Wonder who this hot shot is," Sergeant Posey said to his partner, Croop, and did not wait for an answer. "We're gonna tail his ass and catch him with the goods, or at least see who he is. At the same time we'll give the orders for the guys to bust in on Mr. Ed."

Everybody called Edward Manor Big Ed because he was big as hell. He weighed 300 pounds and was more than six feet tall. He talked as though his tongue was too big for his mouth. He was easy going, but John noticed he looked a little worried today.

"Hey John, wha's up, come on in the house." He let John pass and looked down the street.

"What is going on?" John asked with a little shake in his voice.

"Right after I got your call, I got a tip from one of my friends who's a cop. Said they may be watching and that a bust might go down any time."

"Oh shit. I need to get the hell out of here."

Big Ed laughed at how nervous John became. "Here is your ounce. I already had my stash taken out of here. They'll probably wait until tonight."

John gave him $125 and hurriedly walked to his car. *Damn, I must be a junkie, I should've left this shit and just walked out.*

He took Hargett Street to go towards the Dobbs Building. When he made the left off Tarboro to Hargett he saw a blue, official-looking car pull out of the DMV parking lot.

Oh shit, that's the man, what the hell should I do?

Sarge gave the command for the backup to go in on big Ed. John Colby determined he had to get away if they came after him; he had too much to lose. He thought his heart would break out of his chest, and he began sweating even though the A/C was on.

"Sarge, he's seen us! He's gonna make a run for it."

Sgt. Posey told Croop to take off.

John was surprised his brain started working. The New Education Building had a big loading dock gate that was about thirty feet from the street and once a truck had begun backing down the hill towards the loading dock, it was not visible from the street because of a concrete wall. Every day at 4:00 pm shipping and receiving closed down and the gate was closed. It was his only hope.

He made a right turn onto Person Street and sped two blocks to Lane Street.

The blue lights were closing in on him. He could not let them see him turn into the blind driveway or he would be toast, burnt toast. His business, his future marriage to the woman he adored, the disgrace among his peers, all passed before him. He pressed as hard as he could on the gas pedal. He made the green light at Wilmington Street and pulled into the driveway all the way to the metal gate.

Soon after, the flashing blue lights went flying by.

As the contractor for the New Education Building, John was authorized to have the key to the gate. He raised it and quickly drove his car inside and closed the gate. He looked at his watch. It was 5:15 pm; all his employees would be on their floors. He caught the elevators at the south end of the building and went to the second floor. Looking out the window at Wilmington and Lane Streets, he saw a blue patrol car cruising by. Ten minutes later he saw it again.

The Dobbs, New Education, Revenue and Archdale Buildings could all be accessed from the underground parking lot. You could walk about one and half blocks from the New Education to the Dobbs without going outside. John decided to lay low and walked to the Dobbs Building.

Meanwhile Posey and his partner went back to Big Ed's house while the rookie patrolmen looked for the BMW. They did not find any drugs at Big Ed's house. He told the cops he stopped dealing, that it was too dangerous. When they asked him about the person in the BMW, Big Ed said that all he knew was that his name was Carl, and that he told Carl the same thing, that he had stop dealing.

Sergeant Harold Posey was an imposing man. He was over six feet tall and had black, curly hair that was graying around the sideburns. His dark blue eyes and aquiline nose were prominent on his tanned face. He had been on the force for twenty-five years and could retire whenever he chose.

He thought to himself, *Another waste of tax payer money. The government and the public would be better served if I had my guys looking for drunk drivers; people who kill and maim others.*

As they walked back to the car Sgt. Posey growled, "We been had."

CHAPTER 8

From Grandfather Mountain to Bald Head Island on the coast a severe drought plagued North Carolina and its neighboring states. The area had two mild winters in a row, and the spring rains were too infrequent to make up for the loss. Farmers and other industries that rely on rain were tired of looking at Carolina blue skies. They wanted dark angry clouds that would open up and soak the parched earth from Virginia to Florida. Some people were hoping for a hurricane that would solve the drought.

Greta Wooten sat in her spacious dining room sipping coffee. She was waiting for Pauline to wake up. They spent Friday evening shopping, dining out and having a lot of mother-daughter fun.

She opened the sliding glass door hoping for a cool morning breeze to blow through the house. Cameron Village had grown by leaps and bounds since she and Otis had purchased their two story, four-bedroom house back in the '70s. From Wade Avenue to Clark Street, office buildings, condominiums and a bank had sprung up on Oberlin Road. The Cameron Village Library had been remodeled from its small-city look to a much larger two-story edifice with more computers, meeting rooms and a larger space for children's activities.

Everything Greta owned would soon be going to Pauline if her cancer got worse. She thought of the relatives the deadly disease had claimed. The radiation treatments, the bald head, the loss of weight, no energy. She became depressed. Tearfully she thought, *Damn, why me, and at this time. Just when Pauline is falling in love with a handsome guy who has lots of potential. I won't even be here to play with my grandchildren.*

She heard Pauline stirring upstairs and pulled herself together. When something bad happened to Greta she would ask *Why me* only to have guilt well up in her for what she had done to Otis. She blew her nose. *I didn't kill him, I just paid someone, and shit, he deserved to die. Bastard tried to rape his own daughter.*

That was not true either, from a biological standpoint. At least Pauline knew the truth. After Otis tried to rape her, Greta saw no need to hide it. Greta and James Winton, Pauline's real father, had stopped seeing each other a long time ago, but the three of them still had a good relationship. She was glad James had told his wife about Pauline so if she did die of cancer, Pauline would know where her real father was.

"Mom, where are you?" Pauline yawned at the top of the stairs.

"I'm in the dining room, baby; come on down, I'll pour you some coffee."

Pauline came into the dining room smiling, wearing silk pajamas. She gave her mother a big hug. "How long have you been up? You haven't been down here worrying your pretty little head off, have you?" She hoped she sounded cheery. She had been upstairs worrying. It seemed cancer was a sure death sentence, even if the disease was caught early. You might be fine for a time, but eventually you lost the battle.

The process was emotionally draining. At first you tried to be positive, with *We will get through this.* Once the treatments start, the pain of it all sinks in. The forced smiles, statements of *It could be worse*, then watching it get worse. All the trips back and forth to the clinic, coupled with the ultimate fact that the enormous amount of pain and suffering would be in vain.

Greta looked at Pauline and lost her composure…she began crying. Pauline held her mother and prayed. *God, please help me be strong for both of us.*

Greta kept up her crying for ten minutes, asking *Why me*, and *My God, haven't we had enough cancer in this family?* She loosened her grip, and Pauline guided her to a chair. Greta reached in her pocket for her napkin and blew her nose again. "Okay," she said calming down. That's over with. I'm just so mad at this, and there is nothing I can do. I'm sorry baby, what did you ask me? Oh, how long I been up. I…"

"Mom, if we are going to get through this, let's make a deal. We don't apologize for any of our reactions to this thing. Okay?" She eyed her mother and waited for a response.

"Okay, baby, I promise. Anyway it ain't like I'm ready to drop. I just hate to have to go through all this."

"I know, Mom." Pauline sat near her mother and sipped her coffee. "Mom, let's be calm about this, what if the doctor suggests a double mastectomy, no breasts?"

Greta gasped. "What? Hell, if I want to live, guess I'd just have to do it."

"Of course you'd do it, especially if it will give you a chance to see a grandchild."

"My goodness girl, are you pregnant? Has Tony asked you to marry him? I can't…"

"Mom, Mom, calm down. No to both your questions. I've just been reading that many women who have a double mastectomy live healthy lives."

Like a little kid shaking off a bad taste, Greta said, "Breastless. Yuk."

They looked at each other and laughed. Pauline saw the TV remote on the dining table. "What's the weather suppose to be today?"

"Probably the same way it's been all spring and summer, hot and dry. You want some breakfast, baby?"

"Yes, Mama, I would indeed. How 'bout some of your country ham with red-eye gravy over some grits and scrambled eggs." Pauline's mouth watered.

Greta chuckled. "And would you like toast or biscuits with that, your grace?"

"Biscuits, my dear, and don't forget the peach preserves, please."

A special report was being broadcast from Jordan Lake. "Mom, look at this."

The news camera panned Jordan Lake showing the viewers how low the level of water was. The reporter was saying: "Police responded to the call of some boys who played in the shallow water on the banks of the Jordan Lake. One of the boys felt a chain under his foot, and when they pulled on the chain, they discovered a human skeleton wedged between two cinder blocks."

The camera then panned a shot of the police cars, ambulance and other news media. "I spoke with Sgt. Posey of the Raleigh police department a little while ago and this is what he had to say.

A tall handsome white man filled the screen. The reporter asked, "Sgt. Posey, what can you tell us about this gruesome discovery?"

"Well, Kelly, you guys know about as much as we do right now. It definitely looks suspicious, and I'd say it's probably a homicide. We'll know a lot more once the medical examiner does his thing and we investigate this further."

The young reporter looked into the camera and said, "This is Kelly Rogers for WRAL News reporting from Jordan Lake where the skeletal remains found here suggest foul play."

The ghastly look of Otis Wooten's eyes, an image that lived in Greta's brain, flashed before her.

"Oh," Pauline said disappointedly, "I thought it was a real breaking story. Whoever that person was, has been dead for a long time." She followed her mother into the kitchen. She wanted to keep the mood away from talk of cancer.

"Mom, me and Tony getting serious. He wants to take me to New York to meet his mother, and other relatives."

"I was wondering when you were going to tell me. You've been happy as a lark, and there's a certain glow about you. He must be pretty damn good in the bed, huh?" She laughed.

"Mom!" Pauline was surprised her mother was so candid. She thought of her body wrapped around Tony, his smell, his head between her legs. "Yes, Mama, damn good."

Their laughter filled the house and rode the warm breeze onto Woodburn Road.

⅄

Sunday evening arrived. Clara Whitfield came home with Ashley and Sonja. John greeted them in the driveway and gave Ashley a passionate kiss.

"Oh please, do you guys have to kiss like that?" asked Sonja.

Sonja said the most hilarious things. John picked her up and gave her a long kiss on the cheek. He warmly hugged his future mother-in-law, and they all went into the house.

"I see you cut the grass and cleaned the flower bed. Was hoping you would do that. What else you been doing?" Ashley wanted to know.

He thought about his close call with the police. He had waited until midnight before sneaking his car out of the New Education Building and took the fastest route home down Capital Boulevard to 440 east. John realized how close he came to losing everything he worked so hard for. When he got home, he was still so scared someone was watching him he left the ounce of weed under the car seat.

He replied, "Ain't did much more than that, other than thinking about the good chances I got to get the Albemarle Building."

Sonja went to her room and the three of them went to the family room and sat on the huge sofa that circled half the room.

"Can I get you something to drink mom?" John asked Clara.

"Mom? I got to get use to an ol' man calling me mom. Yes, bring me a glass of wine, son."

John let go a hearty laugh. "You want some, honey?"

Ashley got up. "No, I think I'll take a quick shower. Talk to mom, she'll fill you in on what we've been planning."

John poured himself a glass of wine and sat down with Clara. He had told her before how much he loved Ashley and Sonja but wanted to do so again. "You know how much I love your daughter and Sonja. They mean so much to me and they are all I have. I just want to reassure you of my commitment to them and to you."

"I know you do, John. Both of them always tell me how special you are, so you have my blessings. Now, as for the wedding, we wanted something small with a few of our relatives and friends, and some of your friends and family."

"Well, I have very few friends, so it will be mostly my brothers and two sisters."

"As for the date, we wanted to do it on November 1st, that's a Saturday. Will that work for you?" She asked John.

"Listen, whatever you two decide will be fine with me."

They talked about making the wedding informal; having it catered, and other details that John did not care about. He just wanted Ashley to become Mrs. Colby. When they finished, Clara said she was going to spend the rest of the night with Sonja.

When John came into their bedroom, Ashley was sitting on a chair in front of a mirror brushing her hair. She was naked. They made love all night in every position imaginable.

Time was going by so fast. Pauline had just spent the weekend bonding with her mother and now it was the middle of the week. They decided that surgery was best and Greta would discuss it further with the doctor on Friday. Pauline was taking her so they could talk to the doctor together.

Pauline prepared to meet with her redneck boss and his ass-kissing building manager, Chuck Davis, about awarding the Albemarle Building contract. Colby Cleaning Service was the low bid, and the two of them would no doubt want to award the contract to him. In the past she would argue against awarding anything to John Colby. She would remind them how reckless his company was; the violations of propane tank storage; his slow response to correct problems on his inspection reports. Still at the end of the day she knew they would send the purchasing department a recommendation to award him the contract. So this time she would surprise them.

Man somebody ought to get on her big black ass and ride the evil out of that nigga. After Pauline overheard Colby make that statement to a group of other black contractors, and the hardy laughter of the men, she bristled and despised him ever since. It also made her mad that he acted as if her staff had no clue of how to keep state buildings clean.

His black ass loves white women….well guess I can't say nothing about that since I'm falling in love with a white man. That was the only thing they had in common, but was hardly enough to remove Pauline's disgust for him. She felt the only way to humble his proud ass was to cancel a big contract and show him who the boss was. She thought she had him when her inspector found propane tanks in the Dobbs Building. It never occurred to her or Sam Boswell that John would claim that the tanks were empty; and they had no way of proving he was lying since Sam did not check the tanks.

She chuckled that all Sam wanted was a promotion to head inspector and a bigger office. *Lazy ass state employees. If the taxpaying citizens who pay our salaries knew how lazy we all are, and that state government could be run with half the work force, they would throw us to the curb.*

Pauline pushed herself from her desk and was about to go to the meeting when the phone rang. "Hello, Pauline Wooten, may I help you?"

The girlish male voice said, "Hey girlfriend my food ain't good enough for you no more. What's been happening?"

Pauline laughed, "Hey Ralph, I been kinda busy."

Ralph Simpson was in charge of the cafeteria in the Department of Administration Building. He was an excellent cook and Pauline loved to eat there. Once they got to know each other, he made Pauline feel sorry for him with a sob story about his sick mother who had cancer. He asked her for a hundred-dollar loan; and as appreciation Pauline hardly ever paid for her food.

Ralph Simpson was too fat for his short frame. He was gay and did not try to hide it. His boyfriend was the housekeeper who overheard Tony Bizaro make a bet with his boss that he could get in Pauline's drawers on the first date.

Ralph said in his girlish voice, "Busy? Let me see, has it had anything to do with lover boy Tony Bizaro?" The grin in his voice was tinged with bitterness.

What is this nosey faggot hinting at? "I see news travels fast, and yes that has something to do with it. I was just on my way to a meeting, Ralph. What are you cooking for lunch?" *Might as well eat me a good lunch and go upstairs and see my man.*

"Come on over here and get some of these good fried pork chops and let me tell you some stuff I heard."

Pauline hoped he was not going to ask her for a loan. "Okay, see you around one o'clock, after some of the lunch crowd has died down."

The door to the conference room was opened. "Come on in," her boss Ronald Height said.

She smiled at both of them. *A white bigot with his black dummy.* The thought lightened her mood. Soon Ron would be drinking himself to death in retirement, and their bosses on the fifth floor of the Administration Building would see the error of Chuck Davis as Facility Management director if he got the promotion. Chuck had more experience in how to clean a building. He rose through the ranks, so he knew about floor care, and restroom cleaning. He knew about chemicals and different types of janitorial equipment.

But that was all he knew, just one aspect of maintaining the ninety buildings under Facility Management's care. Pauline had a degree in business management from North Carolina Central University. And though there were many aspects of maintaining a property, from landscaping, plumbing, to repairs and construction, she had what Chuck lacked: administrative and people skills needed to run such a department. She sat down opposite Chuck Davis.

Ronald Height began every meeting the same way: State the facts or problems of a situation and tell everyone how he thought it should be handled. Rarely did anyone disagree with him until Pauline came on the scene. He had a laugh of his own. *These two shit-heads got the nerve to think one of them is going to get my recommendation to be head of Facility Management.* He laughed so hard inside he could hardly keep a straight face.

"Well you guys know we need to decide who we want in the Albemarle Building. Pauline, I know how you feel about Colby Cleaning Service. But he is low bid and Chuck and I agree we send purchasing his name." As soon as he said this, his mouth went into a slight frown for what he knew was to come, a long dissertation on why that was the wrong decision.

"I agree Ron. I…"

"What?" Chuck was stunned and Ron raised his eyebrow in pleasant surprise.

Pauline relaxed them further. "I was going to say that John Colby and I have had our differences but he is the best company for the job."

From that point on the meeting went smooth, at least for Pauline. She then brought up an old idea her boss had mentioned over a year ago about buying uniforms for the inspectors. She handed them a picture of a person dressed in a blue shirt with logo, and nice brown khaki pants, and said the uniforms would make the inspectors more recognizable to the thousands of state employees they saw while inspecting buildings. The inspectors would rebel, claiming uniforms were beneath the position of inspector, but she was confident she could get them to accept it.

Pauline decided it was time to get on the right side of Ronald Height. Unlike Chuck, who believed ass-kissing was what got promotions, she believed proficiency was the way. She was quite aware that Ron might not recommend either one of them, but at least before he retired she would give him a new look.

The three of them discussed other issues. The state of North Carolina used prison labor to do a lot of service work, like landscaping, moving and housekeeping. It was a work release program under state supervision. At the end of the day the inmates were loaded in vans and taken back to prison. One of the problems was their appearance. They wore green uniforms, with the shirt hanging outside their pants or sometimes no shirt at all, only the white t-shirt. They looked sloppy most of the time.

Chuck said, "We need to send the prison a note about making the people they send us look neat all day."

Ron smiled, "You are right about that; on the other hand the staff at the prison is complaining about our lack of supervision. One of their inmates contracted a venereal disease. Somebody in our department must have used one of the trucks to sneak away an inmate to let him have a ride in the hay."

He looked at Pauline. "'Scuse me Pauline, but evidently the poor bloke got burned."

They all laughed for a moment.

Pauline was glad Chuck brought up the appearance of the prisoners. "What you said from the beginning, Ron, still rings true. We need two state workers at all times to be with these people. I've seen too many of them come to work with clear eyes and leave with blood-red eyes."

Chuck saw his boss admiring Pauline and wanted some glory. "I'll research some other work release programs that other states use and see how they deal with these kinds of problems."

Pauline said, "I've already done that Chuck." She passed them two neatly typed folders with the heading typed in bold capital letters that read: *Security for Inmate Labor.*

"Ron, when you get a chance take a look at this. You'll be pleased to find that many of your suggestions in the past are in this report. Especially the one about having two people at all times to supervise the inmates."

"Well, Miss Wooten, you are on the ball this morning. If this is the new you I want more. How 'bout you Chuck?"

Chuck's jaw was busy grinding teeth. "Yes sir, boss, she sure is." He looked at his watch. "Well if we done I got to meet with some landscapers." He said to himself. *Ain't got to meet with no damn body but girlfriend trying to make me look bad. I'm sick of this shit.*

After Chuck left, Pauline told her boss that she had a way the state could save thousands of dollars by cutting waste and putting some of the services like painting out for bid. Ron was genuinely impressed.

While Pauline talked to her boss she noticed his eyes darting back and forth to her cleavage. She wore the two piece business suit she bought while shopping with her mother. It was light brown and hugged all the right places. Her mother picked out a gold silk blouse to wear under the coat so her cleavage would not show too much, but it did not work, because Pauline was heavily endowed. When her mother saw her in the suit she said that Tony ought to rise up some when he saw her.

She now wondered if Ron was rising up. She felt sorry for him. His wife had been sick for years with diabetes and high blood pressure. His sex life was probably like hers use to be, null and void. She wondered; then shook herself, and thought. *Damn girl, do you want the job that bad?*

⚔

Pauline was about to enter the serving line at the cafeteria in the Administration Building and heard her name. Ralph was coming out of the nearby restroom. "Hey girlfriend, let's go to one of the tables, I'll have one of the girls bring you what you want."

Ralph was like a gossipy old lady who could not wait to let somebody know what they heard. "Everybody been talking about you and Mr. Loverboy."

Pauline rolled her eyes to the ceiling and smiled. "We have not tried to hide our attraction for each other, and you know if one state worker know your business all state workers know. Ralph I love your food, but is this what you had to tell me?"

"No, girlfriend. You know me and you go way back and I… ah it ain't really none of my business but I just don't want to see you get hurt by that white man."

Pauline's appetite gave way to frustration. "Can you tell me where this is going? I'm a black woman and he's a white man, and frankly I love him. If that's a problem for folks, I don't care."

Ralph said defiantly, "Well, as a friend I just thought you ought to know he made a bet with his boss that he could get your drawers off on the first date."

Pauline was stunned. It felt like someone had slapped her in the mouth and she was trying to figure out why.

"Before you ask how I know, a friend of mine who works in housekeeping was cleaning the restroom and overheard Tony make a bet with his boss that he could get you in bed on the first date. You know his boss because the guy said you wouldn't even give him a chance."

Pauline's shock gave way to embarrassed anger as she wondered how many people knew he scored on the first date. Tony's boss had lusted after her the first day she saw him at a meeting years back, but she felt nothing for him. He was as arrogant as if he was God's gift to woman. They went out once and that was it. *His arrogant ass is probably saying, nigga wouldn't give a brother a chance, and now lets a cracker get in her drawers on the first date.*

She looked at Ralph, who by the smirk on his face was obviously amused. She thought about slapping him just for the hell of it. She regained her composure. "We've been dating for some time Ralph, why are you telling this to me now?"

Ralph's mother always told him that when he lied he stuttered and his voice got even lighter. "I, ah, well, well I hadn't seen you for a long time, and like, like I said just didn't want to, to see you you git hurt."

⋏

The real reason Ralph told Pauline about the bet was his anger after exchanging words with Tony in the men's restroom. They were both washing their hands.

"Pauline Wooten is a fine black woman and a dear friend. I hope she won't become another notch on your gun, know what I mean?" That's what Ralph had said to him.

Tony Bizaro reached for the hand towels. "You know what, sissy; you need to mind your own fucking business."

Ralph was livid and vowed to get even. He thought it would be nice if he could break up their relationship.

⋏

Pauline, don't be mad at me…" He paused searching for his humble, *I need some love* look. He looked down at the table. "I shoulda kept my, my big mouth shut."

Pauline hardly heard what Ralph said. *Is Tony playing a game with me? Naw, can't be, he said he loved me.* She heard herself tell Ralph he did the right thing and left.

A minute later she found herself exiting the elevator on the 4th floor. The purchasing department occupied the entire floor, buying goods and services for the lowest possible price. She walked towards Tony's office. *Be cool girl, don't make no scene, just ask him is it true.* She had no idea how she would react if he said yes.

Tony's office was on the Lane Street side of the building looking out to the parking lot. He kept his door slightly closed to avoid the distractions of people walking up and down the hallway. Pauline took an angry breath and opened the door.

"Hey baby, what you doing in this neck of the woods," he said. Tony really loved Pauline and knew something was wrong. He got up from his desk, came to her and said, "Sit down, what's wrong, who made you so angry?"

In all the offices there were either two chairs or a sofa for visitors. They sat in the two chairs and Pauline looked deep into Tony's blue eyes. "How much, ah, is it true you made a bet that you could get me in bed on the first date?"

Tony's mouth dropped open into a question but nothing came out. *How the hell did she find out about that? I can't lie to her, she is so sensitive.* "Pauline, where in the world did you hear something like that?"

She knew by the way he avoided the question that it was true. They had become close and knew each other. After the experience with her stepfather, and the few strained relationships with other men that went nowhere, she thought she would never fall in love. Along came Tony Bizaro, saying the right things, touching the right places. He made her scream in bed, waking up pleasure points all over her body. She wanted to slap his handsome face.

"You heard me Tony, did you make a bet that you could get my drawers off on the first date? And not only did I hear you made a bet, it had to be with that pompous ass boss of yours, whom you know I don't like." Tears formed in her eyes.

She lowered her tone, "And tell me Mr. Lover Boy, are you having fun telling him what you've been doing to me? Are you… are?" Pauline could not talk and cry at the same time. She had to get out of his office and stood up to leave.

Tony pleaded with Pauline. "Okay Pauline, baby, please don't leave like this. You got to know I love you. It was a stupid bet, but baby, please, it turned out to be the best bet I ever made."

Pauline raised her voice to a level that went beyond the thin walls and partitions. "Oh, I'm not only a bet but the best bet!" She drew back to slap his face.

Tony could have easily caught her hand, but wanted to be slapped. He wished she would kick his ass, too. How could he be so stupid?

"Pauline that's not what I meant. I…"

"I don't care what you meant. Get out of my way and leave me alone!" Pauline stormed out of the office and almost knocked his boss down. She scowled at him. "Asshole!"

Tony started after her but his boss motioned him back into the office. "I don't know what's going on, but she needs time to cool off."

Tony plopped down in his chair and smoothed his dark hair back. "I don't suppose you would know who told her about the bet we made, how I could take her to bed on our first date?"

Charles Simms sat down. "So that's what this is about. Hell, you know I wouldn't tell her. We were the only ones in the restroom…"

They looked at each other. "That damn housekeeper," Tony said. "Everybody knows that guy and Ralph are banging each other. I ought to go kick both 'em in the ass."

"The damage is done now. Give it a few days. You said you were both in love. Her pride is damaged right now, she'll come around."

CHAPTER 9

J ohn was out and Ashley decided not to disturb him. He told her before that it was difficult for him to sleep when she and Sonja were not there. She did not know the added stress of eluding the police Friday night exhausted him even more.

When Ashley came home Sunday her libido was through the roof making her wonder if John had worked some voodoo or black magic on her. They were together going on five years and she wanted more of him, could not get enough of him.

She rounded up her mother and Sonja and they got into the BMW and went to McDonalds for breakfast. Afterwards she took them to Cary where Sonja would stay for the rest of the day. Ashley did not tell anyone that she was probably pregnant. She missed her period for July and woke up a few days ago nauseated. All the signs were there and she knew them; this would be her third pregnancy, counting the miscarriage. After her massage appointment she was going to the doctor.

She was excited for John and Sonja more than for herself. They would be married soon, and the addition of a child for John, and a brother or sister for Sonja would solidify their relationship, not to mention another grandchild for her mother. *Ashley Whitfield Colby got a nice ring to it....* she thought.

The problem was Frederick Parsons, her arrogant ex-husband. When it was time for Sonja's last visit with her father, Ashley took her, and she and Fred had it out. Sonja told her that each time she stayed with him he would mention the things they could do, and the places they would go. He assured her that she would still spend time with her mother and John, just not as much. Sonja asked why her father could not understand that she wanted to stay where she was.

Ashley demanded that Fred stop all his suggestions about Sonja coming to live with him because it was not going to happen. She was tired of Sonja worrying that she would have to leave her and John.

That's when Fred went into a sulfurous denunciation of Ashley's live-in arrangement with John Colby. He told her it was not healthy for his daughter to be raised in an environment where her mother is engaging in nasty sex with some black man she was not married to. He said a little girl like Sonja did not know what was best for her and should be with her biological father.

Ashley told him that he was not concerned about Sonja; that if the two of them were staying with her mother in Cary, he would not be doing all this. His face turned red when she told him that she enjoyed every minute of her nasty black sex, and that Sonja was crazy about John.

And yet she came away worried, for Frederick Parsons was a determined man; and when he wanted something he would do anything to get it. Even if she had a stronger case to continue the arrangement of Sonja staying with her and just visiting time with her father; if the person or persons who would render the decision could be bought, Fred had the money to buy them.

She was thinking so intently about everything: the wedding; finally having all of John's family together; how thrilled her mother was; hiring another therapist, maybe even two part-time therapists. She thought of hiring a male and female, since some of her female clients told her if she was too busy they sometimes got a male therapist. Her thoughts returned to Fred who would really be outdone if she were to give John a son.

With all those issues running through her mind, Ashley's hands still performed a perfect massage from years of experience manipulating muscles and tendons.

She was now on her way to the doctor's office. A police car was behind her ever since she turned off of Peace Street onto Blount Street heading out to Tryon Road. When she changed lanes, the patrol car would follow suit.

She crossed Martin Luther King Boulevard and noticed the patrolman had been talking on the phone. As she approached the light at Bess Road the blue lights of the patrol car flashed suddenly and began blinking its command to pull over.

Ashley wondered what he wanted; she had done nothing wrong. Maybe John's tail light was out. She pulled into the Exxon gas station on the opposite corner of the feed mill and railroad tracks. She glanced at her watch: 10:45 am.

Officer James Croop ran his hand through his blonde hair. His cheeks were littered with light brown freckles. Friday night, he and Sergeant Posey chased a very similar BMW. They were never close enough to get the tags when they tailed the car from Big Ed's house.

Now Croop had been talking on the phone to Sgt. Posey, who told him the car belonged to John Colby, a janitorial contractor for the state of North Carolina. In all of Posey's years on the force, he had never seen a vehicle disappear the way the BMW did. After losing the BMW, they went back to Big Ed's house and Posey asked Big Ed why he thought the BMW would try to get away from them. Big Ed had no intentions of talking to two white policemen. He did not know.

Sgt. Posey told Croop to pull her over; he would be there in five minutes. Friday evening, the silver BMW with black trim had disappeared in the heart of North Carolina real estate. If that was the car, Posey wanted to know where it went.

Ashley rolled down her window, and pleasantly said, "Officer, did I do anything wrong?"

Damn! She's hot! "Ah, ma'am this vehicle may have been involved in a chase that involved a drug deal Friday evening. If you will just let me have your license, and sit tight for a few minutes, we can have you on your way in no time if there is no problem." While Croop talked in his slow drawl, he thought he smelled a hint of marijuana. They already knew who the car belonged to so Croop ran a check on Ashley while he waited for Sarge.

Ashley's heart began to pound. *Oh crap! What if it was John? They'll get him for speeding, reckless driving to escape police and who knows what else? I told his black ass to stop this shit… oh wait, I'm going to kill him.*

She dialed his cell. She cursed and was about to hang up.

John said sleepily. "Hey baby, whay y'all at?"

"John, the police pulled me over," her voice trembled. "They say your BMW may have been involved in an escape to avoid police, and that drugs may also be involved. John Colby, what the hell is going on? Did you do something stupid?"

John rushed to the front bedroom and looked out the window. *Oh shit! The weed's under the seat.* His knees buckled and he felt weak. "If they find any weed in the car, just say you have no idea how it got there. Tell them that it was me who drove the car and I'll be there in twenty minutes to turn myself over to them."

She screamed his name and Croop looked up.

"Listen Ash, there's no time to explain, just do what I told you…I'm on the way!" *Oh shit! It's all over! Oh my God, please!*

Sergeant Posey arrived and said to Croop. "Whatcha got?"

"She's squeaky clean, Sarge. Thought I smelled weed, maybe he left it in the car. Man, she's hot as I've seen. Check her out."

"I intend to, ain't shit going on back at the office. We did get an ID on that skeleton from the lake, though. Sit tight."

He leaned over to Ashley and agreed with Croop. She had a full abundance of everything in the right places, plus she was gorgeous. "Miss Whitfield, my name is Sergeant Posey; the patrolman told you what may be the case; he also thought there was a hint of marijuana in the air." With a wry smile he continued. "We could ask for the dogs and let them do a little sniffing or you could let us examine a few areas. I might add, because we suspect drugs could be in this car, we…"

She could feel his admiration. "My boyfriend said it was him Friday evening, he's on his way here…may I please talk to you for a minute? My boyfriend will tell you that I don't know anything about what is going on."

"Yes ma'am, you look like an honest young woman, I'll wait for him." He escorted her to his car and told her to sit on the front seat. "By the way Miss Whitfield, if you don't mind, I'll give Patrolman Croop the go ahead to see if he can find the source of that smell of weed." He expected a nod from her and she gave it to him.

Posey had told Croop to look around inside the car and open the trunk. If he found anything he was to give him a nod and go back to his car.

Sgt. Posey thought of the man he saw coming out of big Ed's house. *That black man sho' got himself some woman, reminds me of Helena.*

Helena Posey, his daughter, would be about the age of Ashley, had she survived a terrible car accident. He argued with his daughter over her decision to marry a Hispanic; to him that meant *Mexican, low-life.*

When he told her that all those people want to do is have babies, Helena stormed out of the house and took a curve going too fast…over corrected and slammed into a tree. His wife blamed him for their only child's death and later divorced him. He blamed himself for Helena's death, and for being a stone-headed bigot. He didn't even try to form a relationship with the guy, the man his daughter had said she loved.

Ashley Whitfield's deep dimples and warm smile reminded him of Helena. "Miss Whitfield, what kind of drugs does your boyfriend do?"

"John only smokes weed, he has a saying that some people like a glass of wine, he prefers a little weed." He was listening, so she kept talking. "He said he picked up the habit in Vietnam. I was so happy a few minutes ago, now everything is going wrong, and will probably get worse."

"What were you happy about?" Posey inquired.

Ashley blinked to let some tears fall; she pulled a tissue from her bag. "I was on my way to the doctor to let her confirm a pregnancy. I'm pretty sure. I already have an eleven-year-old daughter and I would be giving her a sibling, and John his first child. I was so excited to tell him today."

"Why do you think your man sped away to elude us? If he is a casual user, he should've had no more than an ounce."

"He probably was scared to death; he made a terrible mistake. Sgt. Posey, please, John is a good man, can you do something to help us? We're supposed to get married in two months." Ashley sniffed and cried.

"Are you asking me to break the law?"

Ashley shrugged.

Posey had gotten the signal from Croop that he found some weed. He wanted to know how much, and told Ashley he would be back.

When he returned he said. "We found about an ounce of weed in your man's car. He should've let us pull him. The most he would've got is an infraction and a hundred-dollar fine. The crime of speeding to elude police pursuit is a Class A misdemeanor, with a minimum of $500 for the first offense."

Ashley envisioned John being taken away in handcuffs to jail, but now it seemed all they had to do was pay a fine. But what if her ex-husband found out or Pauline Wooten did, and decided this was enough to get rid of John? That is what worried her.

With a note of hope in her voice, she asked. "You mean John can pay a six- or seven-hundred-dollar fine and we can go?"

"We'll be taking Mr. Colby downtown for pictures and prints where he can pay the fine. I'm going to let you drive your car. You can ask the guy at the register inside if they will let John leave his ...what's he driving?"

"His black ass will be in a white truck," she growled other words under her breath.

Just like Helena, pretty even when she's mad. Posey was attracted to her.

John pulled into the small parking area of the gas station. He saw no need to lie, especially when they caught Ashley. He walked towards Sgt. Posey's car looking like a complete asshole. Ashley had asked Posey to let her have a word with him before they took him downtown.

She was going to at least smack him as hard as she could, but when she saw how pitiful he was looking, she hugged him and started crying. They held each other for a while. She whispered in his ear, "I'm gonna kick your ass when we get home."

Patrolman Croop opened the back door of Posey's car for John. Ashley was free to leave. Posey knew these were good people and one got caught doing something dumb. He told the attendant at the gas station that John would be back later to pick up his truck.

Posey looked at John in his rearview mirror. His forehead wrinkled and the wry smile returned, he asked John. "Mr. Colby, we were hot on your ass, where the hell did you go?"

Hesitantly John said. "I made two quick rights and simply went around the block, back down Blount Street and made a left on Newbern Avenue, and made it out to 440."

Posey thought about it. When they barreled cross Wilmington Street he remembered looking right, and saw nothing. There was an APB out, so someone would have seen him on that long trek down Newbern Avenue to 440. He grinned. "I don't believe you, but I can't prove you wrong."

It was bad enough John had to go downtown and be fingerprinted. He was not about to tell the police he escaped onto state property. He was hoping no one would get word of his arrest and charges. Would he fight for his contracts if Pauline Wooten said they were going to cancel everything because of his drug possession and flight to elude police? He decided he would; a quarter of a million dollars was worth a fight.

There was an entrance/exit to the Wake County Sheriff's Department from Salisbury Street, which faced the back of the Wake County courthouse. Frederick Parsons was using that exit the same time John was walking out of the Sheriff's Department. They looked across the street at each other. Frederick Parsons paused and frowned. John returned the stare and proceeded to walk to the gas station where his truck was. It was a few long blocks; he did not mind, the fresh air would help clear his head.

Frederick Parsons retrieved his cell and placed a call to Harold Diggs, the Parsons family's long-time lawyer.

⅄

Lenny Williams pressed his naked body into Cynthia Newsome who was wrapped in a towel. They had just made wild, passionate love and Cynthia had finished a hot shower. Lenny nibbled at her ear and whispered. "The reality of you is so, ummh, so much better than my craziest fantasies."

Cynthia let the towel fall as her voluptuous breasts swayed. She turned and gave him a long kiss. "Now let me go, Deacon Lenny or we'll never get to the Dobbs Building."

While waiting for their divorce to be finalized, Lenny and his wife Ruth were able to work out an amicable agreement about the house they owned in

Worthdale. Ruth hated the area and did not want to stay there, so Lenny had the house appraised for sale, refinanced the home for its market value and gave Ruth half the proceeds, about $30,000.

Lenny and Cynthia had been together for a month. Cynthia thought that she would have to tell her niece who was thirteen that she may not be able to come live with them, since Cynthia already had a little girl.

But Lenny would have none of that and told them he was adopting them as his own children. Since that day Cynthia fell deeply in love with Lenny. She asked him as they were getting dressed, "Lenny, you sure it's gon' be okay for you to go strutting back in your church with a woman of the world on your arm?"

"That's exactly why I want you to go back there with me, so I can show those stuck-up rascals my fine woman of the world, and how much she means to me."

Lenny made Cynthia feel special, safe, and secure. She laughed within herself...*Sorry John Colby, you'll never know what you missed out on.*

"What you smiling at, girl?"

"Nothing," she lied.

⚔

Clarence Farmer had been keeping up with the news ever since the skeletal remains were found at Jordan Lake. He made $25,000 on that grisly night fifteen years ago and minus the nightmares he sometime had, it did not bother him that he had savagely killed a man. What did bother him was: Would the cops come knocking on his door? Would they call on Greta Wooten and would she confess she paid a man named Clarence Farmer to kill her husband?

Weeks later his suspicions were confirmed by a follow up story in the newspaper that the identity of the remains was none other than Otis Wooten. He started thinking then how he might weasel some more money out of Greta Wooten. With a few thousand dollars he could trade his car in for a nice pick-up. His car was running so bad nowadays he caught the bus for the short ride to the Dobbs Building. He only drove his car if he had to go a distance from the bus route.

Cynthia Newsome was riding to work with Lenny now so he did not have to worry about picking her up. Clarence joked with Lenny that he no longer had to get hot and bothered by Cynthia, that now she was all his. Lenny had laughed and gave him a high five.

Clarence decided if he could get some money this time he'd go on the lam like Otis did. Otis told him while they were drinking that D.C. had a lot of places to hang out. He thought: *But why would Greta believe me…she'll see through my scam. After all I'm the one who killed him. She knows I'll keep my mouth shut to protect my own ass.*

He kept thinking how he could pull it off and was sure he would come up with something. In the meantime he would lay low and keep his eye on the news. Their paths would cross again; of that he was sure.

Herbert Standoff, deputy secretary to the governor, had called an emergency meeting to reinforce the importance of all departments to continue tightening their belts amidst dwindling state revenue.

"You've heard it before, you'll hear it again. You're hearing it at the federal, state and county level, and you're hearing it across city hall governments throughout our country. You're hearing cut, slash, reduce, lay off. I've just come from a meeting with the governor about the $3.7 billion deficit. Be sure to tell your staff that those who are eligible would be wise to take early retirement.

"Let's face it, the longer you have been with the state, the more money you make, and what is really hurting our budget is high salaries and finding money to pay for our contracts and services."

Ronald Height had brought with him Chuck Davis and Pauline Wooten. Tony Bizaro and his boss Charles Simms were also there. People from the Department of Transportation were there, as well as law enforcement representatives and others who had something to do with their department budgets.

Standoff continued. "If you have any ideas on how your department can save big money, that is thousands of dollars, or if you think we can do something differently and achieve significant savings, then the governor and I would like to talk to you. To give all of us an example how different departments are dealing with budget cuts, I've asked the director of Facility Management, Ronald Height, if he would give us a brief report on what's going on over there."

"Herb, I've asked my capable contract administrator, Pauline Wooten, if she would do that," said Height.

Chuck Davis looked surprised. *I'm the fucking building manager. I should be doing that.*

Pauline had no idea how to win Ronald Height's admiration and get his recommendation for the director's job. One thing everybody knew was that if Ronald Height recommended you for something you got it. Pauline never liked her boss, and knew the feeling was mutual. To be on the same page with Ron and get his approval you had to be a team person with a *Yes I will attitude; yes I will do whatever you say.*

If Pauline thought one of Ron's ideas was not good she did not hesitate to let him know, something that did not sit well with him. Pauline knew that was the real reason Chuck Davis got the building manager's job. Yet, as fate would have it, after she argued with Tony Bizaro about getting her drawers off on the first date, she exploded from the Administration Building hating all men. It seemed they all abused her or took advantage of her.

When she reached Facility Management she was walking full speed. She came around the blind corner near the restrooms and slammed into Ronald Height. She fell backward on her butt. She was wearing a tight blue skirt that was already two inches above the knee. When she fell the skirt rose higher and her boss's eyes seemed transfixed on her silky brown thighs and the short distant to the white panties.

"Pauline, oh wow, are you all right? Wait, let me call for help."

"No, Ron, just help me up." She put her arm around his neck and as he helped her up her breasts rubbed against him. Ron walked her to his office where she sat down on the soft leather sofa.

He had cold bottled water and twisted the top off and gave it to her. "Are you sure I didn't hurt you? You were walking pretty fast."

Pauline Wooten did not realize how ambitious she really was until that wreck with Ron. She had told him, "Ron, I'll be hurt, no, distraught if you don't recommend me to take your position. I know we've had our differences but frankly there is no one that can run this department as efficiently as I can."

Ron smiled. Pauline was a proud woman and when she wanted something she would apply, and deal with the results, good or bad. To ask showed him how bad she wanted to be director of Facility Management. He thought how badly he needed some pussy.

He said, "So you have that much confidence that you can take over."

She finished the bottled water. "Yes, I know I can."

How should I ask for a trade off, my position for your tail? "Well, I have been impressed lately. The uniforms for the inspectors, better behavior from the prison labor, and that idea about putting our painting request up for bid has been well received. But there are still a lot of things you don't know about building services and how they run."

Pauline had fallen in love with Tony Bizaro and figured she could patch things up at a time she chose. She sensed a chance to realize her dreams for giving up her body. She knew it was wrong, but her desire to run the department outweighed everything.

In her mind she apologized to Tony. Excitedly she said, "Ron, you can teach me. We can start working closely. And remember, I will still have your staff and top people to work with me. Ron, I'll do anything, I'm the right person for this."

Anything! He smiled again, more at his dirty thoughts. He asked her if she had lunch and she told him what happened at the Administration Building.

They went to lunch around 2:30 that day and did not return. After eating, Ronald Height told Pauline about his wife's sickness and how long it had been since he did it to her; and how she gave him permission to have extra-marital sex because she could not handle it anymore.

Pauline was genuinely touched when she saw tears well up in Ron's eyes. She took his hand and looked into his eyes. "I said I would do anything."

⅄

Since then Ron decided he would recommend her for his position, especially after how good she made him feel. And it would shock a lot of blacks and whites that Ronald Height, the bigot, recommended a black woman to take over the reins. The thought amused him. He had made his money with the state and decided to go out with a bang. He worked extra hours training Pauline for the job. Both of them ignored the humorous inquiries from other staff.

⋏

Now, Pauline stood behind the podium with the persona of a department director. She told herself not to look at Chuck or she would burst into a laugh at the rejected, dumb look on his face. After all these years of working under Chuck she would soon be his boss.

"Thank you, Ron. Mr. Secretary, at Facility Management we've heard the governor loud and clear. Much of our budget goes to pay for janitorial contracts. For that reason we canceled all contracts for buildings 30,000 square feet or less, and began cleaning them with part-time help and prison labor. These work crews are being supervised by our building inspectors.

"As a result of this move we are presently saving the State of North Carolina $10,000 a month."

Secretary Standoff interrupted with, "Here, here," and applauded. Everybody joined in, everybody but Chuck Davis.

Pauline concluded with her idea to eliminate the painting department and put all painting requests out for bid; a move that would save the state thousands of dollars. She added that the austerity moves made by Facility Management would save $20,000 a month.

When she finished everyone gave her applause. She glanced at Tony Bizaro who smiled warmly and winked at her.

Ronald Height was glad Pauline bumped into him a couple of weeks ago. He worked with her and showed her a lot of the ins and outs of running the facility. He did not have any guilt about giving his recommendation to Pauline in exchange for sexual favors. In fact he was looking forward to meeting her tonight at Candlewood Suites, a first class hotel in Durham, North Carolina.

Chapter 10

Restrooms are the number one building maintenance concern. A restroom is a bio-hazardous waste transfer station. Humans use restrooms to remove their urine and feces. People with viruses, urinary tract infections, HIV and other diseases use restrooms to transfer germs and bacteria. People throw up in restrooms, soiling partitions and walls. For these reasons the restroom is a primary source of infectious disease-causing organisms.

These bio-contaminants if not removed make their way through a building by way of occupant use, air and ventilation systems.

A building with a healthy environment will always have a clean restroom.

It was Thursday evening and John Colby prepared to clean the restrooms on Clarence Farmer's floor, with his special indoor power-washing machine. He made himself feel good that at least he power-washed his restrooms periodically. Most of the companies never did. After spraying down everything in a restroom with a bacteria-removing solution, John washed and rinsed it all to the floor. What did not go down the drain, he sucked up with the wet vacuum. After that, he blew dry the sinks, urinals, commodes, and partitions with the power blower.

This type of cleaning is the only way to effectively remove the bacteria and germs people leave behind. Using traditional tools like mops, wipes, and rags only spreads contaminated soils around which grow, fester and begin spreading, and making people sick. Housekeepers like Clarence make the traditional way of cleaning even worse.

Clarence Farmer was what John called a "dirty cleaner." Upon entering a restroom serviced by a dirty cleaner, things will look fairly well. The faucets and sinks, toilet seat and commodes will be spray wiped to a satisfactory shine. Yet under that shine are millions of germs left behind because the dirty cleaner sprayed a little glass cleaner on the surfaces, gave a few quick wipes with a hand towel and was finished. Many times John inspected restrooms cleaned by dirty cleaners and found blood and fecal matter under the toilet seat. If you spray wipe under a toilet seat with those kinds of stains, you will have only removed what is visible to the eye. The surface would have to be washed, rinsed and dried to remove all the bio-contaminants.

When John power-washed the urinals in the men's restroom, some time the water would be light green to dark green when it hit the floor. When men take a leak, their urine goes other places than just in the urinal. Urine gets splashed on the walls and partitions, especially since men have such different ways of manipulating their penises to get that last drop out; from shaking to squeezing to milking.

Dirty cleaners never wash the walls or partitions around a urinal. Most of the time, even the inside of the urinal is not washed; that is why long rust-looking urine stains run from top to bottom. All a dirty cleaner will do is spray and wipe the chrome, the top of the urinal and any other visible signs of dried urine. In the Dobbs Building there were many restrooms that had two sinks and two commodes in the ladies' restroom; and three sinks, two urinals, and two commodes for men. A spray-wiping dirty cleaner will clean both restrooms of this size, including mopping the floor in fifteen minutes, less if they are in a hurry. Spray and wipe, squeeze and mop. Go.

When dirty cleaners mop the floor they don't sweep the floor before mopping, so they pick up everything they can with the mop. Some even mop two restrooms never rinsing out the dirt from the first restroom. The germy result is contaminated soils that settle in the grout, in corners and under commodes. John blasted a lot of hair from under sink counter-tops and around commodes. Much of this bacteria-laden debris is pushed there with dirty mops. The intent of the dirty cleaner is to push the debris out of sight.

When workers get sick from viruses on the job, it usually starts in the restroom.

He finished the smaller restrooms on the north end of the third floor and headed toward the south end. Clarence was removing a full bag of trash at the elevator while talking to Lenny. John stopped. "Wha's up guys?"

They returned the greeting.

Clarence asked, "How my restrooms look, boss?"

"I gotta tell you Clarence, they look bad." There was no need to tell a dirty cleaner what was wrong and how to correct it. They will listen to what you say, maybe try to improve, but will soon be spreading germs again. Just tell them it looks bad and do a better job. That was the procedure for dirty cleaners. One other thing dirty cleaners have in common: they don't last long on part-time jobs. John would get rid of Clarence soon or Clarence would quit. It never failed.

Lenny asked John, "You heard about all the layoffs, and early retirement going on in these buildings John? I thought it was just our building, but the guy from the Archdale Building told me at the dumpster that there are a lot of vacant office spaces over there too."

"It's also going on in the New Education Building, that's why I tell you guys to keep our buildings looking good. You never know what the state is thinking." He changed the subject. "How are you and Cynthia getting along?"

"Hey guys, I'm outta here. Y'all got these fine dames to talk about, I'm gone. I'll tighten up on the restrooms, boss." Clarence disappeared around the corner going to the north end of the building since John was on his way to the south end.

"Man, we get along fine, the way we going at each other I wouldn't be surprised if she don't pop up pregnant soon."

Both of them being horny men, they had a hearty laugh. "Clarence is right," John said. "We got some fine women, and I aim to get as much of mine as I can. My daddy said sex was healthy for you."

Lenny said amen, and then looked excited. "John why don't you and Ashley come to church with us this Sunday? I'm going back to show that two-timing wife and crooked preacher how much I thank them for driving me into Cynthia's arms."

John thought about it. "Well, we haven't been to church in a long time."

"Think no further then. Morning service starts at 10:00 am."

"Ashley said the other day she thinks Cynthia and her could be good friends."

"We'll wait till y'all get there. I'll e-mail the address to you. Reverend Earl may be a scoundrel, but he's a very good preaching scoundrel."

John laughed. "The crooked ones are the best preachers."

Lenny agreed and John was on his way to the south end restrooms. He was surprised that his arrest for an ounce of marijuana and speeding to evade a police pursuit had gone unnoticed. The first few days after the incident, sleep eluded him. He worried someone might read a report in the crime section of the *News and Observer* Triangle Section: John Colby, a contractor for the State of North Carolina, was arrested for possession of drugs and speeding to evade police. He checked the paper every day since Monday and there was nothing.

When he got home the evening of his arrest, Ashley shoved him into the wall and made him promise her, and mean it, that he was not going to jeopardize his business and their life together messing with weed any longer. She began crying and telling him how bad it could be for them if Frederick found out. John did not tell her Fred saw him coming out of the Wake County Sheriff's office.

He was silent the whole time, realizing how true her words really were.

After all, the little voice in his head had told him a thousand times what could happen. When she finished he pulled her to him and promised he would not buy any more weed.

He told her he would never risk losing her and Sonja, and his business over weed, or anything else again, and begged her forgiveness. It was a commitment he intended to keep. John loved Ashley and her child too deeply to ever risk breaking them up.

The ladies' restroom on the south end had five stalls with commodes and three sinks. Each time John made his rounds detailing restrooms the sinks would be the dirtiest. Evidently there were a lot of coffee drinkers on the south end of the building due to the dark brown coffee stains in the sinks. Ladies cleaned their coffee pots and rinsed out the filters, staining the cheaply made sinks.

You could whiten the sink enamel a little with Clorox but before the day ended, they had a brown coffee color again because employees kept up the mad assault on sinks all day long. The plumber was always being called to unstop a sink, because of coffee grinds.

When John finished a floor, he stored his equipment in that floor's storage room. He heard the dirty cleaner vacuuming in a nearby office while he waited for the elevator. He thought. *Oh Clarence look like he hiding some dark, ugly secret or that he's always up to something. Tha's a no good nigga if I ever seen one.* John chuckled and got on the elevator to the fourth floor. It was almost time for Ashley, her mother and Sonja, to pick him up.

He wanted to speak to Cynthia before he left.

John was happy for Lenny and Cynthia. He knew they were now inseparable just like he and Ashley. When he got off the elevator, the quietness was eerie. It was amazing the noise of people during the day and the absence of that noise at night. The elevators were in the middle of the building and the offices had doors to shut out the noise of the long hallways.

His heavy voice would echo down the hallway. He yelled, "Cynthia Newsome… Cynthia!" He waited; then a door to the hallway opened.

"John Colby, is that your big mouth, I'm down here."

She was working in the suite of offices on the south end near the Insurance Commissioner's office. As John approached, he noticed her shorts were a little lower now that she was with Lenny, but that was all. Cynthia had it and nothing was going to stop her flaunting it.

John smiled and said, "Ashley's picking me up in a few minutes…hadn't seen you in a few days. Thought I'd stop by and see how you doing. Saw Lenny, he's happy as a lark."

They both laughed. "That man is something, John, but he's so sweet. Hate to say it, but I'm glad he broke with his wife. A woman can always use a good brother."

"I hear you," John replied. "Wanted to tell you we'll be coming to church with you guys Sunday…"

"That's awesome, how'd all this happen?"

"Lenny invited us; I called Ashley, so all of us are coming, Sonja and Ashley's mother."

"Super, at least I'll know someone other than Lenny. I just finished, let me put up this stuff and I'll walk down and say hi to Ashley." Cynthia stopped talking and gave John a warm look of affection.

"What?"

"Thank you for not taking advantage of me. You know you could have led me on and banged me any time you wanted to. But you resisted all my sultry advances." She giggled at her description, and then was serious. "I just want to say thank you for being true to your woman. I believe my deacon will be true to me like that. Do you, John?"

"Lenny is a Christian man. All he needs is a woman to love and who will love him back. I think y'all were made for each other."

"You mean like you and Ashley."

"Exactly." His cell phone rang. It was Ashley so he told her he was on the way down. As the elevator arrived, John hugged Cynthia and whispered, "Thanks for saying that about me. Lenny doesn't know how lucky he is."

Cynthia was happy to hear that in return.

John's crew was waiting at the loading dock. Ashley was driving the infamous BMW. She smiled and waved. When Cynthia came to her side of the car, Ashley gave her a warm grin and said, "Hey girlfriend. My man treating you right, giving you timely raises and providing healthcare benefits?"

"Naw girl, he ain't gave me a raise in years and working me like a dog."

It was funny to everybody. Before buckling up, John leaned over to the back and planted a big kiss on Sonja, and grinned at his mother-in-law to be, who knew about his arrest and fines. He said to Cynthia, "I'm going to tell Lenny to take you to the altar Sunday for lying."

"That's right," Cynthia said looking at Ashley. "We'll definitely wait for you before we go inside the church, so I can have somebody to talk to."

Lenny appeared at the loading dock and came down to meet Ashley's mother. "Please to meet you, ma'am."

"Likewise," Clara nodded friendly.

Ashley said to Cynthia as she eased the car into reverse, "We got to get together some time."

Cynthia replied. "We will, one day next week, call me." She reached for Lenny's hand and they walked back into the building.

Ashley told John as they headed to Edenton Street, "They look so sweet together. You know Cynthia was sweet on you don't you?"

John lay back in his seat for the twenty minute drive to Wendell and said with pride, "I seem to have that effect on women."

"Booooooo!" they exclaimed loudly.

It was almost 9:00 pm and Pauline Wooten was on the telephone talking to Tony Bizaro. "You hurt me, Tony, and it will take time to heal; my pride has been wounded. Just give it a little more time." The truth was she did not want to be screwing two men at the same time. In two hours she was meeting her boss for their second interlude.

When Ron crashed into her, and she caught him looking hungrily at her thighs and panties, ambition seized her. It seemed all men wanted to use her. So she thought that day…looking up at Ron, *Use yourself girl. I know what I want and know what he wants.*

Tony pleaded. "What has happened baby is done. It was a stupid bet. I even told Charles that he won and gave him back his hundred dollars. You know we love each other." He moaned her name. "Pauline, baby, I need to hold you, kiss you and be inside of you."

The thought of him doing those things made her wet. "We can go play tennis Sunday if you want to." Tony was excited and said that was a start.

She had been dressing while talking to Tony. When she hung up, she was ready to go lay down an installment on her director's position.

Ron was no comparison to Tony when it came to lovemaking. Pauline would act as if Ron's lovemaking was driving her crazy. He would come so quickly, she felt motherly, or wifely. On the other hand, when she was with Tony, he would have her on fire until she had multiple orgasms before he finished. Ronald Height had an ill wife that gave him permission to have sex on the outside. Pauline was providing all that in exchange for a few important words from him to the right people.

She did not feel dirty. In fact she wondered how many women gave powerful men some pussy for a position. She frowned; this time she would tell Ron for their next get together, he should bring some kind of proof that he was putting the ball in motion for her take over. She wanted to see a letter from him to someone in the governor's office that Pauline Wooten was his choice for director of Facility Management.

She had thought about inviting Ron to her place and using a hidden camera to tape their affair, just in case he was another man trying to use her. But if the tape got in to the wrong hands, her career would be over, and Tony a memory. She could not take that chance. She was willing to take the risk, give up her body and trust Ronald Height to come through on his word. Her mother did not know what she was doing with her boss and Pauline planned to keep it that way. Her mother had enough worries with cancer.

Sgt. Posey was taking Officer Croop on his first investigation. It was a murder investigation. The skeletal remains of Otis Wooten had been identified and the medical examiner in Chapel Hill said the victim was probably stabbed to death before being thrown in the lake.

It was Friday morning just after 10:00 am. They rang the door bell of Greta Wooten, who had been standing in the mirror brushing her short grey hair, and admiring her figure. For a sixty-six-year-old she gave herself a B plus. It was the deadly disease lurking inside of her that was the problem.

The doorbell ranged. She opened it and had an immediate feeling of dreadful news. "Yes, may I help you?"

Posey flashed his badge and held it for a few seconds in front of her face. "My name is Sgt. Posey, this is Officer Croop, may we come in?"

She led them into the living room where they sat down.

Posey said, "Mrs. Wooten you probably heard on the news a little over a month ago about human skeletal remains being found on the banks of the Jordan Lake." He noticed Greta Wooten's eyes bulge for a moment and thought she looked weak all of a sudden. "We sent the remains to the medical examiner in Chapel Hill, and by way of dental records we've determined that the remains are those of your husband, Otis Wooten."

Greta fell back in her chair and took a long deep breath. For a moment she saw Otis's eyes opened in death and blood circling around the butcher knife in his chest. "I don't know what to say. After he tried to rape his stepdaughter, the police went on a big search for him, but he was never found."

Posey replied, "Yes, I read about that. And you never heard from him again, telephone, e-mail, nothing?"

Greta regained her composure; she was telling the truth; she never heard from Otis again. "Nothing."

Posey looked at Croop.

Officer Croop asked, "Mrs. Wooten do you know of anyone who had a grudge against your husband...anyone who might have wanted him dead?"

"I won't lie; I wanted him dead after what he did to my daughter. But he never came on the scene again and the years made me forget that ugly period." She wondered if they believed her.

Posey stood up to leave. "Did you have any life insurance on your husband, Mrs. Wooten?" He knew she did.

"Why yes, a $150,000 policy that I never collected. You don't think I killed him, do you?"

"No ma'am, we always have to look for motive. Thanks for your time Mrs. Wooten, we'll be in touch."

They parted at the door. Officer Croop said, "What you think, Sarge? Look like she might be hiding somn' to me."

"I don't know, you may be right. Mr. Wooten's sister said she was a gold-digger; that she married the guy 'cause he had a promising NFL career, then busted his knee in training camp, gave up on life and became an alcoholic. We just have to keep digging till we come up with something."

Greta watched the mild-mannered sergeant and his goofy-looking sidekick pull away from the curb. She had dreaded this day ever since she and Pauline watched the breaking newscast of skeletal remains found at Jordan Lake. She kept worrying if it was Otis and now she knew.

Her mind was plagued with "what if" questions. What if they located Clarence who killed Otis, and he confessed one Greta Wooten paid him to do it? She did not want to think about jail time.

The only comforting thought she had since they discovered Otis's bones was that Clarence Farmer might be dead too. She was not sorry Otis was dead; she just had no idea she would be haunted so much. At church services and funerals over the years since she paid to have him killed, a howling conscience would quietly remind her over and over that she was a murderer, and that she was going to pay for her sins.

While Otis worked at the post office during their marriage, Greta worked for Simpson and Simpson Law Firm. The father died six years after Greta retired. She would call the son, Terry Simpson, and get him to get her a death certificate for Otis and collect the $150,000. She would also give him instructions for updating her will. She had a similar life insurance policy in the same amount for herself, and she owned a home worth $200,000.

Greta also had $50,000 in liquid savings. So with all that, her car, clothes and jewelry she could leave her daughter an estate worth a million dollars. The thought made her feel better, so she decided to focus on getting her financial house in order and hope like hell the police investigation would turn up no leads.

After Otis tried to rape Pauline and then could not be found, Greta lost all contact with Otis' siblings. Sgt. Posey said the city would be calling her soon to see if she wanted to give the remains a proper burial. He told her a sister and brother died and that he spoke to Otis' sister who suffered bouts with dementia and expressed no interest in the burial of her brother's remains. Posey told Greta that the only remaining sibling said the entire Wooten family was against him marrying a gold-digger, to which Greta shrugged and said the two families never got alone.

She dialed her lawyer. She would add one more task for him to do: Arrange to have Otis Wooten's remains properly buried.

⚹

John and Sonja sat at the table eating pancakes, while Clara tended the stove. "Dang Mom, what you put in these thangs?" John asked with a greedy chuckle. He washed his sixth pancake down with a glass of orange juice. "These cakes so light they melt in your mouth."

He looked at Sonja who had just eaten two pancakes and asked: "Where is your mother?"

"She must be still in the bathroom. I don't think she feels good. She was throwing up," Sonja said licking syrup off her fingers.

"Hmmn," Clara pondered. "Early morning sickness may mean a brother or sister."

"Oh, wow," exclaimed John and abruptly lost himself in the fantasies of fatherhood.

Sonja laughed and said. "Look at Colby, daydreaming of a son."

The three of them laughed so hard they were unaware of Ashley standing in the door way. She said with a weak smile. "What's got you guys so tickled?"

"Never mind that." John turned to look at her. "We want to know, are you pregnant?"

Ashley's face lit up. She had rescheduled her appointment with the doctor after the weed debacle and the doctor confirmed her pregnancy. Another life had been growing inside her for five weeks. Ashley waited for the right moment to tell the people she loved so dearly. She grinned and said loudly, "Yes, I am pregnant, John Colby. I'm pregnant, everybody! Yea!"

John rushed to her, hugged her tightly and kissed her with passion. When he let her go, he said with tears in his eyes. "Oh baby, you've made me the happiest man on Earth."

Clara Whitfield dabbed at her eyes. Sonja came jumping in their arms hollering she wanted a little brother. A marriage, and now a child to plan for; they were all one happy family.

Very soon a turbulent train of events would disrupt their lives like never before.

CHAPTER 11

The Slammer is an informative weekly newspaper published on Fridays in seven states. Their focus is local crimes and arrests, plus other crime related news and information. The paper prints crime news that other local newspapers avoid.

Sam Boswell spilled coffee on his white uniformed shirt. He read the arrest three times: John Colby, janitorial contractor, arrested for one ounce of marijuana; and speeding to avoid police pursuit. The notice listed an address in Wendell, North Carolina.

He hurried to Pauline Wooten's office. She looked up suddenly. "My goodness Sam, why you flying in here like that?"

"Boss, you won't believe this." He had highlighted the arrest notice and handed her the newspaper. "Your boy been arrested for one ounce of weed and speeding to avoid a police pursuit."

"Say what?" Pauline took notice immediately.

Sam chuckled and was about to say something, but Pauline quickly raised her hand to silence him. She was dumbfounded, and like Sam, had to read it more than once.

Pauline said with a look of great satisfaction, "Sam, I need to keep this paper. You've given me what I need to finally get rid of Colby Cleaning Service. It's almost lunch, take the rest of the day off."

"Dang, I knew you'd be happy, but not enough to give me the rest of the day off. Have a great weekend then, I'm gone. Thanks, boss."

"No, Sam. Thank you." She thought of her top gun position soon. "Your official promotion and raise should be coming soon. I'll see to that."

"That's what I'm talking about," Sam said.

Pauline relished in planning the demise of Colby Cleaning Service. Not only would she end his career, she would rub his arrogant face in the mud. After properly notifying him of cancellation of all contracts she would call a contractors' meeting to put all of them on notice that criminal behavior would cause them to lose their contracts. She would use Colby Cleaning Service as an example. The news would please quite a few contractors because they were always being outbid when Colby went after something hard; not to mention their jealousy of his service having cleaner buildings.

Before buzzing Ronald Height and Chuck Davis, Pauline called to verify the report and make copies of the page the notice was on.

Chuck Davis wondered what Pauline wanted. She said it was important. Lately it seemed to him that Pauline was spending a lot of time away from her desk. And everybody at Facility Management was talking about seeing Pauline and Ron together more. At meetings Chuck became aware of Ron agreeing with everything Pauline said. He could not fathom Pauline making out with the director to get his nod for the position, but had to admit the signs of a possible affair were all there.

Chuck wanted Ron's job just as bad as Pauline. *Too bad I ain't got a pussy,* he thought as he entered Pauline's office. "Hey, Pauline, wha's up?"

"Sit down, Chuck." She handed him the newspaper. "Seems there's another side to our expert contractor, Mr. John Colby." She said it with as much sarcasm as she could muster. Their boss strolled in and took a seat beside Chuck. He smiled warmly at Pauline. "Hey Chuck, ready for the weekend?"

"Yeah, Ron, I am," Chuck replied, astonished at what he had just read. He handed Ron the copy. "Damn, John Colby into weed."

Pauline added. "If that's not bad enough, he could have killed or maimed somebody driving recklessly to escape the police."

Ron leaned over and laid the copy on her desk. "Who gave you this?" he said incredulously.

Pauline held up the newspaper. "Sam picked it up from a convenience store in his neighborhood. The paper prints a lot of local crime news and information that the *News and Observer* omits. I called Raleigh police and they confirmed the story."

Ron said. "Well, I have not seen a problem like this in thirty years. I've never had to deal with a contractor getting busted for criminal behavior."

Pauline broke in. "If there is no protocol we need to establish one now with this case. We cannot and should not allow persons who exhibit criminal behavior to do business with the State of North Carolina."

"Well put, Pauline. Maybe we do need to cancel all Colby's contracts." Ron knew that was what Pauline wanted to hear. For a second he felt her warm black body on him and saw himself riding her like the black guys in the videos he watched riding horny white gals. He continued. "We need to incorporate the statement you just made in his cancellation notice, and include it in all future specifications of contracts."

Now I know they fucking each other. Ron ain't never agreed with Pauline so quickly on something so serious. Chuck spoke up. "Hold on guys. Don't you think we need to review the specifications of the contract to make sure there is no standard procedure and that we punish accordingly? If there is no precedent and we take a man's livelihood he may sue the state."

Pauline thought about the relationship the three of them had. *How times have changed. Before it was Chuck agreeing with everything Ron said. Now it's Ron agreeing with everything I say. My, my what a little pussy will do.* She giggled inside. "Sue us for what, Chuck? He's the one breaking the law. We're trying to protect our employees from a man who may have a drug problem, and who has no concern for the law. He recklessly speeds away from a police chase endangering lives in the city of Raleigh."

Chuck thought. "He can sue us for excessive punishment. In all these kinds of cases the victim pleads guilty and pays the fine, avoiding court cost. If we cancel and he pleads his case to purchasing; hell, you know those softies over there; he could have a case."

"Well, what do you suggest we do?" inquired Ron.

Chuck rubbed the bald spot on his head. A warning would not be severe enough. "Hell, I don't know."

Pauline did not want to jump on Chuck too hard. She suspected he thought something might be going on. She was with the boss all the time, a change so dramatic from just a month ago. Say the wrong thing and get on his nerves, he might see if he can confirm his suspicions.

She tried a different approach. "Chuck, the state is going through a serious budget crisis, and no matter how much you may respect Colby's Cleaning Service, the guy is making about $250,000 with us now. The award of the Albemarle would take him close to a half-million dollars. We are terminating John Colby's contracts for a very good reason, and I say we cancel and show Deputy Secretary Standoff how we can clean these buildings for half this amount; by cleaning them with part-time help and prison labor, just like we are doing in some of the other buildings."

Ronald Height liked the idea, and frankly did not care about anything they were talking about. On a new diet and new medicine, his wife was making a good recovery. His affair with Pauline would end sooner than he wished. But for a while longer he would jump on her every chance he got, so he wanted to keep her happy. She longed to get rid of John Colby and he decided to give her what she wanted.

"Chuck, let's go with Pauline's decision. We cancel all his contracts and alert all contractors to the fact that the State of North Carolina will not tolerate this kind of behavior. We have to have standards."

He stood up to leave, and so did Chuck. He said, "You the boss, Ron. Whatever y'all think is best." He walked out the door with great hatred for both of them.

Just before Ron left he whispered to Pauline, "The next time we get together I have a surprise for you."

She smiled. "Can't wait."

When he was gone, she reared back in her chair and said aloud: "Enjoy your weekend Mr. Colby, and hold on to the help wanted ads in the Sunday paper; before next week is out you'll be in the unemployment line."

⋏

The Moore Square District is a registered historic district located in downtown Raleigh, North Carolina. The district is centered on Moore Square, one of two surviving four-acre parks from Raleigh's original 1792 plan. The park was named after Alfred Moore, a North Carolina judge who became an Associate Justice of the Supreme Court. The district includes East Hargett Street, once known as Raleigh's "Black Main Street" due to its large number of black-owned businesses.

City Market opened across the street from the park on October 1, 1914. From that time to the mid-'40s the market flourished. Farmers from the eastern part of the state came regularly in their trucks and horse-drawn carts, filled with produce, poultry, seafood and flowers. Many of the women loved the baked goods. On Saturdays families would gather in the park for picnics and to be with friends.

In 1983, the gothic style architecture of the City Market Building, the cobblestone roads, and the surrounding history of Moore Square itself earned the area a place on the National Register of Historic Places.

Moore Square may not be a place for farmers anymore but the area is still alive. The city of Raleigh has held Artsplosure in Moore Square for the last thirty years, drawing 80,000 people. On the first Friday in every month during the summer and fall, live bands gather in the area to perform.

Every bus that travels downtown makes a stop at Moore Square Station. It serves as a transfer facility for Raleigh's bus system known as CAT, for Capital Area Transit.

Clarence Farmer could have made a connection to a bus that would drop him off right at the Dobbs Building. It was 4:30 pm, so he had plenty of time and decided to walk the few blocks to the Dobbs building to give him time to smoke some weed.

Clarence's car was running so bad he rarely used it. He needed more money. The drug dealers in his area were making $120 a day. It took him three hours a night for five days a week to make $120, but he was too old and too scared to deal drugs.

Clarence made sure there were no cops riding around on bicycles and lit the blunt while walking past the Capital Building. He slowed down. It was Friday and he decided that some time during the weekend he would call Greta Wooten's number and flat out ask if the police had been to her house. He would play it by ear looking for a place to ask for some money to leave town.

His mind fixated on how to scare her into giving up at least $15,000. She could afford it. He wondered if she got anything from an insurance policy on Otis. It dawned on him that Greta Wooten might not even be alive; that all his planning and thinking may be in vain; that was why he had to call her. People like Greta Wooten never moved and their phone number was always the same.

When Clarence approached the three story red brick building known as the Seaboard Building, he saw two black women sitting and talking in a black Lexus. The older woman sitting on the passenger side watched him curiously, so he stared back.

He got nearer and could not believe his eyes. *Damn, ain't got to call her, Greta Wooten is alive as hell!*

Pauline and her mother had come from a late appointment with Greta's oncologist, and they had stopped by Facility Management for Pauline to pick up some papers. She parked on the street since her parking lot was busy with inspectors arriving and the daytime staff leaving.

Pauline said to her mother, "Why is that ugly ass man staring at you so hard? Oh, he has on a Colby Cleaning Company shirt; he must work in the Dobbs Building."

Greta's heart quickened and she became fearful. She never forgot a face. The sneaky-looking man looked older and heavier, but it was Clarence Farmer, the man she paid to kill her husband.

For the first time in months, the late August evenings were cool with temperatures in the 70s, so Pauline's windows were down while she and her mother talked.

Clarence could not believe his stroke of good fortune. "Greta Wooten, is that you?"

Pauline noticed how nervous and uncomfortable her mother had become, but did not say anything.

Greta acted as if she did not know the murderer; maybe he would go away. Hesitantly, she said. "Well, yes I am Greta Wooten, but I'm afraid, aah, do I know you?"

A devious chuckle escaped Clarence's lips. "Yes, you *do* know me." He put emphasis on *do*. "I'm Otis Wooten's cousin. I use to do some yard work for you years ago; don't you remember?" He laughed. "'Course I'm older and uglier, but I'm Clarence, Clarence Farmer.'"

Greta thought. *I can't believe this shit. The cops inform me the bones they found at Jordan Lake belong to Otis, and now after almost fifteen years I run into the sorry ass rascal I hired to kill him.* She made a lame attempt at surprise. "Oh Clarence, I thought you moved to Greenville to start a landscaping business."

Clarence shrugged. "Well, a few things did not pan out, so after a few years I came back to Raleigh…you need anybody to cut your grass?"

"No, no, I have a company that does it now." In spite of the cool breeze, she was finding it hard to breathe. She lied, "Well, it was nice seeing you again, Clarence."

Clarence looked at Pauline, nodded, and then aimed his beady eyes into Greta. "It sho' was nice seeing you too. I'll be in touch." He walked across the street to the Dobbs Building singing, "Summertime and the living is easy."

"Wow, what a creepy looking guy; and Mom, you look so rattled. Are you okay?"

"Yes, I'm fine, child. Just shocked to see someone related to Otis. Go get your papers and let's go home." *What the hell did he mean, I'll be in touch?*

⅄

The area for the choir at Bethel Baptist Church was behind the pulpit, so that choir members observed everything that took place during the service, including who came in the door. Next was the pulpit with the same view, except that the podium was in the middle of the pulpit. The pastor sat behind the podium in a lot of black churches and did not have the same observation as the choir until he stood up.

To the right of the pulpit were three pews for the deacons and other important men of the church. To the left of the pulpit were also three pews facing the deacons where the mothers of the church, pastor's wife and other important women of the church sat. The congregation was seated in three sections of long pews that began a few from the communion table and extended to the back doors which was the main entrance.

Just before entering, John overheard an usher tell Lenny that wherever he got Cynthia to let him know so he could trade in his old lady. The choir was about to sing when Lenny entered with seven guests, three of them white.

Sunday at 11:00 am was still the most segregated hour in America. Black people in black neighborhoods were not accustomed to seeing white people in their churches.

The choir director's back was to the congregation. The choir did not start on cue, and when some of them nudged each other and look surprised; he turned his head, in unison with every other head in the three rows of pews, to see what caused the stir.

Ruth Williams drove her husband into the welcoming arms of Cynthia Newsome. She was shocked to see Lenny so bold, and noticed with disgust that he had reserved a whole pew.

Reverend Timothy Earl Johnson could not see and raised himself to look over the podium. When he saw Cynthia holding on to deacon Lenny's hand, his thought rendered a chuckle. *Deacon Lenny, you can have Ruth back for that fine thang.* He stared at the white beauty behind Cynthia, and then felt Ruth's look of disdain.

He stepped to the podium; his voice, deep and powerful. "Let the church say amen."

The congregation said amen.

Lenny grew up in the church and everybody liked him. They deplored what his wife did to him and labeled the affair with the pastor a shame and disgrace. When the news broke, the Deacon Board put Reverend Johnson on notice that he would have to go. He understood and in three weeks Bethel Baptist would be searching for a new pastor.

Reverend Johnson continued. "We're glad to see deacon Williams and his lovely entourage. Might I say, welcome to all our visitors. We pray you will be blessed by our service." He turned to the choir. "Choir, let's praise the Lord this morning. I believe we need a closer walk with the Lord. Amen?"

The congregation said amen, and the choir sang "Just A Closer Walk With Thee."

John loved the song and recalled how his dad would sing it at Pentecostal Holy Church in Goldsboro. When he finished the church would be on fire and shouting would break out everywhere.

While John enjoyed a favorite old song, Lenny stared hard at Ruth Hodges Williams. As the choir sang, he nudged Cynthia and whispered, "Let's stare her down."

Cynthia smiled and said. "That ain't right, deacon Lenny…but I'll do it for you."

They stared hard at the side of Ruth's face; so hard in fact that after a couple of minutes, their mental telepathy reached into her ear and made her head turn slowly to their waiting eyes. They shook their heads at her in shame. Ruth jerked her head back to the choir. She despised Lenny.

Ashley, her mother, Sonja, Cynthia, her daughter Tasha, and Linda, Cynthia's niece, were all having a good time rocking their heads back and forth to the music like everybody else.

The next twenty-five minutes of service included prayers, announcements, another song from the choir, an offering; and a sole stirring solo by a man who sang "I Would Rather Have Jesus."

After the solo, Reverend Johnson began his sermon. "In this life trouble can come suddenly, and like the roaring waves of the sea, that come one after another; sudden disasters can come to us one after another. Our lives can go from happy and normal, to suffering and turmoil as quickly as lightning can flash from the sky.

"In times like these we need to do what King David did when he found himself facing overwhelming odds. David said, "I cried unto the Lord and He delivered from all my fears."

The congregation said *amen* without being asked.

John liked the message. Lenny was right, the man could preach.

Reverend Johnson went on to tell how trusting God, and putting all your faith in Him, one would be able to face those waves that come in their lives. One would be able to overcome their problems, and defeat their enemies.

Once service was over the pastor waited at the door to greet the congregation on their way out. He shook John's hand and the rest of his crew, and thanked them for coming.

Cynthia smiled at Reverend Johnson. "I enjoyed your sermon, Reverend."

"Thank you, I'm so glad you came," he said to Lenny. "You two make a good-looking couple, Deacon. You did real well for yourself."

Lenny grinned at Reverend Johnson. "Well you always said God works in mysterious ways. You probably won't enjoy Ruth, as much as I'll enjoy Cynthia."

People nearby grunted and chuckled.

John treated everybody to Golden Corral. A special bonding had begun between him, Lenny, Ashley and Cynthia. Ashley was to pick Cynthia up Thursday for lunch at K&W in Cameron Village.

CHAPTER 12

The loading dock at the New Education Building was too small for a trash dumpster and a dumpster for cardboard, so John had to haul the cardboard to the Dobbs Building which had two large dumpsters, one for cardboard and one for trash.

The space beside the cardboard dumpster would often be taken by a worker from Facility Management who would park his truck and go into the building to kill time in the cafeteria or hide out in a mechanical room.

Whereas August ended on a cool note, early September arrived with hot temperatures. It was 9:00 am on a warm and muggy Monday morning. John arrived at the dumpster with a load of cardboard and cursed the state vehicle that was parked in the space next to it. Now he would have to get as close as he could to the front of the dumpster, and squeeze around the vehicle to get the cardboard inside.

The motor was running on the van and he saw a white Facility Management worker on the passenger side of the vehicle. Then a black worker appeared with food, coffee and a newspaper. John said, "Oh good, you guys 'bout to move?"

The black man rolled his eyes, angry he would be rushed. "No." He got in the van, and the two men sat there with the engine running to provide them a cool environment while they ate their breakfast and read the newspaper.

John shook his head. Their behavior was representative of most Facility Management maintenance workers. They drive nice state vehicles, and park at different state owned properties, taking up needed space while they pretend they are working, when the most they do is un-stop a toilet, fix a door or change a ballast in a light fixture, or less; turn on a switch on a heating/ air conditioner unit. During the winter, John frequently observed their trucks parked outside with the engine running while they would be inside attending to non-important things. They cared nothing about taxpayer dollars for all the gas they wasted; they cared more about returning to a warm truck. These same, lazy employees curse the state once they learn they've been laid off due to the budget crisis.

John squeezed around the maintenance truck with the last handful of cardboard. He pulled his truck into the space beside the long dumpster for trash and garbage. He went into the Dobbs to wash up and then went across Salisbury Street to Facility Management to check his box.

A half-hour later he returned to his truck and saw the black maintenance worker get out of his truck to brush the breakfast crumbs off his pants. He said to himself: *Look at those lazy ass buzzards. Eating breakfast and goofing off before the first break.*

He had ideas on how the state could save millions of dollars in a few years if they changed the way they purchased and manage their janitorial contracts. Now that the state faced a huge budget deficit they might want to listen.

He thought about his buddy Earl, of Horn Janitorial Company, and dialed his number to see if he wanted to take an early lunch at Bojangles on New Bern Avenue.

"Hey Earl, how you doing, partner? You still blowing the competition away?"

They laughed. Earl replied, "Yo John, ain't no happenings. Everybody tight on spending that money. The state put the lid on bids, so ain't no competition to blow away. You lucky you were low bid on the Albemarle."

"Yeah I was, and the good Lord knows I show needed that award…'bout to get married and taking on a …."

"Man, I was wondering when you gon' say that. Being saying to myself I know John ain't gon' be no fool like that cracker who let something like Ashley get away."

"Well, thank you my brother, and you right. Ashley is beautiful inside and out. Let you know more about the wedding date later. Been a long time since we sat down and chewed the fat. You got time to do an early lunch at Bojangles?"

"I got some supplies to deliver. How 'bout eleven?"

"Cool, see you then, Earl."

Earl was right. John was lucky to get the Albemarle Building. With that income he would be out of debt by the second half of the three-year contract.

All the janitorial contractors doing business with the Department of Administration had contracts that had expired. The budget problems shut down the bidding process. That's why John agreed with Earl that he was lucky to get the Albemarle Building. Nobody knew what the state was thinking, or when the bidding process would resume.

Sorry contractors took advantage of their expired contracts and did no more than dump trash and spray-wipe restrooms. When people in their buildings complained, they replied their contracts had expired and they were only helping the state out until contracts were re-bid.

John thought such attitudes were despicable. As long as the state paid the contractor the same amount of money before the contract expired, and was continuing to do so, the contractor should be held accountable. Their behavior was larcenous and their buildings accumulated more dirt, germs and bacteria with each passing day.

Colby Cleaning Service was the only company still stripping and waxing floors, power-washing restrooms, and shampooing carpet at no extra cost. It seemed to him that the contract administrator should be happy with what he was doing instead of always looking for an opportunity to cancel his contracts.

When Ronald Height started taking small accounts from contractors and began cleaning them with prison labor and part-time help, all the contractors worried the state was going back to in-house cleaning to save money. John lost two small contracts and worried like everybody else.

Then abruptly as it had started, it stopped and contractors continued cleaning their buildings even though the contracts had expired. An inspector who had known John for a long time told him it was a dumb idea for Facility Management to cancel some contracts and start cleaning the buildings with prison labor. When contractors lost their buildings, they took all their equipment with them. Consequently, Facility Management spent money buying vacuum cleaners, barrels, mop buckets and all the other equipment needed to maintain a building, so the savings could not be much.

Another problem was how hard the Hispanics and prisoners were on equipment, causing more expense. And most frustrating to the inspectors who supervised the crews was communication. When they tried to tell one of their Spanish-speaking workers how to do something, their only English was "Sorry, no English."

John arrived at Bojangles a few minutes before eleven o'clock and went inside to wait for Earl. He ordered a wing dinner, dirty rice and ice tea. He took a seat by the window.

This Bojangles was located in a black neighborhood and served as a meeting place for retirees and people out of work who had nothing to do but gather at the restaurant to catch up on the latest bad news. Most of the men knew each other and conversations stretched across tables making the restaurant a noisy environment. "Obama ain't got no balls." John heard a man say to a friend at another table. "He's suffering from the scared-eye syndrome?"

His friend looked puzzled. "What the hell is that?"

"The scared-eye syndrome. You remember way back when it was a crime to look a white person in the eye. Ol' cracker be rattling off commands and demands to the black man who be looking at his shoes; shaking his head saying *yes sah, yes sah.* That's what Obama is doing, saying *yes sah* to them white asses in the Republican Party."

Everybody chuckled, including John. He heard the same thing wherever he went. People were sick and tired of President Obama caving in to demands of white Republicans who cared only for themselves, their families and their wealthy friends.

"Well, he's a liar too," another man chimed in. "Said over and over during the campaign he would not extend the Bush tax cuts on the wealthy. Then after he gets the needed votes to become president, he extends the tax cuts.

His ass won't be getting my vote next time. He's like all the other crooks in Washington; makes excellent promises then don't do shit. The only difference is his color."

Wow, the vitriol is thick in here. Shame Obama can't hear it. John saw Earl walk in and go to the line to order.

When Earl came to the table, John said, "Good to see you Earl. How's the family?"

"They're fine, John, hope yours are too."

William Earl Horn was short, had wooly grey hair and brown eyes.

"This place is loud with anti-Obama rhetoric," John said.

"Can you blame 'em? We all voted for the first black president and his message of change, and now he's pissing on us."

"Whoa," John said. "Ain't you seen all the television ads of Obama pushing his jobs bill and telling Americans to get behind him and call their people in Congress to get on board and pass it?"

"Yeah. Too little too late, as the saying goes. Obama lost faith with the masses when he gave billions of taxpaying dollars to banks and Wall Street. Then after he rescued the greedy crooks who caused all our financial problems, he gave billions more to banks and corporations to make loans and hire people. And what did they do, John? They fixed their books and did little to help the economy."

"Guess you right on that. Now guys like John Boehner; other rich Congressmen, and the tea party buffoons are doing everything in their power to make Obama a one-term president."

Earl gave an affirmative nod and changed the subject. "Your boy Max Cleland sho' was interested in your girlfriend after he saw you with Ashley's daughter at the proposal conference."

"Man, that nasty rascal went to Ashley for a massage and wanted her to work around his scrawny little dick. She…"

"Say what?" Earl almost choked on the spicy, dirty rice.

"Yeah, Ash called me and said, 'Guess who I just threw off my table.' She did not know who he was until he started getting nasty. Then she remembered me talking about a redneck named Max Cleland who lost some contracts to me. And get this Earl, sucker asked her was she intimidated by his size."

Earl could not believe his ears. "Should have known he was up to no good when he asked me about her during the tour of the Albemarle Building. What did Ashley tell him?"

John laughed. "Told him my man had a lot more than that little thing, and threw him out."

They laughed so hard, the Obama bashers stopped their gossip and looked in their direction.

Earl finished his tea. "I knew the cracker was foul. Didn't know he was a pervert too."

After their meal John asked Earl to go with him to his truck because he did not want to be overheard. Once inside he said, "Earl, we go way back. We even smoked a little weed back in the day."

Earl smiled. "Yeah we did. Kinda wish I had me one now. They ought to make that shit legal."

John agreed. "To make a long story short, I got caught with an ounce of weed."

"Why you sneaky rascal, I thought you had stopped."

"Well, I have quit now. It really got to Ashley the way it went down and I promised her that was it."

He told Earl everything that happened and that if Pauline Wooten got wind of it she would use it to get rid of him. John spent thirty minutes telling his friend about a revolutionary way of cleaning state buildings; a plan he hoped to present to the state one day. What John needed was another janitorial company that would help him execute the plan. He told his friend he wanted that company to be Horn Janitorial, and asked if Earl was in.

Earl said, "Count me in. With that plan I'd be making more than I am now."

"Great, I knew I could count on you."

They talked for a while longer, and then promised to stay in touch.

⋏

Wednesday morning arrived with shocking news. Ashley tore open the envelope, from Wake County Family Court. *Frederick Parsons, you son of a bitch.* She screamed. He had filed for sole custody of Sonja and a hearing had been scheduled for October 3rd, a month away.

John ran into the living room. "Ashley, what's wrong, you scared the shit out of me."

She handed John the summons. He read it twice and sat down on the sofa. "There's no way the court will let him have sole custody. Sonja has been with you all her life. How could they suddenly decide she needs to live with that bastard?"

Ashley plopped down beside him. They were both in their robes. Twenty minutes earlier John was grinding on Ashley from her back side. He told her the doggy position was easier for pregnant women. Both of them hollered as John pulled her to him, driving himself as far as he could go.

Now this.

Ashley remembered how angry Fred was when he promised to take Sonja away from them. "I know why he's doing this. He can't stand to see me with a black man. I told him that if you were white he would keep the arrangement we have. Do you think we need a lawyer?"

"Gee, I don't know. You would think Fred's lawyer would have advised him that the odds are against him to win."

"The thing is, when his pompous ass wants something, he listens to nobody," Ashley said.

"I say we wait until the hearing. The court will not make a decision on one hearing. We'll know then if we need a lawyer. Are you going to tell Sonja what he's up to?"

Ashley thought. "Guess I'll have to tell her, because I'm not taking her to visit him ever again. If he wants to see his daughter he'll have to come pick her up."

John dressed for work.

Each month he went through all his storage areas, checking and making sure there were no problems with the vacuum cleaners and other equipment.

Ashley was on vacation and had notified all her clients that the office would be closed for a week. She was looking forward to spending Thursday with Cynthia. They would leave the kids with Cynthia's niece while they went to K&W in Cameron Village.

John parked his white cargo van and went to Facility Management to check his box. Most of the inspectors were busy at night supervising work crews, and had little time to inspect buildings and fill out inspection reports. Still, contractors were advised to check their boxes once or twice a week.

It was lunch time and things were quiet in the building. In John's box was an official looking letter that made him nervous. He went to the snack bar in the Dobbs, sat at a table, took a long breath, and opened the letter. It read:

Dear Mr. Colby,

It has come to our attention that you were arrested on September 16, 2011 for possession of marijuana and speeding to avoid the police.

The State of North Carolina cannot and will not tolerate such reckless behavior from contractors. By speeding to avoid police, you endangered the lives of our citizens. There is also the possibility that you are a drug addict.

Therefore, the State of North Carolina will no longer do business with Colby Cleaning Service. You have 15 days from the date of this letter to remove all your equipment and vacate the buildings you currently clean.

The letter was signed *Pauline Wooten* with a copy going to Ronald Height and Chuck Davis. The purchasing department also got a copy.

John took another deep breath, hoping to control his emotions. He knew this could happen but thought he was in the clear. He read the letter again while grinding his teeth in rage at Pauline's words: drug addict, endangering lives, vacate property. *Bitch finally got what she wanted. Probably somewhere now gloating.*

He despised her with every fiber of his being, in spite of the fact had he not gone to Big Ed none of this would be happening. *If it ain't one thing it's another.* That's what his mother said when things went wrong. How would he tell Ashley? More bad news was the last thing she needed but he knew she would be the first one he told.

There was no need to service his vacuum cleaners so he got in his truck and headed home. With each passing moment the weight of the news became heavier. How was he going to pay his bills, his mortgage?

I got to fight this cancellation. Maybe I can plead with Chuck Davis or the director. After all, this is my first offense and no one was hurt.

As he drove down New Bern Avenue on his way to the 440 Expressway, depression seized him like never before. His Plan B, the one he discussed with Earl, would save the state money, but now there was no guarantee they would accept the plan; and even if they did it would take time.

Financial counselor Suze Orman advised people to have an eight-month emergency fund. John had enough funds to last about three months. After that he would be bankrupt. He knew all this could take place if his crime was made known. Still, he was not prepared for the pain, fear and embarrassment he was feeling. Without his contracts he had nothing.

Devastated, he walked into his house. Ashley came from the bedroom where she watched "Days of Our Lives." Immediately she knew something was wrong.

"What is it now?"

"Our worst fear has come to pass. Pauline Wooten found out about the weed." Earlier, Ashley had handed him her letter of bad news, now he did the same and handed her the notice.

She sighed. "When it rains it pours." She thought for a moment. "Shit, if they found out, maybe Fred knows too and he'll try to convince the court I'm living with a drug addict." She yelled at John for the first time in their relationship. "I told you over and over to stop that crap! Now look! John Colby..." She began to cry.

They were standing in the middle of the kitchen. John came to her, tried to hug her for comfort, but Ashley would have none of it. She pulled away.

He managed to say, "Ashley, please, I'm sorry. I know I should have listened. You...you and Sonja deserve better. I... I'll understand if you want to leave me."

Ashley turned suddenly and slugged his jaw as hard as she could with her fist, making him fall backwards. "Leave!" she screamed. "I'm carrying your baby; my daughter loves you, and all you can do is suggest we leave!?"

She stormed back into the bedroom and slammed the door.

⅄

Pauline returned from lunch and checked the box of Colby Cleaning Service. Her cancellation notice was gone. She smiled. *Yes!* She called Sam to her office.

"Yeah boss, wha's up?"

"Sam, I'm going to put a note in each of the contractors' mailboxes alerting them to an emergency meeting on Monday at 10 am to discuss some important issues. Some of them might not check their boxes, so I want you to call everybody on this list to make sure they're here. Make sure you say it's mandatory and do not mention what the meeting is about."

"Will do. So you finally got rid of Colby?"

"Yes! Finally."

Chapter 13

After Ashley slammed the door to their bedroom, John slept in the guest room, tossing and turning. He worried, and hated, and wallowed in guilt. Finally at midnight he took three sleeping pills even though the directions said take only one. He fell into a deep sleep and did not hear the door open the next morning.

"John." Ashley called his name again.

She was ashamed of herself for hitting the man she loved so hard in the face. He was so good and loving to her and Sonja. They were living rent-free because John would not take money for any expenses related to the house. During their five years together she'd saved $40,000. Money they would now need.

When he did not answer, she walked to the bed and shook him. "Honey, wake up."

"Huh...hmmn." He turned to face her.

"Oh my goodness! John... baby I'm so sorry...oh wow, look at your face... wait, ooh."

John was startled at the attention. His jaw was swollen and the lower part of his eye was puffy. But he felt like shit inside, so might as well look like shit.

Ashley returned with a cold wash cloth and knelt by the bed. "Baby, please forgive me. I didn't know I hit you that hard." She placed the cloth on his jaw and some of her tears dropped to his face.

John took her hands and kissed them. "Don't worry about that. It's not as bad as it looks. I bruise easy, always have. Can we just make up and start figuring how we're going to calm this sea of trouble that's come on us?"

Ashley removed the cloth and kissed his bruised cheek, his forehead then pushed her tongue into his mouth. She stretched out on top of him and they stayed that way for a long time.

At last Ashley sat on the edge of the bed. "You remember what that, aahh, what's his name, Reverend Johnson, said about trouble coming into your life, like waves of the sea; one right after the other. He said we need to be like King David who cried unto the Lord and trusted Him for deliverance. Maybe that's what we need to do."

"Wow, you were paying attention, huh?"

"Yeah, I was. I really enjoyed myself, and so did Mom and Sonja. Maybe we need to find us a church."

"We do. Until that time we can go to Lenny's church."

Ashley kissed him again and got up from the bed. "I came to tell you I'm going to Mom's house to pick up Sonja, and then we're going to spend the day with Cynthia."

"Okay, tell Cynthia what's going on. I'll call Lenny later."

When she got to the door, she turned and looked at the man she was crazy about. "Honey, when I hit you, I was so mad when you said you would understand if we wanted to leave you. We'll never leave you. Promise me back."

John sat up. "I promise you Ashley Whitfield. I will love you until the day I die and beyond…and that as long as I live on this earth, I will never leave you."

They came to each other and embraced. Their vows joined them in a love that would last forever.

Slowly releasing him, Ashley reach inside John's pajamas. "Stay home baby, I'm coming back for this."

John grew quickly and moaned as Ashley walked out the door laughing.

"Baby, you can't leave me like this," he yelled.

ʎ

Clara Whitfield lived in a two-story brick and stone home near Ashley Woods. Her four-bedroom home sported hardwood floors and featured a spacious, casual living room with wood fireplace for those chilly nights in Cary. The master suite with sitting room was on the second floor with a door that opened into a beautiful sun room with a wide view of the backyard.

Ashley marveled at the home her mother said would be hers one day. Clara had always dreamed of a home like this, and paid cash for it when her husband died. As Ashley pulled into the driveway it was comforting to know that the three of them could live with her mother if things got bad.

Sonja was at the door waiting. "Mom," she jumped into Ashley's out stretched arms. "I miss you and Colby."

"Oh sweetheart, we miss you too. Have you been having fun with Grandma?"

"Yeah, we went to the mall, swimming… we went to the zoo in Asheboro."

Ashley hugged her mother. "You two been on the go, huh?"

Clara knew everything that had been going on. She could not believe Frederick Parsons would try to get sole custody of Sonja. As for John losing his contracts over weed, she told her daughter not to be too hard on him, that a lot of older people smoked it. She laughed and said she did it a few times, but it made her crave food.

Ashley could not believe her mother. They laughed when Ashley said she told John to stop, not knowing her mother might be a bad influence.

Once they were in the car about to leave, Clara said, "Together, we are family and together, we can overcome anything."

"Thanks, Mom. Love you."

"Love you, Grandma," Sonja said.

Lenny's house in Worthdale off Poole Road was a simple brick, A-frame house. It had three bedrooms and two bathrooms, and a small kitchen. Lenny marveled that, when it was just him and Ruth, the house was full of tension. And now with someone in every bedroom, the house was full of joy.

They were all excited about spending the day together. Cynthia opened the door grinning. "Hey girlfriend. Hey Sonja, how's my girl?"

"Hey Miss Cynthia. I'm fine." Sonja then ran to the girls who held out their hands for her to join them on the couch.

Cynthia said to Ashley. "Ain't no need for us to sit around, I'm ready if you are."

"Let me go pee," Ashley said.

"Mom!" Sonja shook her head, as they giggled at Ashley rushing down the hallway.

When Ashley made the left onto Poole Road, heading to Cameron Village, Cynthia noticed a somber mood come over Ashley. " Okay, what's wrong?"

"John lost his contracts."

The news was numbing to Cynthia and she said nothing. She and Lenny were just talking about the extra money they could make during the holidays by working more at night with Colby Cleaning Service.

Finally, Cynthia managed to say, "Did you say what I think you just said… John lost his contracts?"

Ashley said yes and told Cynthia what happened. By the time they reached Cameron Village, reality set in. Cynthia was wide-eyed, and in a state of disbelief. "This means I ain't got no job!"

Cynthia wanted to see where Ashley worked so they parked near her office.

Ashley said to Cynthia. "You don't seem surprised that your boss smoked weed?"

"Not really. I smoke weed and I seen John's eyes kinda red one night; and Clarence, that sneaky-looking guy on the third floor, said he saw John's truck parked near Big Ed's one night. Big Ed sells the best weed in town."

"Cynthia, you better stop smoking that stuff before you get into trouble like John did."

"Oh no girl, I mean I used to smoke weed. With deacon Lenny always on my tail, I ain't got no time for weed."

They laughed hard and Ashley was glad they were together. Cynthia had an easy way of making you feel better.

Cynthia was impressed when they entered the waiting room for clients in Ashley's office. "Girl, this is a nice office. Is this is where your clients come first?"

"Yeah, and we got two nice-sized rooms through this door, and a restroom in the back."

Cynthia commented on the extra room. "It's nice you got space for another therapist."

"Yeah, I do." Ashley pondered a thought. "You'll soon be unemployed. You could take the course for massage therapy, get your license; work here and share a small percentage with me of the clients you get."

"Sounds good, only one thing. I ain't got no money to pay for a course, and don't want to ask Lenny. He's done too much for us already."

A light bulb went off in Ashley's brain, again. "I'll pay for your course, per your signed agreement that you will work out of my office for at least four years."

Cynthia laughed. "You and John just alike, always thinking how to make some money."

"Still, you need to think about it. I'm pregnant and will be hiring someone soon. So it means once you get your license you have a place to work."

"Okay, we'll think about it." Cynthia replied. "Right now let's go eat, I'm starving."

"Me too. Besides we need to figure out a way to help John."

The two beauties walked to K&W restaurant drawing every available eye in their direction, especially the men. They ate their lunch laughing and talking, learning more about each other and how much they were alike.

As they sipped their tea, Cynthia saw the somber mood returned to Ashley's being. "Is there something else?"

"My ex-husband filed for sole custody of Sonja."

"Say what? So you decided to let me have a load of bad news before, and after we ate?"

Ashley gave a half smile. "Like the preacher said, bad news comes in waves." She gave Cynthia the details and what life was like with Frederick Parsons. And just like before, Cynthia was aghast and wide-eyed.

She said to Ashley, "You and John got a lot going on. We got to find a way to get through all this and come out on top."

Ashley was touched by the way Cynthia identified with their problems by saying *we*. "That's so sweet of you to say *we*. Thanks."

"Girl, you ain't got to say thanks. John is special. Hope you don't mind me saying it, but your man could have been banging me left and right but because he was so in love with you, he refused …he's so… so honorable."

They laughed at her description. "Yeah, John is fine and sweet. I love him so much."

They spent the rest of the day going to a few shops and then out to Crabtree Valley Mall. When they returned to Cynthia's house, the girls were in the yard teaching Sonja how to play hopscotch.

⅄

John lay around the house all day napping, watching the news, and re-runs of "Gunsmoke" and "Bonanza." He heard a car door shut and went outside. Sonja saw his face, and said, "Colby, what in the world happened to you?"

As John scooped up Sonja, he saw the discomfort on Ashley's face. "I got stung by a bee yesterday."

Sonja was tired and sound asleep by eight o'clock.

Ashley came out of the shower naked and climbed on top of John who had been laying in wait, naked himself. She whispered in his ear, her breath warm and penetrating, "I told you I'd be back for this." Ashley moaned, lowering herself to consume him. Finally when she couldn't go any further her body erupted in a volcano-like explosion. She leaned forward, pressing her breasts into his chest and sucked his neck to keep from screaming and waking up Sonja.

John blacked out, or thought he did.

⅄

Monday morning arrived; the conference room at Facility Management was buzzing with what the meeting could be about. Everyone was there but John Colby.

Max Cleland said across the long conference table. "Hey Earl, where is your boy?"

Earl Horn had a foreboding feeling when he did not see John. He thought about what John told him at lunch that day in Bojangles. He told Max he did not know.

Pauline Wooten appeared and the conference room grew silent. Sam Boswell closed the door. It would be a short meeting. Pauline remained standing. "A situation occurred recently in which a contractor we do business with was arrested for possession of an ounce of marijuana and speeding to avoid a police chase.

"That contractor will soon be without any contracts."

Everyone looked at each other and realized it was John Colby.

Pauline said, "I can see by your faces you know who it is by their absence from this meeting. So yes, the State of North Carolina canceled Mr. Colby's contracts."

A buzz of conversations broke out amongst the contactors and for a moment, Pauline let the shock sink in.

Max Cleland looked at Earl and gloated, then asked a question. "The bid prices show I'm next in line; does this cancellation of Colby's contracts mean I'll be awarded the Albemarle Building?"

"I will check with the director and the building manager, but I see no reason you should not get the contract." Max was ready to explode with glee.

Pauline cautioned him. "Please be aware we are looking at other measures of cleaning so there is no guarantee."

The group of twenty contractors became quiet again.

"Let me be clear," Pauline said emphatically. "The State will not tolerate criminal behavior, and when appropriate we will cease doing business with the contractor and cancel all accounts as we have done in this case.

"Are there any questions?" She waited five seconds. "Okay, thanks for coming. Be sure to sign the sheet Mr. Boswell has confirming your company's presence at today's meeting."

Max Cleland was elated with the news and wanting to make fun of John's friend said, "Earl, you might blow the competition away, but are you blowing something else, like your buddy?"

Some of the contractors giggled. Pauline heard the comment and shook her head at how John Colby crucified himself.

Earl was pissed and replied loud enough for everyone to hear him. "That ain't hardly as bad as I hear what you did…trying to intimidate John's girl-friend with your little dick while on her massage table."

Everybody gasped, then chuckled, or laughed out loud. Max Cleland turned red, rolled his eyes at Earl and quickly removed himself from the building.

Earl laughed inside. *Take that you sorry ass cracker, fucking redneck bastard!*

Pauline heard the comment too and warned Earl with a grin in her voice. "Mr. Horn, please hold that kind of language for another place."

Earl went to his truck and dialed John's cell. "Hey John, we just had a meeting a while ago…"

John interrupted, "The meeting was about rubbing my face in the dirt and Pauline's command to you guys that you'd get the same treatment if you followed my lead."

"Damn, that's exactly what happened, how did you know?"

"Even though I was canceled, they still put a notification in my box about the meeting. The note didn't say what the meeting was about, but I knew."

Earl told John about his exchange with Max Cleland and they had a big laugh. He asked John if he needed him to do anything and John said not now, maybe later.

◢

Greta Wooten lay exhausted from the chemo treatment she received for her cancer on Thursday evening. She and Pauline agreed with the doctor that the way to go was double mastectomy. Pauline assured her mother they were go-ing to beat her breast cancer, but Greta was not so sure. The doctors said the same thing to her relatives who died from the disease, and Greta's attitude was that it was only a matter of time.

Time was what she needed to get her financial house in order. The doctor had said that it could take up to eight months to recover because of her age, so Greta decided to take chemo treatments for a month. She would have the operation as soon as she took care of some business.

Her lawyer did give her some good news. She would be able to collect on the insurance policy she had on Otis. He was still working to update her will. The thought of that brought back Clarence Farmer's disgusting words: "I'll be in touch."

The telephone rang but Greta did not recognize the number, so did not answer. Twenty minutes later the phone rang again. It was the same unfamiliar number. She wondered, *Who is this, please don't let it be that little weasel.*

She picked up the phone but did not say anything.

Clarence Farmer nervously said, "Hello, Mrs. Greta, this is Clarence."

Speak of the devil. "Yes!" She said angrily. "Our business is over, Clarence. I'm not feeling well and you should make this your last call. Good bye!"

Before she could hang up the phone she heard the words *convicted of murder.* "Say what? Convicted of murder, you're the one that…that did it."

"Yeah, I did, but only 'cause you paid me to. I'm ready to confess what I did to Otis, and why. At least in prison I'll be getting all my food free, and health benefits free. I need dental work now and cannot afford it."

Greta's worst fear was about to happen. He wanted more money. And once that was gone she was sure he'd be back for more. She fought back. "I can tell the cops you're lying, that I had nothing to do with Otis's death. Where's your proof?"

"Well, I got Otis' wallet. The cops will want to know how I got it. Some of Otis's belongings are still in a backpack in my closet, and I took two pictures. When he went on the lam, he went to D.C. and I found some receipts from the rooming house in his bag. And I betcha, if it's possible to look at your bank account fifteen years ago the cops will find a $25,000 withdrawal."

Greta wanted so badly to be done with Clarence Farmer. He was the only one who knew. "What do you want?"

Yes! Be cool. "Fifteen thousand is all I need to get back to Greenville and live out the rest of my days."

Her voice shook with hatred. "Seems like I heard a shitty line like that before. How do I know you are not lying? You blow the money and then come creeping back for more. If I do it you'll have to turn Otis's stuff over to me."

Excitement filled Clarence's wicked veins. He was almost there. "I'll be glad to turn the stuff over to you. When do you think you will have the money so we can end this affair?"

"Affair!?" A murderous rage entered Greta's voice. "This is not an affair, this is all a bad mistake. But I can tell you this, if I do this and you come back to me a third time, I'll kill your sorry black ass myself."

Clarence knew this would be the last time he would be able to go down this road. There was no doubt in his mind she had the guts to do it.

He asked her again. "So when can we do this?"

"Call me in two weeks!" Greta slammed the phone down before Clarence could say anything.

A minute later Greta's phone rang again. She was too weak to scream, so she growled. "Now you listen you son of a...'

"Mom, mom, whoa, it's me, your only daughter. Good grief, who got you that mad?"

"Oh, I'm sorry; hey baby. Aahh, it's nothing. Just some sales guy, and this medicine got me weak and my nerves are bad."

"Ooh, you poor baby. It's almost lunchtime. I'm going to Lowe's Foods and get you a sandwich and soup."

"You sure you can break away? That sure would be nice."

The way things were going with Pauline and her boss, she could do anything she wanted. "Sure I can. Besides the only thing going on around here is the buzz of Colby Cleaning Service losing his accounts. I'll see you in an hour."

"Okay baby, bye-bye."

Everything was falling into place for Pauline. When January 1 rolled around she would be director of Facility Management...that is if Ronald Height kept his word, and she believed he would. When she moved into his office in January, she would keep her door closed for a few months until the staff and other visitors to her office got used to the name and title on the door.

Her fantasy would come true. The media would cover the story, and local news stations would want an interview of the first black female to hold such an important position. Pictures would be taken at Ron's retirement party of him shaking her hand and passing on the reins.

Managers and supervisors within Facility Management would be doing things to win her favor. Jealousy would pervade every fiber of Chuck Davis' being, but he would be afraid to cause trouble. And best of all her salary would jump to $55,000 a year, a $20,000 promotion.

It was also good she and Tony were seeing each other again. He stopped by her apartment a few days ago and made love to her. She did not want to be giving her body to two different men, but Tony was so persistent. She could not wait for her sexual interlude to be over with Ron. He told her in the office that day the next time they got together he would have a surprise for her. Three days after that they got together and all he said was *Just trust me,* he was working on something and wanted it to be a done deal before he told her. They would be seeing each other Monday night. If he would not give her concrete proof this time, Pauline knew he would be just another man using her.

What really made Pauline happy was the relationship her mother had with Tony. She was sure they would both gang up on her whenever she and Tony would have a fight. Their goals were the same: Greta wanted to see her daughter married before she died; and Tony wanted to make that happen.

When Pauline arrived home from Lowe's Foods with the sandwich and soup her joyful spirit waned. She thought, *If only Mom could be healthy.*

Chapter 14

Ashley Whitfield wore a flimsy t-shirt she borrowed from John, minus a bra. Her red shorts rose high on her tan thighs. She was working in her flower garden on a balmy, early fall Friday, when a car pulled in the driveway. She did not look up; she knew who it was.

Frederick Parsons had come to pick up Sonja. She knew he was watching her and finally she turned and walked towards his car, her breasts gently bouncing. Frederick Parsons became aroused, remembering the times in their bedroom. He would not admit to himself the regret that tore at him for letting her go, and that he longed to have her back, knowing it would never happen.

He may have been aroused, but Ashley was pissed. "How can you do this to Sonja, Fred? You know she would rather stay with us. Why don't you just admit it, you're jealous I fell in love with a black man."

"I told you I was going to take her away from you and I am. She'll understand later. You'll be free to come spend time with her whenever you want. Now where is she, you knew I was coming."

The windows were open and John and Sonja had been watching. They heard Fred when he raised his voice and asked for her. John said to Sonja, "Don't worry, you can make it through today and Saturday, and Sunday we'll pick you up."

"I'm gonna be sad the whole time I'm there, Colby," Sonja said with poked out lips.

John picked Sonja up and tenderly hugged her. They walked to the waiting car, and Sonja fought back tears while hugging her mother. Ashley whispered, "Be strong baby, we'll see you Sunday."

Ashley removed her sunglasses and gave Fred a scowl…grabbed John's hand and they walked towards the picnic table under the tall poplar tree. For a while, they processed their thoughts in silence.

Then John said. "Go to work with me tonight. You can bum around, talk to Cynthia to kill some time while Lenny and I close some loose ends. After we're done we can all go grab a bite to eat."

Ashley got up and sat in John's lap. "I love you, John Colby. Actually I'm crazy about you."

⚑

Later that evening Lenny said to John, "Man, where you gon' put all this equipment? You got barrels, mop buckets, four buffers, and who knows how many vacuum cleaners and maid carts, whew."

John wearily replied, "Have to cram it into my two storage buildings, put what I can under the house, and if necessary buy another storage building."

They were standing at the loading dock with the gate up when Clarence came out with his trash for the dumpster. He heard John tell Lenny he had one more week to get everything moved.

John told his employees that his contracts had been canceled, but that he hoped through appeal to reverse that action. He knew there was no chance he could keep his accounts, but he did not want his employees to quit before the contracts were over.

Clarence Farmer went back to the third floor with his mind made up. Tonight would be the last time he came to work for Colby Cleaning Service. In one more week he was to call Greta Wooten to get his hush money. With fifteen grand, he would do the same thing Otis did: disappear. The only difference was, he was not going to hide. If the cops found a reason to talk to him they could come to Greenville.

Once he got the money he would trade in his raggedy car for a used pickup truck. That way he could still earn money as a handy man/landscaper.

He was proud of his convincing performance over the telephone with Greta Wooten. He thought, *I should receive an Academy Award. To think that old broad would believe my life is so bad I would turn myself in for murdering Otis.*

He laughed to himself, and then thought of where he would ask Greta Wooten to bring the money. The newspaper carried an article about the deep cuts the State of North Carolina was making in every department. The article listed the Capitol Police, the agency charged with protecting state property, a victim of the budget cuts. There would be fewer, if any, patrols of buildings because of the cut backs, and by then Colby would be long gone from the Dobbs building.

Clarence decided the safest place to meet Greta might be at the Dobbs loading dock sometime after 10:00 pm. He could get the money, turn over Otis' belongings, walk back to Moore Square and get the last bus to his rooming house.

▲

Ronald Height could not believe how much he enjoyed his secret sex with Pauline Wooten. However, he was annoyed with his libido. After the first round with Pauline he could not have an erection strong enough to do the things he would like to.

Recently while browsing the Internet he saw an advertisement that said what he wanted to hear: *Last As Long As You Want.* The main ingredient was 1000 milligrams of yohimbe, along with DHEA for testosterone, an herb called horny goat weed, and one gram of l-arginine. He tried it around the house and it worked. His penis had gotten so hard it throbbed. Tonight he would do to Pauline what he saw the brothers doing to white girls in the porn movies he watched at home.

He fantasized over and over how the night was to go. Get her hot as hell, and then mow her down. He would then take a break, show her the surprise and finish her off in a second round. And it was all about to happen.

Pauline came out of the bathroom naked and smiled at Ron. "I'm all yours," she lied, and wondered what her mother would say if she knew.

There was a sense of urgency in Ron's voice. "Come here, Miss Wooten."

While Pauline lay on her back Ron got on top of her and began kissing her everywhere. When he came to her lips, they kissed each other like dear friends, no tongue. His mouth stopped on her black nipples for a brief moment. His destination was the valley below, and suddenly he went there, surprising Pauline. He had never done that. Even though she was drained from being with Tony Bizaro a few days ago, Ron's mouth made her moan. There was an added thrill of sorts that it was the director of Facility Management whose head was down there. She had miniature eruptions.

Once Ron was inside of Pauline, she had another surprise. He lasted four times longer than his usual five minutes. When he finally exploded, sweat was pouring off both of them and Ron gasped for air and rolled off of her.

Pauline said, "My goodness Ron, what have you been taking, you trying to kill me?"

Pauline's words made Ron feel strong. He thought to himself, *Just wait till I come out of the shower and jump on you again.*

Ronald Height kissed Pauline on the cheek and put his robe on. He went to his briefcase to get an envelope. "Here is your surprise," he said smiling. "I'm going to take a quick shower; back soon."

Pauline sat up, putting some pillows against the headboard. The letter was addressed to Deputy Secretary Herbert Standoff. It read:

As you know I will be retiring December 31. I have personally been working with the person I think is the one to replace me. I have spent more than a hundred hours showing her the ropes.

You and so many others know her as Pauline Wooten, our present contract administrator. She has the education and background, and as stated she's been trained by me.

With much confidence I recommend that the State of North Carolina promote Miss Wooten to be the next Director of Facility Management.

Sincerely, Ronald Height

Pauline trembled. A surge of excitement took over her being. In three months she would be director of Facility Management. She read the letter again. She had seen Ron's signature a thousand times. The letter was authentic. Ronald Height knew enough people in the Department of Administration to get his way on certain requests. He worked with the governor's staff on many projects and events held at the Capitol or on Fayetteville Street Mall. More importantly he was a friend of Deputy Secretary Standoff. His choice for the next director was guaranteed.

The shower refreshed Ron and he returned ready to realize the second round of his fantasy, his genitals empowered by a new-found herb. Dressed in a robe he sat at the table and poured two glasses of champagne.

Pauline got up, and while putting on her robe, said, "Oh Ron, you don't know how happy this makes me. Thank you, you won't be sorry."

She came to him and sat on his lap. "Wow, from what I feel, you ain't through with me yet."

They laughed. Then Ron became serious. "I had my doubts at first of you or Chuck being able to take over. Who knows, a little racism might have existed in that judgment. I'm glad you ran into me that day."

Pauline sipped her champagne and got off Ron's hard penis. She wondered what he had taken, as she sat down in the chair opposite him.

Ron continued. "My wife is recovering well and thank God for that. That means that our affair will have to end."

"Does your wife suspect you're having sex with someone?"

"I don't know. I told some good lies, but Ruby knows me. That's why I have to stop. You don't find many women who will give their husbands permission to get sex from someone else due to their sickness."

Pauline was happy to hear their sexual relationship would soon be over. She had what she wanted and her boss was happy. She stood up, letting her robe drop to the floor. "I'm going to shower like you did; back in a second."

Ron smiled. "I'll be under the sheets waiting."

Their second round was like the first, except this time Pauline was so happy and appreciative to her boss for keeping his word, she let her mind and body be involved with what Ron was doing to her. She gripped him tightly, saying loudly in his ear. "Oh yes, Ron, yes, thank you!"

It took Ron forever to arrive; finally he entered space and the galaxy beyond.

After their lovemaking they had coffee and Ron checked them out of the hotel. Ron let Pauline leave first. See ya tomorrow, Miss Wooten."

"Okay Ron. Thanks again."

Ronald Height lived on the outskirts of Clayton and took the 440 Beltline heading east. Mentally he was feeling good, macho. He thought, *I wore her out tonight. Had Miss Wooten moaning my name.* He laughed to himself and decided he would have to get a bit more of her, now that he could perform the way he wanted to.

Physically, he was worn out and wished he had not drunk the wine and coffee. It was giving him a bad case of heartburn and gas. By the time he reached the exit for Highway 70 East his heartburn changed to severe pain in his chest and he was alarmed. Before he could get off the curve that took him to Garner, his foot slipped off the gas; he was dizzy. His head and chest pounded; the car slid onto the grass and he slammed on the brakes. Ronald Height choked on his last breath and died of a massive heart attack.

⋏

Tuesday morning arrived. John Colby parked his truck along the brick wall at the Dobbs, so he would not block other delivery trucks. He and Ashley decided it would be worth a try to appeal the decision to cancel his contracts. It was his first offense; he paid the fines and no one was hurt.

It was 9:30 am. Pauline's door was ajar, so John tapped lightly and walked in.

"Yes, Mr. Colby," Pauline said impatiently.

John sensed she was on edge about something so got to the point.

He said, "This run-in with the law was my first offense. I paid the fines and nobody was hurt. I was not driving recklessly as your letter said. Fast, yes, but not without regard for traffic signs and red lights. I want to file an appeal to reverse this decision to cancel my contracts."

Pauline had been awakened at 2:00 am by a call from Deputy Secretary Standoff. He said that Ron suffered a heart attack and was dead. Pauline dropped the phoned in disbelief and cried. Secretary Standoff kept calling her name until she picked up the phone. He told her to meet him in his office at 7:30 am. She almost dropped the phone again when he told her that he was accepting Ron's recommendation and that she was now the new director of Facility Management.

She had not slept since his call. There were too many thoughts running through her brain. And now here was someone she could not stand, talking about appealing a decision.

She looked at John with disdain. "I can tell you now your appeal to Facility Management is denied."

"I thought I would give you some respect and come to you first. Should have known that would be a waste of time. I'll see what your boss has to say about my request."

Pauline gloated. "I am the boss. See, you have not heard. Ronald Height is… is dead." It was hard for her to say the words. "You are looking at the new director of Facility Management. If you want to submit an appeal to the Department of Administration, you can, but I'm sure they will uphold my decision."

John inched forward towards her desk, leaned over and looked Pauline Wooten in the eyes. "Tell me now, why do you hate me? You know I'm one of the best companies the state has…something you should appreciate."

For a minute Pauline thought she was going to have to call for help the way Colby stared at her with his big eyes. With a smirk she said, "It's the way you always got to keep talking how things use to be under Sarah Jenkins. And I heard what you said to your friends about somebody jumping on me and riding the evil out of me."

Pauline's face went from smirk to scowl. "And now that I'm the director, you can kiss my ass, John Colby."

John thought about slapping her but instead he countered with, "Well, I can see your promotion has made your head bigger than your ass."

"Get the hell out of…."

John slammed the door. Before leaving the building he stopped in the men's restroom. Chuck Davis was washing his hands.

"Hey Chuck. Just had a fight with your new boss. Damn, can't believe she's suddenly the new director."

"You! I can't believe Ron is dead. They say he died out by Highway 70 early in the morning...had a heart attack. That's all we know."

"Chuck, I need a favor. I can see an appeal to that cancellation notice I got is useless now. You think you can contact Standoff on my behalf so I can have until the end of October to... as Miss Wooten said in her notice...vacate the premises?"

"Sure John, don't see why not. I was against the cancellation but Pauline and Ron overruled me. I'll call you back later."

"'Preciate it Chuck. Wished you were the one getting that position."

"Thought I had a shot one time, but then Pauline and Ron started getting cozy. She was spending a lot of time in his office. Ron's change towards Pauline and blacks in general softened; making a few of us around here wonder if any hanky panky was going on, know what I mean?"

John chuckled. "Well, pussy'll do that to a man...make him change, forget who he is...he start doing things he never thought he would do...especially a good piece of pussy."

"I know that's right," said Chuck, laughing as he left.

John sat in his truck digesting the half hour just spent at Facility Management. Pauline Wooten was the boss. It was time to implement Plan B. His future with the State of North Carolina was over. She was already seeing to that.

Plan B was plain and simple. He would take the last checks from the State of North Carolina and buy another restroom cleaning machine and begin a service that concentrated on cleaning restrooms and maintaining floors. Those who managed real estate, government properties, and others responsible for the cleaning of their buildings would be shown how to reduce their housekeeping budgets by having the most critical areas of their properties professionally cleaned using new, money-saving technology.

John was hopeful that he could make enough money to keep paying his bills. If the loss of income proved to be too much to overcome by slow growth of his new service to businesses, then he would file for bankruptcy. Plan B also called for finding a way to share his revolutionary plan on a new way to clean state properties.

Damn, I was almost there, he thought. The Albemarle Building would have brought him $11,000 per month. This was the one account he longed for. It was suppose to be the catalyst for becoming debt-free. All his back taxes, credit card bills and small loan balances would be paid off.

To make matters worse, he was scheduled to marry Ashley in November, and within a few days they would be in court fighting Frederick Parsons's child custody suit.

His cell phone brought welcome relief from his troubling thoughts. He looked at the number. "Hey baby, wha's going on?"

Ashley said, "Guess who's coming by for a massage this afternoon?" She waited, knowing he had no clue.

John laughed. "Okay, okay; I give up already."

"Sgt. Posey. He told me that day we were waiting on you that he might call me for a session. I had a cancellation when he called so he took it."

"Well, I'm pretty sure he's not like that pervert Max Cleland."

"No, I don't think so either. I kinda like him. If I get the same good vibes like before, I'm going to ask if he would like to meet mom."

"You women ain't happy unless y'all meddling in somebody's affairs."

"Be quiet Colby," Ashley said laughing. "Mom's lonely and I can tell he is so… Anyway, whatever. How'd it go with you this morning?"

John told her what happened, then said, "I just hope Chuck Davis calls me today with approval of my request to have until the end of October to leave."

"Don't be down, honey. We can make it without your income if we have to. What we need to keep our mind and prayers on is defeating Frederick Parsons in court."

⅄

Meanwhile, Pauline Wooten got up after John slammed her door, opened it and put a DO NOT DISTURB notice on the door, locking it when she closed it back. She sat down to her computer and clicked on the website for News 14 Carolina.com. The station's focus was local news 24/7.

The station carried a picture of Ronald Height. Under the picture were the words in capital letters: *Facility Management Director Found Dead by Motorist.* Ron's smiling face unnerved her. She clicked on the story and felt sick. There was another picture of Ron slumped over the steering wheel. His car was on the grassy section of the exit ramp to Highway 70. A motorist had found the body, and while waiting for police took the picture on his cell phone. News 14 had gotten hold of it.

Pauline saw the picture and gasped. She leaned over the trashcan to puke, but the only thing that came out was the coffee she had been drinking since Secretary Standoff called her with the news of Ron's death. She rinsed her mouth out with the bottle of water she had on her desk and finished reading the story.

The police had no comment as to where Ron was coming from. It appeared he was on his way home. It seemed to police that the victim died of a heart attack and that was all they said. The rest of the story was about Ronald Heights's career with the State of North Carolina.

What worried Pauline was an investigation that would uncover her affair with the director, and whether or not that affair led to her getting the director's job. Her staff would be first to crucify her. Their sneers and gossip would be too much. She had a nauseating thought. *The men will really disrespect me and might even start saying I fucked Ron to death.*

She wondered all morning if their last sexual interlude had anything to do with his heart attack. The metamorphosis that took place in Ronald Height's libido was amazing to say the least. The first round had surprised her, but the second round lasted almost an hour, exhausting Pauline. Ron rolled off her gasping for breath like he did before, only this time worse.

Pauline was too worried. Her previous fantasies about the positive coverage from the media concerning her promotion were replaced with visions of a scandalous expose of a black woman who was willing to screw her way to the top. She got up from her desk to pace the floor.

Ron told me he always reserved the hotel room with cash, so probably the only person that knows is the lady who reserved the room. Maybe I should go give her a few hundred dollars to stay silent. She looks like she can be bought…Ron, Ron, why did you have to go and die!

She thought of Ruby, Ron's wife, and how much she knew. Then, Tony Bizaro. She was in love with him, but if the affair was uncovered, he would drop her like a hot potato. She thought how she did her best to humiliate and embarrass John Colby. Now it looked like she might get a taste of her own medicine. Usually when she had a serious problem, she would talk it over with her mother. But how could she burden her mother? The radiation treatments were wearing her down enough.

Pauline's thoughts got the best of her, so she went home to rest. Before she left she sent a memo to the staff of Facility Management alerting them to a meeting in the morning at 10:00 am.

Chapter 15

John spent the rest of the week taking inventory of all the equipment he would not need for the short time he had left with the State of North Carolina. He made a note where everything was located. Lenny was right; he had more equipment than he knew what to do with. If finances got really bad he was sure he could sell it all and get $30,000.

He moved a lot of equipment to his storage areas at home; the rest he stored at the Dobbs Building since its loading dock was more accessible than the one at the New Education Building He was moving his floor scrubber machine to the Dobbs Building when his cell went off.

"Hello."

"Hey John, Chuck. Good news, got your request cleared through purchasing. Told Standoff what a good company you've been for the state and that I was sure Miss Wooten would not mind if we extended your time to the 15th of November."

"Thanks Chuck, I owe you one."

"No problem. Well, I'm off to lay ol' Ron to rest today. Have a good one, John."

"You too Chuck. Thanks again." *Wow, how suddenly your life can change*, John mused. *How suddenly your life can end.*

⚙

Edenton Street United Methodist Church was celebrating its bicentennial. Since 1811, the church had seen the Civil War, two World Wars, a host of conflicts and tragedies like the Great Depression, and more recently 9/11.

Today the historic church was doing what it had done thousands of times before for its members. The funeral of Ronald Height was being held. State officials, employees and friends gathered to pay their final respects. The staff of Facility Management was given its own section behind the family.

Secretary Standoff gave a special eulogy just before the sermon. He had asked Pauline if she wanted to give any remarks, but Pauline felt she might get too emotional and cry. In a strange way she and Ron had become good friends. She asked Chuck Davis to do the honors.

At the grave site, final rites were given and Ronald Height was lowered to the bottom of the grave. People began dispersing, while others milled around and gave final sympathies to Ruby Height and the family. Pauline told her mother and Tony to wait while she spoke to Ron's wife.

Ruby Height was sitting down, and Pauline bent slightly, forcing herself to look into the warm eyes that greeted her. "Mrs. Height, I wanted to tell you how sorry I am. We will all miss Ron."

Ruby smiled, squeezed Pauline's hand and motioned her to lean closer so she could whisper in her ear. "I know what you and Ron were doing. Thanks. You helped him when I could not. There will be no investigation."

Pauline was flabbergasted. She almost tripped when leaving. Greta and Tony noticed how shaken Pauline looked. "You all right?" Tony asked.

Pauline nodded yes and they proceeded to the car in silence. Now she knew why there was no further mention in the news of what may have happened to Ron. There was a long obituary in the *News & Observer* with a photograph. Pauline remembered what Ron told her about Ruby's parents and siblings. Her grandfather, Hermot Lee Meriwether, had been a power broker in state politics, and was a powerful member of the Masonic Grand Lodge. Her father, who was still alive, had the same connections. He had an extensive career in law enforcement and had retired as director of the State Bureau of Investigation; her brother was a lawyer for the city of Raleigh. The obituary listed heart attack as cause of death. Ruby Height did not want a scandal revolving around her husband's death and had her family quell an investigation.

Pauline said to herself, *Maybe I've been worrying too much and now I won't have to bribe the receptionist who reserved the room for our affair.* She took a long breath, exhaled and lay her head on Tony's shoulder as he drove. This would be a secret she would have to live with. Only a few people knew and they wanted it to remain a secret. It was time for her to start thinking about being the Director of Facility Management.

⚸

John, Ashley and Sonja went to church with Lenny and Cynthia. Bethel Baptist Church had a new preacher and they all enjoyed the service. Afterwards they left Sonja with Cynthia and her girls while they went to lunch with Clara, and her new friend, Harold Posey.

Sergeant Posey was happy the ounce of weed found under John Colby's automobile seat led to his new friends. Clara was on his mind all the time. She was so thoughtful and affectionate. It had been a while for both of them when it came to sex, so they took their sweet time enjoying each other.

He liked Ashley the very first day he saw her, and was glad she introduced her mother to him. He was fast becoming a part of the family, something he had been missing for years.

Posey befriended John, remembering his reluctance to do it with his daughter's Hispanic boyfriend. John was the man Ashley was madly in love with. He saw it in her eyes when she looked at him. He learned how hard John worked over the years but never had the chance to really grow big because the finances were not there. He could not believe there were times John was grossing $40,000 to $45,000 per month, and banks still would not loan him the big bucks. Evidently banks decided his success was a fluke and he would not last.

Posey took a swallow of beer and said to John, "Now that we're becoming friends, John, it's about time you told me where you disappeared that day."

John laughed. "I can see you ain't gon' be satisfied until I do. Promise Ash you won't take me in."

Ashley and her mother smiled. Posey promised.

John told him about the brick wall that made the entrance to the New Education loading dock invisible from a certain part of the street, and how he pulled his car all the way to the gate and watched police fly by a few seconds later.

"Oh, you mean that if I had my head turned sharply to the right I would've caught a glimpse of you?"

"Relax, Sarge, it's all over," John said laughing.

Ashley said to Posey, "Harold. We have that custody suit hearing coming up Wednesday. Do you have any connections in the family court division?"

"I'm afraid I don't. We've come across a few domestic cases where parents or live-in couples get in fights over children. We handle any violence or crime, and refer the abuse and other social issues to the right people in the county."

Clara said, "Fred Parsons needs a swift kick in the ass."

"I still do not believe any judge in his right mind would rule in his favor," John added..

"I just hope you're right," Ashley chimed in.

Posey asked Ashley how she had prepared for the hearing.

"Fred and I signed a waiver to forego the mediation process. I had to send to the court a list of reasons and evidence of why I'm contesting Fred's sole custody case."

"What are your reasons for contesting?" Posey wanted to know.

Ashley snarled. "I said Frederick Parsons is an arrogant racist buffoon, and is incapable of providing the loving environment Sonja needs."

They laughed in amazement. Clara said, "No you didn't, did you?"

"Okay, I did not say it exactly that way. But I did say his actions are motivated by jealously and possibly racism."

"Possibly my foot," John interjected. "You should've seen his hateful look that day I dropped Sonja off. Sonja hugged me tightly like she always does and I can tell it got to him."

Clara repeated what John said. "You've taken care of that child from birth; the judge has to rule in our favor."

John and Ashley had a feeling that Fred might try to make it appear Sonja was in a bad environment. John confessed to Ashley that Fred had seen him coming out of the Sheriff's department the day he got fingerprinted.

John sipped his lemonade and nudged Ashley to look at who was walking their way. It was Max Cleland with his snooty, old-looking wife in tow.

Max said derisively, "Well, if ain't John Colby. Got to thank you for that Albemarle, the new director just let me know I would be getting it. And just think, all for a little puff, puff." He put his hand to his lips like he was smoking weed.

Ashley and Clara stood up at the same time and threw their drinks into Max's face. "Go to hell you son of a bitch," Ashley growled.

Max's wife gasped in horror. Posey grinned. Other patrons were amused and appreciated the excitement.

John vowed he would find a way to get Max once and for all. He hated losing $11,000 to a man who disrespected his wife-to-be, and now had the gall to try and humiliate him.

Posey said, "Would you ladies like more tea?" They all had a big laugh.

⚓

Cynthia looked into Lenny's eyes, that is when Lenny was not looking into his plate for another piece of Bojangles chicken, or a mouthful of dirty rice. "Ain't that something Lenny, me and you falling in love."

Lenny swallowed and said, "Yeah, but I got no regrets."

Cynthia pushed her foot across the floor and ran it down the calf of Lenny's leg. "I missed my period for September."

For the first time Lenny stopped eating. He looked at the woman who made him moan and holler in the bed. He could make love as long as he wanted to. He always remembered his former wife telling him to hurry up; and often would close his eyes and say *Thank you, Jesus.*

He said to her. "Wow, I pray to God you're pregnant. Nothing would make me happier."

They were on their way to work. Monday had come and gone. It was now Tuesday evening. When Clarence did not come to work Monday, Lenny told John he and Cynthia would do the floor.

Lenny went back to eating. Cynthia was not hungry and was looking around. She said, "Well I'll be if it ain't ol' sorry ass Clarence in the flesh."

They waved at him. Once Clarence Farmer had his three-piece chicken dinner he came to their table.

Lenny said, "Hey man where were you last night?"

Clarence shrugged and acted aloof. He no longer needed Colby Cleaning Service. "Well, you know how it is, man. Come a time when you need to move on."

Cynthia wondered why Clarence was acting so uppity. "That's true, Clarence, but it would have been nice to let John or Lenny know, especially seeing how they let you get away with some sorry cleaning."

Clarence grinned and widened his sneaky eyes. "My, my, kinda late to be going supervisor on me, ain't it?"

Lenny finished his meal. "What you want me to do with your last check?"

"Oh yeah, forgot about that. You got a pen?"

Cynthia opened her purse. *Nigga forgot about his check?* She asked, "Clarence you find another job?"

Clarence sucked the chicken off the bone, wiped his greasy hands and reached for the pen. "Naw, got a little investment ready to pay off. When it does I'm going back to Greenville to live out my days." Clarence wrote his address in Greenville where the check was to be mailed.

They parted wishing each other well.

Later that evening they told John what happened and he was not surprised. Most everybody that quit with no notice or concern for their employer were usually black and low-life like Clarence.

The shift was over and the other employees had gone home. John was finished, and hit the close button on the loading dock gate.

Cynthia said, "Tell Ashley we'll be praying for you guys tomorrow."

"Will do," John said.

⋏

Pauline Wooten was livid when she arrived for work at 8:00 am. She checked her e-mail and there was a notice from the purchasing department that the request to give Colby Cleaning Service until November 15th to be out of the building was approved. She dialed Chuck Davis's number and told him to come to her office.

It was a wonderful feeling having Ron's office which had a big window facing Salisbury Street. The room was big enough to hold a small meeting.

Unlike her old office with two chairs and small desk, she now had a big, cherry-red mahogany desk, leather chairs for her visitors and a large black leather couch. Along one of the walls were a table with chairs, two computers, and a file cabinet. Ron use to tell everybody it was his work station.

Chuck Davis walked in to see what his new boss wanted. "Yeah, Pauline, what's going on?"

"Chuck, did you contact purchasing requesting John Colby get more time to pack his bags?"

"Yeah, I did. A very good company who I think was treated unfairly asked me if he could have a few more days to get all his equipment out. I called Secretary Standoff; he ran it by purchasing and it was approved. Is there a problem?"

"The problem is I would have never given him more time, and as contract administrator, that decision should have been made by me."

Chuck Davis was not going to be intimidated by Pauline Wooten. He did not give a damn about her promotion. He learned from a person in Standoff's office that Ron had recommended her to be director before he died. He had his suspicions about the cozy relationship the two of them developed all of a sudden.

Piss me off and I'll ask did you fuck Ron to death for his position. He growled, "Well, boss lady, it's done. Is that all you want?"

Pauline gave him a hard look. "You're right, I am the boss, and from now on don't make any final decisions on things I need to know about."

Chuck grunted and walked out.

⚔

John, Clara and Sonja walked from the parking lot on Salisbury Street to the front entrance of the Wake County Courthouse. After going through the metal detector they walked to the directory to see where Family Court was located. They caught the elevator to the 5th floor. Before the elevator closed, a black woman with blonde hair rushed in.

John looked at her hair, and remembered a picture of Beyoncé sporting blonde hair on the cover of a magazine. He thought, *Twenty years ago it was us brothers processing our hair into waves like the white man…now it's sisters sporting brown, red, and blonde hairstyles, colors normally seen on white women.* He wondered if black women were making some type of statement. To him blonde just didn't look right on a sister, especially if she had a dark complexion.

They walked in to a mini-court room. Frederick Parsons and his lawyer, Harold Diggs, were already seated at one table. Ashley and John sat at the other table. Three long, brown pews ran the length of the court room where family, character witnesses and other concerned parties sat. Clara and Sonja sat on the front row behind John and Ashley. Since Sonja was almost eleven years old and very intelligent for her age, the judge allowed her to be in court.

Frederick Parsons leaned back in his seat, certain of victory. Through powerful contacts in the Masonic Grand Lodge, he got Judge Henry Van Waltrip to hear the case. Waltrip told Fred he would need good evidence for him to rule in his favor, especially in light of the child being with her mother all her life. Fred assured him they would be ready.

Judge Waltrip entered the court and everyone stood. He nodded for them to sit. John noticed his *I gotcha back* glance to Fred. Ashley said Fred knew powerful people and was good at getting his way. John started feeling uneasy.

Judge Waltrip began. "I see both of you have waived the mediation process. Today is the pre-trial hearing. Both sides will have thirty minutes to present your evidence. We'll begin you with you, Mr. Diggs."

"Your honor we won't need thirty minutes. Our evidence is already before the court. We can prove that Sonja Parsons is being raised in an environment that is not conducive to her health and well-being. John Colby, the boyfriend of Miss Whitfield, was arrested for an ounce of marijuana. He recklessly sped through the streets of our city to escape police, instead of obeying their command to pull over.

"I cringe at the thought of Sonja being in the car with him and a terrible accident occurring, or what could have happened to one of our citizens.

"Because of this reckless behavior we have learned that Mr. Colby has lost all his contracts with the State of North Carolina. This means he will have no income. He was already deep in debt, and was levied more than once by the Internal Revenue Service for failing to pay his quarterly taxes.

"These dire circumstances could drive Mr. Colby to use more drugs. He could very well become abusive. We would ask the court to notice the complaint by a mall security guard that involved Mr. Colby assaulting a teenager because he bumped into Miss Whitfield."

John sat in his chair, pissed that he could not get up, kick Fred in the ass and slap his lawyer's face for trying to make him into a desperate drug addict who beat up a minor. The guy John remembered giving a few punches was every bit of six feet and 200 pounds.

He and Ashley expected Fred to go this route but John did not expect him to go this far. *Maybe next they'll say the funny-looking birthmark on my thigh is a sign I'll begin molesting Sonja.*

Harold Diggs concluded. "We would ask the court to award sole custody of Sonja to her biological father because of Mr. Colby's negligent behavior. Thank you, your honor."

Ashley wanted to scream. She regretted not having smashed Fred's head with a frying pan that day he told her it was time to rev up the old eggs and get on with giving him a son.

The court reporter stopped typing when Diggs finished. Judge Waltrip looked at Ashley. "Miss Whitfield."

Even though she was pregnant, Ashley looked stunning in her purple dress. The top of the dress revealed her high cleavage and gave her the look of a sexy lawyer playing a court scene.

Judge Waltrip looked over his wire-rimmed glasses to take in more of her. He said to himself, *This babe is fine as ever. Fred's a shit-head to let her get away. I see why everyone calls him an asshole now.*

"Your honor, this custody suit is about me and my daughter. I hope the court will notice Frederick Parsons' lawyer spoke only of my boyfriend's recent misfortunes. The picture he paints of constant drugs in the home is totally untrue. If you ask my daughter who is right here if she ever saw Colby smoke weed she will say no. In fact, I've been with him over five years now and I've only seen him smoke once or twice.

"The loss of income, the debt, is all real, but we can handle that. We are getting married in November in spite of these few misfortunes. You will see from my income statement that I make $10,000 to $12,000 a month, so our problems are not as severe as this lawyer implies."

Fred grinded his teeth when he heard Ashley say they were getting married; he had no idea Ashley was making that much money. He had been too busy looking for dirt on John.

Ashley's voice became cold. "Truth be told your honor, we believe this suit is racially motivated. Frederick Parsons is jealous I'm in love with a black man, and he's taking this route to punish me."

Diggs objected. "Your honor, we would ask Miss Whitfield to refrain from unfounded accusations of my client. He is only interested in the well-being of his daughter."

Before Judge Waltrip could respond, Ashley said with contempt to Diggs, "If your client is so interested in Sonja's well-being why would he want to take her from the mother she has been with all her life? Why would he want to do the very thing that would make this child miserable?"

"She loves her father, but the thought of her staying with him and having only visiting rights for me is already having a bad effect on her. She worries all the time. And what proof have they given to the court that John smokes regularly? They are making all these allegations from one incident."

John and Clara had the same thoughts. They were proud of Ashley and the way she expressed her disgust with Fred's move to take Sonja away from them.

The judge looked at Diggs and then Fred. "Gentlemen, the lady has a point. Do you have any evidence other than what happened on…" he paused to look at the arrest record… "other than what happened on July 15th of this year?"

Frederick Parsons shot John a devilish sneer.

Harold Diggs was confident. "Your honor, we have a witness that will testify John Colby regularly bought marijuana from him. Unfortunately, he could not be here for pre-trial. We do however, have a signed, notarized statement of one Edward Manor, better known as Big Ed, who supplied Mr. Colby with drugs."

Ashley looked at John helplessly. John decided while listening to Diggs that they would have had to pay Big Ed to signed a statement like that. An ounce of marijuana lasted him two to three months. He didn't want anybody to know, so he smoked alone. He motioned for Ashley to come to him. He stood and asked the judge if they could have a minute. Waltrip nodded yes.

"Tell the judge this man is lying, and that we need a couple of days to respond and to possibly hire a lawyer."

Ashley made the request and Judge Waltrip went into his authority mode. "Miss Whitfield, this court no doubt would have ruled in your favor. Taking a child, who is deeply reluctant to leave a woman who has cared for her, all her life, is certainly frowned upon by the court.

"It seems however that your former husband does have credible evidence that the environment in which Sonja spends most of her time may not be conducive to a normal upbringing.

"Mr. Diggs, do you have any objection to a second day of pre-trial?"

"No, your honor, in fact we will be able to have our witness appear at the next hearing."

"Today is Wednesday and Friday I'm busy. Therefore we will re-convene at 10:00 am Monday morning." The court reporter stopped. Judge Waltrip rose to leave and everyone stood.

Harold Diggs looked at Ashley apologetically. He did not want to file this suit for the exact words Ashley had used when she described the case: racial motivation and jealousy. But what was he to do? He was the family lawyer, he told himself. The real reason was his firm was in need of cash. And since Fred was determined to go through with it, he would charge him the maximum.

As they left the court, John let his crowd go ahead of him. He said to Fred, "Your daughter loves you now, but should you win because of lies and bribery, she is going to end up hating you. What a fool you are, Parsons. You lost the mother and if you keep this up, you'll lose your child."

Fred was speechless. He frowned, knowing the words were true but his hatred and regret drove him. He would keep it up until he took Sonja away from them.

▲

That evening Harold Posey, along with Clara, came out to John and Ashley's place. He wanted to know everything that happened. When they finished briefing him, he said, "So their star witness is a drug dealer who goes by the name of Big Ed. And John, you swear he'll be lying if he takes the stand."

"Harold, I was ashamed. Smoking weed is somn' I did alone. An ounce lasted me forever. I saw his fat ass…"

Sonja alerted Colby to her presence. "No cursing, Colby, you've been a bad boy already."

They all chuckled at Sonja's wit.

"Okay Miss Sonja," John continued. "I saw Big Ed only about three or four times a year. If he is going to testify for Fred that he regularly sold to me, it will be because Fred offered him money."

Clara asked, "Whatcha thinking, Po?"

Ashley laughed. "Po? What's going on with you two? And Harold, what sweet little name do you have for her?"

Posey gave Clara a lusty look. "If you must know, every now and then I call her 'Sweet Thang.'"

Everybody laughed so hard, for a moment the custody suit was forgotten.

⚔

While they were laughing, Clarence Farmer was dialing Greta Wooten's number. She said to call her in two weeks. It was a few days early but he did not want any surprises. He had already been to a used auto dealer on Capital Boulevard to pick out a 2008 Ford Ranger.

Greta Wooten saw the number and cursed. She was cold as the North Pole.

"Well, if ain't the ol' lying murderer, calling in his bribe."

Her words ticked Clarence off. "Whoa, hello to you too. You got the money?"

Greta had been in a depressed mood all week and didn't give a damn what she said to the weasel on the other line. "Yes and no. Yes, I have the money, but it won't be clear to use until another two weeks."

"Another two weeks! Woman, I quit my job 'cause you said you'd have the money in two weeks."

"Clarence, the way this cancer is doing me, I could care less about your problems. I'm only doing this to be rid of your sorry ass once and for all. Two weeks!" She hung up.

"Damn you, bitch!" Clarence screamed into the dead line. Now he would have to pay another month's rent. He dialed Lenny's number.

"Hello," Lenny said.

"Aaah, Lenny, this is Clarence. Don't mail that last check to Greenville. I'll pick it up Friday."

"Okay Clarence. What's the matter, investments didn't pay off?" Lenny tried to return the arrogance Clarence showed at Bojangles.

Seems everybody is a smart ass today. "Naw, investment still good, just making a few adjustments."

After Lenny hung up, Cynthia asked what he wanted.

"Said not to mail his check, he'd pick it up."

Cynthia mused sarcastically, *Wonder what that sorry ass negro is up to.*

CHAPTER 16

John told Posey that Goldsboro was famous for chopped pork barbecue and that he would bring him some. He took the 70 East bypass and headed to Wilber's Barbecue where he ordered five pounds with bread and slaw.

Nostalgia seized John each time he drove down Leslie Street on his way to the house where he was born. On Christmas day there would be gangs of people roller-skating down Leslie Street, on their way to Elm Street. There, more skaters would join the long line and the fun would be on. The sound of the skates hitting the pavement, the legs gliding back and forth in military-like precision, and the long line of arms swinging in rhythm was a thing of beauty gliding up and down the hilly street.

Beale Street was also a treasure trove of memories. The Colby boys and the Jones boys who lived one door away would get together with the other kids to roam the neighborhood, stealing plums and peaches off people's fruit trees. If that got boring they would go smoke rabbit tobacco. John's mother boiled rabbit tobacco and made a strong tea she used to fight colds. Jason, John's brother, swore it cured him of his asthma.

John pulled into the driveway of 311 Beale Street.

His mother and her friend-caretaker were sitting on the porch in the rocking chairs. They both sat on pillows. It seemed rocking chairs induced reflection and good conversation.

Mabel Colby grinned and said, "My son the businessman, how's my boy?"

John bent over and kissed his mother. Just looking at her and touching her made him feel better. He hugged his mother's friend and thanked her for taking care of his mother. After they all talked a while the friend went inside to make tea and start supper.

John moved his rocking chair close to his mother and blurted out, "Mama, me and Ash need some serious prayer. A lot of things have been happening to us, stuff I've been keeping to myself."

His mother smiled. "I know, you ain't been coming clean on everything."

"How you know that?"

"You know how the Lord speaks to me. Been kinda troubled in my spirit when my thoughts go your way. Why don't you tell me all about it."

John spent the next hour telling his mother everything: about the weed, police arrest, the lost of his business, and Ashley's involvement in a bitter custody suit. At one point they moved into the living room which was more comfortable. His mother's friend brought them tea.

When he finished his mother contemplated everything he said, took a deep breath and exhaled. "Son, God can bless you when all the odds are against you. He can move the wrong people out of the way, and move the right people in your way... Oh glory, hallelujah."

John watched his mother get happy and tears filled his eyes to see how close she was to God. He was so thankful for Christian parents, and knew his dad was looking down from heaven.

"Oh yeah," Mabel Colby continued. "My God can have you at the right place at the right time. He can make your enemies become your friends. Don't you worry 'bout nothing. Job lost all his wealth but in the end God gave him more wealth than he had before. We gon' pray that God will do this very thing for you and Ashley."

After they prayed, John heard his mother's caretaker stirring in the kitchen like his mother use to do with the pots. While his mother was catching him up on news of the family, the smell of fried fish floated into his nostrils. For the first time in weeks John felt a sense of relief; that somehow they would come out on top. Like King David, they would trust God for deliverance.

⅄

While John was in Goldsboro seeking divine guidance, Ashley was in Wendell making calls. She was telling Cynthia about the ugly picture Fred's lawyer painted of John.

"Why that scoundrel," Cynthia retorted. "What John need is some support. We can't have that cracker... oops, sorry Ash."

Ashley chuckled, "Don't apologize, I agree."

"We're not gonna let him get away with that. I'll tell Lenny. We'll be there Monday."

"Thanks, girlfriend, knew you'd get my drift."

"I got it baby. See ya Monday."

Ashley had a thought and made one more call.

⚔

Harold Posey wore jeans, a red hoodie, and brown work boots. He did not look like a detective. He drove his old '98 Ford Ranger. He was off duty and nobody knew what he was up to.

The police knew drugs were being sold at Big Ed's house but they could never catch him with the goods. Did Big Ed have a paid informant on the force? That was the question everyone asked. Posey's goal was to cruise back and forth on Tarboro Road, watching the house. He would case the neighborhood to see if Big Ed had any lookouts, guys who would hang out within the block where the house was located and watch for cops, ready to warn Big Ed. If Posey saw a chance to catch Big Ed with customers inside he would barge in.

It could be dangerous; he might catch somebody who wanted a fight rather than go to jail. He might be outnumbered, not knowing who might already be in the house. It was a chance he was willing to take to help Clara's daughter retain custody of sweet little Sonja.

His instincts told him Big Ed was no rat. If he was going to testify against one of his customers, it had to be for money. When Posey found out that Frederick Parsons and Judge Waltrip were Masonic Lodge brothers, he was convinced the deck was rigged against Ashley. Maybe he could level the playing field.

He did not see any lookouts so he parked on Hargett Street facing west so he could pretend he was reading the newspaper and watch the traffic in and around Big Ed's house in his rearview mirror.

During the first hour he saw a few people knock on Big Ed's door. Once the door opened there was a screen door. Somebody said something behind the screen door and the people would leave. There was zero automobile traffic.

Posey toured the block again to break his boredom. This time there were suddenly two people he saw hanging out within the block. When he passed by the side of Big Ed's house along Hargett, he saw a young girl sitting idly on the porch across the street. She was not there his first time around the block.

Posey stayed on Hargett, crossed Tarboro and parked in the same space. He did not have to wait long. A blue SUV pulled alongside Big Ed's house, and a tall black man with a heavy mustache and beard emerged. He removed a bag from the back seat and strung it across his shoulder. When he got to the door someone inside opened it right away.

Posey knew the supplier had arrived with goods in his bag. He could have the police there in no time and catch both of them. He thought about the outcome of a bust. It would look good at the precinct that he was the one who caught Big Ed and his supplier.

On the other hand they would make bail and continue their business until their trials.

He was going to take the law into his own hand. Posey forgot about barging in on Big Ed while he had customers. He was going to bang on Big Ed's door as soon as his supplier was gone. He had not told John, but his view on marijuana was quite liberal. His peers would demonize him for letting a supplier get away. He did not care. He thought weed should be legalized and taxed, instead of wasting billions of dollars trying to stop something people were going to do regardless of what the law said.

The tall black man who could have passed for a college professor came back to his car without the bag. His car was facing west on Hargett as was Posey's. He crossed Tarboro Road and went past Posey's truck. From the out-of-state license plate Posey knew it was a rental. Drug dealers stopped using their own vehicles to conduct business. If they were caught while using their personal vehicles, their transportation would be impounded.

Posey got out of his truck, and waited for the light to stop the traffic on Tarboro Road. He jogged across the street with his head down. Before the girl watching the house from across the street could do anything, Posey was banging on the door as hard as he could.

"Big Ed! Open up the door now or it's coming down! Police!"

Posey had his weapon drawn. The door opened. He flashed his badge at Big Ed who was frowning. A woman in her sixties with grey hair looked at him with disdain. Posey looked around.

"Remember me, Mr. Manor?" Posey had come through the front door. When he looked at the table near the side door entrance he saw the bag the tall black man had carried, under the table.

Big Ed said, "Yeah, I remember you. This ain't your normal bust is it? Where's your company?"

"Who else is in the house?"

"Nobody, just me and my sister you see here."

"Get rid of her," Posey demanded.

The sister leveled more disdain on Posey with her mean eyes and thick lips.

Big Ed motioned with his large face for his sister to go upstairs. When she was gone Posey put his gun up. "I've learned you are supposed to go to court on Monday and testify that John Colby…yeah, remember him, that he was a regular customer. Don't lie to me or I'll call for that company you mentioned and have them remove that bag under the table over there, and take you and your sister downtown. And before you answer think about this. I got a good look at your supplier, he went right past me. I could have him located and picked up within the hour. I'd say your business here would be finished. While you are thinking that over, let's sit down where the bag is."

It did not take long for Big Ed to figure out what Sgt. Posey wanted. "A businessman by the name of Fred Parsons knocked on my door and offered me a deal I could not refuse. One thousand dollars to sign this piece of paper saying John Colby was a regular customer, and another grand, for coming to court Monday and testifying. Two thousand for just that? I like John but not enough to turn down a deal like that."

"How many pounds in this bag, Ed?"

Big Ed licked his lips and his voice trembled. "Four."

Posey looked inside. There were six tightly wrapped bundles. "Looks like six to me. Why you got to lie, you think I wouldn't look in it?"

"Sarge please, I don't know why I lie, I can't help it. Whatchew you want me to do?"

"Answer my first question, was Colby a regular customer?"

"No, he wasn't, I thought I answered that already. I saw John about three times a year, that's all."

Posey put three pounds of the tightly wrapped weed on the table. "Here is what you will do Monday in court. Don't worry about the punk who paid you two grand, he'd rather lose that little money than be convicted for bribing a witness. Once you do what I tell you, I'll bring the other three pounds back, and this will be between you and me."

Posey told Big Ed what to do and left with the bag that had three pounds of weed in it.

ᛘ

Sunday came and John and Ashley stayed home from church. They had been going to Lenny and Cynthia's church but decided to rest up for their day in court.

When they got off the elevator on Monday, the hallways were crowded with far more people than before. John thought some important custody battle must be going on. As he got closer to their court room he recognized some of the people from Lenny's church. He smiled and wondered why some of his employees were milling around. A few of the church members told him the Lord was with him.

John held the door for Ashley, her mother and Sonja. He asked Ashley if she knew what was going on and she said she told Cynthia what had happened last week.

While walking to the front of the courtroom, Lenny and Cynthia waved. The pews were full. Before Ashley sat down she scanned the crowd and spotted her. She smiled. *Good she made it.*

Frederick Parsons considered the crowded court room. *All these cheer leaders are not going to help you Ashley, my judge will see to that. Money and power!* He looked back at his star witness Edward Manor, and knew he would win.

The judge walked in and everyone stood. Frederick Parsons looked dumbfounded. Judge Henry Van Waltrip had morphed into a short, grey-haired white woman.

Judge Mildred Hester had a round face with a double chin. She was too heavy for her short frame and seemed impatient. It was her day off. She told everyone to be seated.

Judge Hester began. "Mr. Parson, I can see your look of surprise and wonderment as to my presence. Judge Waltrip suddenly took ill Friday evening after a dinner engagement. It was too late to postpone, so here I am. I've read the transcript, so we may proceed."

Of all the time to get sick, Fred thought. *Still, I can prove Colby is a regular user. Good I paid this fat nigger behind me to come to court today.*

The judge said to Ashley, "Miss Whitfield since you requested more time, we will begin with you."

Ashley was as shocked as Fred to see Waltrip was not there.

"Your honor, this custody suit is about taking my daughter away from me. On Wednesday of last week, Mr. Diggs painted a false picture of me and my daughter living with a drug addict. He made that statement based on a signed declaration from a man they say will testify that my husband…"

The people crowded onto the long church-like pews clapped and cheered. Frederick Parsons was irritated. His lawyer looked amused. John Colby blushed.

"Order in the court, please!"

"I'm sorry your honor. I meant to say my *boyfriend,* we've been together so long, I feel like he's already my husband."

Parsons gave Diggs a sarcastic smirk; he was fed up. He stood. "Your honor, can you ask Miss Whitfield to suspend her romantic history and get on with it."

Judge Mildred Hester gave Parsons a testy look. "Yes, Mr. Parsons, I can, but I'm not. Continue, Miss Whitfield."

"Thank you, your honor. To refute these accusations and innuendoes that me and my daughter are living with a drug addict: I've ask a few people who know John Colby to say a word or two about his integrity and character."

John gave Ashley a puzzled look. She only told him there would be people there who would support them.

The judge told Ashley she would allow no more than five minutes for each character witness. If the case proceeded to trial she would swear each witness in. For the sake of time, each person would be expected to tell the truth and be brief. Ashley was allowed three witnesses. She had wanted to call four, but would have to let Lenny speak for himself and Cynthia.

Lenny Williams took the stand. He gave his name and told the judge how he had worked for Colby Cleaning Service for four years and had never seen a hint of John being a drug addict. He related how the money helps him pay his mortgage and buy food; and that for the last four years he grossed $12,000 a year just working part-time. There were murmurs of agreement from some of John's employees when Lenny said a lot of people owed a lot to Colby Cleaning Service for providing them an income.

Then Lenny cleared his throat and glanced at John and Ashley with a smile. "Your honor, the fine lady I'm with and who will also testify to John's integrity has consented to be my wife too…"

The crowded little courtroom cheered again.

Judge Hester rolled her eyes to the ceiling in exasperation. "Order in the court, please."

"We just want to say that John Colby is no addict, and more important than anything I'm saying Sonja Parsons is crazy about him."

John was touched by Lenny's support.

Ashley stood, turned and looked at the crowd, and nodded to Harold Posey. She was glad she befriended him that infamous day. He gave all of them a sense of confidence. Her mother was falling in love with him.

Posey had been on the witness stand many times testifying in cases for the prosecution. He looked relaxed in his dark blue business suit. He stated his name and profession.

"Your honor, I have not known Mr. Colby that long. But what I do know when I see one, is a drug addict. This man is not an addict. An addict is a person who use drugs every day and more than once a day. They will do anything to get their fix, and their one goal in life is to be high.

"As a Raleigh police detective I've seen the rich, judges, lawyers, and doctors get caught with a small amount of drugs as Mr. Colby did. These people pay their fine and the case is closed. Mr. Colby was scared and made a bad decision to speed away from a police chase. The following day he realized what a mistake he made and turned himself in."

I love Harold's choice of words, John thought.

Posey concluded. "Mr. Colby paid his fine. And your honor, let me end by saying whoever is without sin let him cast the first stone. I was in Vietnam just as John was. Marijuana was plentiful and it was potent. I smoked it almost every day."

The crowd let out deep sighs of surprise. Clara held her head down and chuckled.

"And as I was about to say, your honor, I turned out okay, as did many others who still use it. People like this should not be termed addicts, or made to seem they are not responsible adults."

Upon leaving, Posey smiled at John and Ashley. When he got near the little gate that led to the seating area, he gave Big Ed a *you know what to do* look.

Cynthia was sitting behind Big Ed and caught the look. She whispered loud enough so he could hear her. "Big Ed, shame on you. We can't believe you gon' testify against John."

Big Ed was uneasy. *If I say somn' against John, this crowd may lynch me.*

Ashley made one more turn to the crowd and smiled at Sarah Jenkins. It was taking her a while to get to the stand, so John turned to see who it was.

His mouth dropped opened. He stood and walked to Sarah. They hugged each other tightly, tears filling their eyes.

Finally John said, "Sarah, is it really you?"

"Yes it's me, now go sit down, I got something to say."

Frederick Parsons threw his hands in the air in an act of desperation.

Sarah Jenkins identified herself and looked at Fred's lawyer with contempt. "John Colby is one of the best persons I have ever had the opportunity to work with while I was contract administrator for the state of North Carolina. He was one of our best contractors. For a long time the state of North Carolina was paying Colby Cleaning Service $39,000 a month. Over the years, and considering he's still in business, the man has generated millions of dollars for the local economy. That fact alone should be enough to redeem this man from any charges."

The crowd of witnesses were stirred once again. *Here, here; yes, you got that right*; and *amen*. Judge Hester exhaled and chastised the crowd with a hard look. They were quiet again.

"Your honor, what I've said is no small feat considering that in the twelve years I worked with John, he was unable to secure any major financing. I don't think he could be addicted to drugs and manage his business the way he has, helping so many people.

"Finally, your honor, let me be as candid as Detective Posey. I smoked some pot before and so have many others. Remember, President Clinton smoked too, he just didn't inhale."

Judge Hester chuckled with the crowd.

"Thank you so much, your honor. I know you'll do the right thing."

Some of the crowd stood and clapped. John stood and gave Sarah another hug and whispered for her to wait for him.

"People please! Miss Whitfield, your half-hour is about up, do you have any closing remarks?"

John Colby looked at Ashley and wanted her. Not only was she beautiful and tough. She was smart. Fred Parsons knew Ashley was squeaky clean, so he decided to go after John. So the woman he loved played Fred's game and brought in people that would make John look good.

Ashley stood and felt his eyes; she looked at him. John's lips said, "I love you." She nodded, and yearned for him like she did that first night.

"Thank you for your patience, your honor. John Colby is a good man. I'm carrying his baby, and we will be married next month. I've cared for this child," she looked back at Sonja, "since the day she was born. She would be miserable if the court would separate us on such a bogus charge, motivated by racism and jealousy."

Diggs was about to object to his client being called a racist, even though it was true. Ashley stopped him and said she was finished. Everybody in the crowd gave Ashley a standing ovation.

Judge Hester allowed them a few seconds, then repeated herself. "Order in the court. Mr. Diggs, you have thirty minutes and may begin." Diggs had to do his job.

"Your honor, Miss Whitfield has brought together some good people who no doubt are very fond of Mr. Colby and I'm sure they are all telling the truth. Yet there may be a side to Mr. Colby no one knows. We said to the court last week that we can prove Mr. Colby is no casual user. We have a witness here today who use to sell marijuana to Mr. Colby on a regular basis and will testify to that if I may call him to the stand now."

"You may."

Big Ed walked to the stand. He glanced at John. Fred Parsons was eagerly awaiting the response of the biased crowd when they would hear John Colby bought an ounce of weed twice a month. Judge Hester said, "State your name and profession for the record, please."

Big Ed's thick lips pursed into a confident smile. "My name is Edward Manor, better known to my business associates and friends as Big Ed. At present I'm retired."

Cynthia let go a big *boo-h* sound under her breath. The crowd snickered.

Judge Hester silently prayed to be finished. "Order in the court."

Diggs was as tired as Judge Hester, so he got right to the point. "Mr. Manor, you know the boyfriend of Miss Whitfield, John Colby, am I correct?"

"Yes sir, I do."

"Isn't it true that you used to sell an ounce of marijuana to Mr. Colby at least two times a month for a number of years?"

"No, that's not true at all."

"Not true!" Frederick Parsons yelled. "You, you…"

Diggs told him to sit down and apologized to the court. He leaned over and whispered to Fred. "You don't want to say something that will incriminate yourself. Give up. You lost."

Frederick Parsons cursed. *That fat ass, black nigger is getting away with my money.* Nevertheless, he knew Diggs was right. If he continued he could wind up charged with bribing a witness.

"Your honor, my client would like to drop this case."

The crowd broke out into cheers and clapping.

Judge Hester rebuked the crowd, "Order in the court!" She had already made up her mind to rule in Ashley's favor regardless of what their witnesses said. She had heard enough custody suits to know this was no more than the effort of an angry, former husband seeking some sort of revenge.

"Mr. Parsons you will be charged court costs. You have wasted two days of the court's time. It's easy to see you are mad as hell and filed this suit out of hatred and revenge. Your lawyer has not said one negative word about Miss Whitfield, and there has been no testimony about her being a bad mother. This case is dismissed, and court is adjourned."

The court reporter stopped typing. Judge Hester left, relieved to be finished with the emotional misfits.

The crowd of support for John began milling around and talking to each other. Frederick Parson's back was to the crowd and he got up to leave, thoroughly embarrassed. He wished he had listened to his lawyer.

Sonja noticed her father all alone and headed toward him. The crowd noticed and stopped talking.

Sonja touched her father on his leg and he turned around, looked down and picked her up.

"Don't be sad, Dad. Just because I want to stay with Mom and Colby don't mean I'll stop loving you. I still want to visit you and spend time with you like we use too. Okay?"

They kissed each other and Fred fought back tears. "I'll be fine, darling, and will call you soon."

When Fred put her down and Sonja started back towards her mother, the crowd resumed their talking.

John and Ashley thanked everybody while making their way to the special guest. Ashley hugged Sarah. "Thanks so much for coming. It means so much to us."

"Especially me," John said while hugging and kissing her on the cheek.

Sarah told Ashley, "I should be the one thanking you for letting me know what was going on. Besides, John and I had a special relationship. We cried the blues on each other's shoulders; know what I mean?"

Ashley's dimples grinned at Sarah. "Yeah, I do. Why don't you and your son come out to our place for dinner? You could spend the night."

"Sarah, that would be great. We can talk about old times," said John.

Sarah Jenkins looked disappointed. "I would love to, but the only way I could get my son to bring me was I had to promise we would leave for home after the hearing."

John shook the son's hand and thanked him for bringing Sarah. The son left to bring the car around to pick up his mother. Ashley and Sonja said goodbye to Sarah, and told John they would wait for him in front of the courthouse.

John said to Sarah, "Thank God I got a chance to see you again. I think about you often, and how much I owe you for the good things you did for Colby Cleaning Service."

They walked slowly, Sarah holding tightly to John's arm. She replied, "I owe you more. I always enjoyed our time together, especially when you were doing you know what."

John laughed out loud.

Sarah chuckled. "I must have been going through a horny, change-of-life stage when I retired; and I could not have had a better person than you to help me get through it." They made it to the street where Sarah's son was waiting. John hugged his dear friend again and they wished each other well.

Once he got back to Ashley and Sonja, he grabbed Ashley and kissed her. Sonja said, "Let's go home, you two."

Meanwhile, Harold Posey was driving his pickup truck to Big Ed's house. Clara was with him. She sat close to him, the way Ashley sat close to John when he was driving. She leaned over and bit his ear lobe.

"I'm in love with you, detective. Do you know that?"

Posey blushed. "I kinda thought you were." His arm was resting on her thighs. "I'm in love with you, too."

"What did you do to that man, Po? Fred and his lawyer were clearly expecting Big Ed to say yes. When he said no, we could not believe it. We all know you did something, we just don't know what it is. So spit it out, detective."

By the time Posey finished telling Clara what he did, he made a right off Tarboro Road onto Hargett Street and parked near the corner like before. He told Big Ed what he would do and what time. Before he could cut his engine off he saw Big Ed coming toward his truck.

Big Ed looked under the tool box on Posey's truck like he was told; took the bag and came around to Posey's side.

"You a man of your word, Sarge. Thanks."

"You did a good job, Ed. Take care."

When he was gone Posey said, "You want to go out to John's place and celebrate our victory?"

Clara put his hand up her dress, all the way to her moist panties. "No, I want you to take me to my house and make me scream."

CHAPTER 17

Pauline was happy she made the decision to award the Albemarle Building contract to Cleland Janitorial Service. Max's company was not as good as Colby Cleaning Service, but they would do a much better job than the last company. Before her boss died she was trying to impress him and Deputy Secretary Standoff with the idea of using state workers and inmates to clean the buildings to save money. Now that she was director, she did not want that responsibility.

She was winning everyone's respect at Facility Management. She met with all department heads and their workers to encourage loyalty to the state and to the citizens of North Carolina by working diligently in whatever they were hired to do. She assured them that they could count on her to look after their benefits and rights as employees.

She decided to raise Sam Boswell's nose a notch up her ass by promoting him to assistant building manager. Chuck Davis would not like the idea, but she did not care. Sam Boswell had been loyal to her while she was contract administrator. She chuckled at the thought: *guess everybody in management need a dependable go-fer.* Sam asked her when she was going to hire another contract administrator. She told him it was no rush since the Department of Administration had closed the bidding process.

Like always, when things were going good on the job and her relationship with Tony Bizaro soared, it was again her mother who worried her. Pauline was upset with her for putting the surgery off until after Thanksgiving, but her mother insisted there were things she had to get done first, so Pauline relented.

She wondered if her mother was hiding something like she was. They were talking that evening after the police stopped by to tell Greta that the bones found at Jordan Lake belonged to Otis Wooten. After telling Pauline about the visit, Greta got up to go to the bathroom, and Pauline thought she heard her mother say, *I hope that's all they find.* But when Pauline asked her what she said, Greta said, *I hope that's the end of it.*

While daughter thought of mother, mother was thinking about daughter. Pauline's sudden promotion to the top job at Facility Management was a big surprise. Greta knew her daughter had the ability to handle the job but there was no indication that it would happen so suddenly. It made her wonder if her daughter was carrying a dark secret.

Greta remembered a few times she wanted Pauline to take her out, go shopping or to dinner, and Pauline would say she had a lot of work. She never said that before. And there was one time Tony complained to her that he thought Pauline was being a little stubborn forgiving him, especially after he told her the truth about what happened. Greta told Tony to be patient; she had been hurt before, but she would come around.

When Greta voiced her surprise to Pauline about her promotion, Pauline said that Ron mellowed out and began treating people with more respect, especially blacks. She said she was surprised too, but learned Ron had recommended her for the position before he died.

Even if she was carrying a secret, it could be no darker than her own.

Greta woke up feeling good for the first time in weeks. All her business had been finalized sooner than expected. Even though Otis had been dead for years she was advised at her law firm to continue paying the premium all along, especially since it was a small amount. For that reason they paid the $150,000 insurance policy in full.

Her lawyer had taken care of her will and she had signed it. She was greatly relieved to know that her daughter was heir to a nice estate and portfolio worth a million dollars, should her cancer take a turn for the worse. And what was best of all, her baby had a man who was sure to marry her.

She thought: *Now my baby won't be alone.* There was only one thing left to do: get rid of Clarence Farmer once and for all. Before her cancer took all her strength, she was willing to pay Clarence the $15,000 to keep his mouth shut and disappear.

Once her insurance policy money cleared, she shocked Clarence by calling him. Pauline decided she would not renew her lease that expired at the end of December. The decision made Greta so happy. They both agreed there was no need for her to pay $1200 a month for an apartment when her mother would need someone in the house with her after surgery. They even talked about Tony moving in. Pauline was back and forth from her apartment moving small items back home, and the last thing Greta wanted was for Pauline to be there should Clarence Farmer call.

They set up to meet near the loading dock of the Dobbs Building. Clarence told her it was safe there after 9:00 pm; that there were no capitol police patrols. Greta felt a little leery doing something so criminal near her daughter's job, but she agreed to meet him Thursday at 10:00 pm. She reminded him again that he would get nothing unless he turned over what he said he had that belonged to Otis.

By Friday she would be able to relax and focus on her disease, Pauline and Tony.

Max Cleland was set to go in the Albemarle next Monday. It was Tuesday evening. He had just gotten off the telephone with his building manager who would be delivering the equipment and supplies to the building on the weekend.

John Colby and his girlfriend may have gotten some laughs at his expense, but he was the one with the last laugh. He thought, *What a shit head. Risk everything for some damn weed. That's just like a nigger. They got a reputation for fucking, but they ain't got no damn sense.*

The thought was so funny he laughed aloud and said to himself as he left his office en route to a Bible study at his church. *Thanks again asshole, I'll be thinking about you while me and the family will be spending some of that $11,000 every month at our vacation home on the beach.*

Wednesday morning found John Colby taking a break in the janitorial office located in the basement of the New Education Building. He had just finished stocking the men's restrooms on the north end of the building. His day man who handled all the custodial duties in the day had to rush his three-year-old daughter to the hospital. John only had a few days left with the State of North Carolina, so decided to fill in.

He looked at the walls and desk and saw many notes in Spanish. There was a Spanish/English calendar and magazines left on the desk. He reflected how times had changed. All of his nine employees who worked in the New Education were of Hispanic descent, except the day man who was black. It was the same in the Dobbs building; all six evening part-time employees, and the day male and female housekeepers were Hispanic.

In the 1990s and early 2000s, all John's employees were black. He recalled having far more stress then, than he currently had now with his Hispanic employees. Black employees missed too many days from the job and their work was mediocre. They often quit without giving notice which drove John insane with having to suddenly replace them. When John tried to show them the right way to clean, or warned them about missing days, their attitude turned to contempt. They got mad or irritated and acted as though he should be honored they were working for him. He got in heated arguments with many blacks who had no respect for his position as their employer. He found great relief in getting rid of them.

On the other hand, his employees of Hispanic descent were totally opposite. They came to work, and if they had to miss a day, they would ask if one of their buddies from another floor could fill in so a day's pay would not be lost. They never quit the job without letting John know in advance, and most of the time would already have an *amigo* to take their place. Their cleaning was better and John did not have a problem with their attitude when he had to correct them. His biggest problem was communication, which he preferred over all the other problems he had with his own race.

He chuckled at the thought of the few white employees he had over the years. They were embarrassed first of all that they had to be hired by a black man. Once John told them what to do and how to do it his way, their tenure was short-lived. They couldn't stomach a low-life job under someone they considered a low-life employer.

Over the years many of the blacks that quit with no notice, or raised hell and got fired, would see John years later and ask him if he had any job openings. John figured they finally realized his dollars were as good as the white man's dollars. Those employees that John remembered to be lazy and came to work when they chose to, got John's patent reply. He told them his Spanish workers came to work every day, and when they quit, they had someone to replace them. They understood, and told John to keep them in mind, which never happened. Their needs were hardly worth remembering.

Twenty-five years of experience he thought. *It's not suppose to end like this.* Years of competing with other companies; the thrill of the award, the agony of coming so close, and losing out because some company decided they could do it for less. Even the stress of managing people and training them how to clean was something he would miss. Cleaning state buildings was all he knew. The bid process was shut down and the economy was struggling. It might be a while before he would be able to bounce back.

His mother called him and said the words that kept every Colby child going when times got bad and their back was against the wall. She said, "Don't you worry, John Colby, God knows all about you. Keep your head up; you a Colby, you can make it."

He knew he could make it, but how? He was putting the finishing touches on his plan to have Colby Cleaning Service clean all the buildings under Facility Management's care.

Under his cleaning project state employees would be involved to help reduce the cost of daily trash collection, which was the major expense of any janitorial contract. The Department of Administration, along with Facility Management would have to issue an edict to all state employees requiring them to comply with the new cleaning rules and regulations.

In each building there would be a central location for employees to bring their trash. If a new trash can liner was needed there would be a dispenser for that. A new liner was to be used only if necessary. This method would eliminate one of the most time consuming jobs of daily cleaning, which is trash collection. The current method of office trash collection was for the housekeeper to enter each office, or stop at the hundreds of cubicles on each floor in search of trash. Once they had a full barrel of trash the housekeeper usually took the full bag and placed it near the elevator. Once all the trash was collected, the housekeeper then took it to the dumpster.

Many times on each floor there might be twenty to forty cans that don't need emptying, or have very little trash; no more than a piece of chewing gum or a few sticky notes. If the housekeeper did not have to spend at least an hour and a half each night collecting trash in medium to large-sized buildings, it would translate into a savings of thousands of dollars per month. The housekeeper could then focus more time on dusting, vacuuming and better restroom cleaning.

John called his plan *Revolutionary Cleaning Project* or RCP, because of the major changes that would have to take place in order for his plan to work. Even some laws of North Carolina would have to change. At present the State of North Carolina was required by law to put its product and service requests, over a certain amount, out for public bid. John was convinced that if he showed the state how to have a cleaner work place for its employees, and save millions of dollars a year, they would make an exception for janitorial services. Besides, laws were made, changed and struck from the books. At each stage someone benefits and someone loses.

Of course John's plan was to benefit himself, while some janitorial companies would be losers. The great benefactor of his plan, however, would be the State of North Carolina. Each year thousands of employees miss time from work due to gastroenteritis and conditions like the stomach flu, sinus infections, and other infectious diseases contracted while they were at work, most likely in the restroom. Productivity goes down and the state ends up paying for sick leave and medical costs.

This repetitive scenario goes on year after year because most janitorial companies do not effectively remove the viral pathogens that lurk on all surfaces in restrooms. These companies hire inexperienced people who could care less about the health of state employees. What they want is to be finished as fast as possible. Thus, armed with glass cleaner and paper towel, they wipe their way through each restroom, pushing and moving bio-contaminants to new positions.

Only Ashley knew of John's secret investigation into the cleanliness of restrooms in the buildings under Facility Management's care. A purchasing agent had told him once that it's always good to have some dirt on folks, especially your enemies. He got the idea after Pauline Wooten's letter canceling all his contracts. There was not enough time to go into all the buildings, so he tested five large buildings, five medium-sized buildings and five small buildings.

To perform the test he purchased an ATP meter, a device that makes it possible to monitor how clean surfaces are by detecting the level of microbial contamination on surfaces in just seconds. The meter measured Adenosine Triphosphate (ATP), which is the universal energy molecule found in all animal, plant, bacterial, yeast, and mold cells. Once surfaces are clean, all sources of ATP should be significantly reduced; the higher the reading, the more contamination present.

His contractor's badge made it easy for him to get in buildings early in the morning before employees arrived, to do his test. In each restroom he took swabs and tested small portions of the floor, partitions around the commodes, toilet seats, and other surfaces that people touch. Each time in every restroom in all the buildings, the readings were off the charts. In some of the restrooms he saw fecal matter on the wall behind the commodes, and in the ladies' restroom, more than once he saw blood stains in and around the sanitary napkin holders.

If John saw a janitorial closet that was unlocked he peeped in and encountered dirty rags hanging on barrels and very little supplies to clean with. He saw filthy mops soaking in almost- black water, which meant the housekeeper intended to use the same slimy, germ-laden water to mop the restroom again. Some contractors had no conscience and no clue what hygienic cleaning involved. He took pictures on his cell phone.

In John's Internet research of viral pathogens and other bacteria, he learned that there are over thirty different types of Staphylococcus (Staph) that can infect humans, however most infections are caused by Staph Aureus which colonizes in the nasal passages and is also found on skin, or in the gastrointestinal tract.

These viral pathogens in a dirty restroom are exacerbated by a process called aerosolization, or "toilet sneeze," because the flushing of a toilet is like a person sneezing without covering their mouth. When a toilet is flushed it produces a menacing cloud of aerosol droplets that stay airborne for up to two hours and travel six to eight feet up and out from the toilet. The greatest aerosol dispersal occurs when the water from the flush meets the water in the bowl. These droplets cannot be seen by the naked eye, but are full of a wide variety of the bacteria found in human respiratory systems.

If a toilet bowl is dirty with rings under the rim, bacteria and viruses can cling to the ring and be ejected during flushing. John read that microbiologists have shown that bacteria that have dried on surfaces may remain infectious for days, weeks, and in some cases months; and that this dried bacteria can be picked up by air currents and vibrations and become re-aerosolized as infectious particles in restroom air.

He thought of the Dobbs Building which had poor circulation in the restrooms. When someone had a bowel movement the smell would remain in the air far too long. If an employee walked into one of those multi-stall restrooms after a person with a stomach virus or some other staph infection who had just vomited, or had diarrhea, then flushed the toilet, that employee could easily be infected.

John's evidence was replete with videos, pictures, and charts about the dangers of an unclean restroom, and the correct way to remove the soils that contain bacteria and make people sick. His problem was who to contact. He wished he had gotten the idea before Sarah Jenkins retired. Now that Pauline Wooten was head of Facility Management it would be almost impossible to get an audience with the right people.

That thought depressed him and he began rummaging through the desk drawers to make sure there was nothing of value left. When he was almost finished he came across a letter from the Social Security administration dated 2007. The letter was about an employee of Colby Cleaning Service. The social security number that John submitted did not match anyone in their records. The money that the department had collected was $800.

Part of the letter read: *We cannot put these earnings on the employee's social security record until the name and social security number you reported agree with our records. This letter does not imply that you or your employee intentionally provided incorrect information about the employee's name or SSN. It is not a basis, in and of itself for you to take any adverse action against the employee, such as laying off, suspending, firing, or discriminating against the individual. Any employer that uses the information in this letter to justify taking adverse action against an employee may violate State or Federal law and be subject to legal consequences. Moreover, this letter makes no statement about your employee's immigration status.*

John smiled and threw the letter in the trash, and thought: *What y'all mean is keep sending that money, that's all we care about, and if you fire this person and we stop getting this money, we might come after you.* He finished cleaning out the desk and took the elevator on the south end of the building to the seventh floor.

His cell phone rang while he was stocking the men's restroom. He looked at the number. "Hello, Mrs. Colby, how are you today?"

Ashley laughed. "Hey honeybee, guess who I just hired as a therapist to help out, while I carry our baby?"

John loved the sound of her words, *our baby.* "Who'd you hire?"

"Her name is Patricia Ann Lucas. After I finished interviewing her, she noticed an old copy of the *News and Observer* on my desk with the story about Ronald Height's death. She worked nights at Candlewood Suites in Durham, where she remembers he checked in on at least three occasions. And get this honey, there was a black lady that arrived a few minutes later every time."

"Whoa…did she describe her?"

"You know, I asked her what she looked like. She reads the paper every day and said it was the same black lady in the news a few days later who was reported to take Ronald Height's place."

John mused about an affair between Pauline and her boss. Maybe this was a chance to get some dirt on the woman who made it her mission to get rid of him. "Did she say anything about the police visiting her for questions?"

"I asked her that too, and she said no. You think I ought to ask Posey to look into it?"

"No, baby. Harold already broke some laws to help us out in that custody suit. It may be that she was never contacted by police because someone does not want an investigation. And if that's the case and Harold goes asking questions, he might get in trouble."

Ashley paused for a second, considering what John said. "Maybe you're right, the article did not report where Ronald Height had been, only that he was on his way home in Clayton. Don't tell me his wife did not know where he was."

"Yeah, I hear you," John said. "Pauline Wooten was being banged by the director of Facility Management."

Both of them laughed at the revelation.

Ashley recovered first. "And honey, more than likely they were making out the night he had a heart attack. Wow!"

"Wow is right. We need to keep this information to ourselves for a while. You think the therapist…what's her name, Patricia, has been talking, 'course I know you just met her, but does she look like the gossipy type?"

"No, I don't think so. We spent almost three hours together. She gave me a massage so I could see if she was good enough for my clients. She's got really good hands, and after the massage we talked some more. She told me she was gay and that she and her girlfriend keep pretty much to themselves in their Durham apartment."

The news left John stupefied. "This is all happening for a reason. Oh well, are you finished for the day?"

Ashley sighed like her daughter Sonja. "Colby, you getting old. Remember I told you Cynthia was cooking lunch. Sonja is around the corner at the Cameron Village library, listening to storytelling. I'll pick her up and we'll go have some fun with Cynthia and her gang. When we leave Cynthia, we'll be home." She giggled sarcastically. "Think you can remember that, dear?"

John retorted, "You won't be calling me old after I jump on you tonight."

"Looking forward to it, old man."

John laughed. "Love ya, baby."

"I love you too, John Colby."

Chapter 18

Thursday evening arrived. John told Ashley he was going downtown to finish going through some storage buildings and check a few other things. He backed his truck to the loading dock of the New Education Building. After loading some barrels and vacuum cleaners onto his truck, he decided to go to the Dobbs. Since his truck was loaded and it was such a short distance he walked. It was nine o'clock.

He started in the second floor storage room. December would make eight years Colby Cleaning Service had been in the Dobbs Building. Over time he used some of the storage rooms to store barrels, vacuum cleaners and other equipment he rarely used. He was going through one barrel separating rags from dust mop heads when he came across a small plastic shopping bag from Vitamin World.

"Well I'll be damned, looka here," he said out loud. Inside the bag was a small pipe made especially for smoking weed, and almost a quarter-ounce of marijuana in a sandwich bag. He remembered losing it a few years ago. He was making room in one of his storages at home and loaded some barrels onto his truck. His intent was to take the weed with him but he misplaced it and could not find it. He gave up after searching hours for it, and hoped nobody would find it.

John smiled. *This shit will probably knock my socks off.*

He had not smoked any weed since the day he promised Ashley he would stop. The desire to smoke was strong at times but he managed to resist the little voice in his head. He thought, *At least I didn't buy the shit.* He put some weed in the pipe and headed for the north end exit.

Construction repairs to the concrete walking bridge over Salisbury Street had been going on for the last two years. A metal gate was there with a big red sign that said *Keep Out.* The gate was not locked so John opened it and took a few steps onto the bridge. The loading dock area to the Dobbs was dark. Lenny had forgotten to turn on the lights when he left.

John fired the pipe up and took a long pull. The aged marijuana burned his throat, permeating his lungs. He coughed hard a few times until tears rolled down his cheeks. After recovering he took a few more hits and inhaled more slowly.

⚜

Time approached for Greta Wooten to meet Clarence Farmer for the last time. She put $15,000 into a brown envelope and stuck it in her bag. She had a leather jacket with deep pockets she bought especially for carrying her .38 revolver. As a single mom she was advised by people at her law firm to take a course in the use of firearms. She did not think she would need it, but took it to be safe.

She was happy the meeting was taking place tonight. Pauline and Tony were coming over Friday after work and spending the weekend. She was looking forward to that because Tony told her that he was going to ask Pauline to marry him. She prayed God would let her live to see Pauline married, and hopefully one day give her a grandchild before she died of cancer.

Greta was thankful for one thing: the police had not come back to ask her more questions about Otis. She hoped that chapter was over and that it would go in the books as unsolved. None of this would be happening if Otis Wooten had not busted his knee. She visited him in the hospital after the injury. His left leg and part of his thigh were wrapped in bandages, elevated in a sling. Her dreams of life with the rich and famous were over…and so was her love for Otis.

Her deep regret was that she did not divorce him. If she did, everybody would call her a gold-digger, a truth she did not want to accept at the time.

At least Otis got paid $100,000 for his brief stint with the Dallas Cowboys. He also got a good job with the post office and they were able to buy the nice house in Cameron Village that would someday belong to Pauline.

Greta went to the kitchen to get a bottle of water. She cursed. The kitchen trashcan was full because she forgot to bring the trash to the street. She had time to bag all the trash and put it in the trunk of her car. The Dobbs Building had a dumpster and she would make Clarence put it there; that was the least he could do.

▲

Clarence Farmer rode the bus down Newbern Avenue. His destination was the stop across the street from the Dobbs. His cell phone time was 9:35 pm. In his shoulder bag was an envelope containing Otis Wooten's wallet, an expired driver's license, and an old identification badge from the post office. There was also a worn out Polaroid picture of Otis, his eyes opened, with a butcher knife in his chest. He would give it all to Greta Wooten; he was tired of it anyway.

Poor Otis, he thought. *It's all your evil wife's fault. How could I refuse twenty-five grand…and just think; now I'm collecting fifteen more g's like a late life benefit.*

He signaled the bus driver for the next stop. By this time tomorrow he would be sitting pretty in Greenville, North Carolina.

A bus pulled around the curb from Wilmington Street, just as John was about to go back inside. He moved behind the concrete column. He had seen buses go past that stop many times around ten o'clock on their way to Moore Square but rarely did they stop. He decided to be nosy.

The bus dislodged its passenger from the side door and moved on. John saw Clarence Farmer crossing the street. He had on a black hoodie and blue jeans. At first John thought he might have gotten hold of someone's badge and was coming back to steal something, but Clarence walked to an open area near the loading dock and lit a cigarette.

John looked at his watch. It was almost ten o'clock. Clarence was obviously waiting for someone. *What is this sneaky weasel up to?* John asked himself.

Just then a blue Honda Civic showed up and pulled alongside the dumpster that was enclosed by a wooden fence. Clarence hurried to the door and got in. John could not hear the conversation; he could only make out a woman driver from where he was watching.

Greta frowned at Clarence and said. "You have Otis' belongings?"

Clarence gave her the envelope and Greta looked through it. She saw the picture and grunted. "So you took two pictures?" Before he could answer, she snarled. "Remember one thing, I will kill you myself if you come crawling back for another dime."

Clarence growled back. "Just give me the money, woman. By the way, been reading about your high-society daughter and all that money she's making with her promotion and all…bet you ain't told her 'bout our little secret, have you?"

Greta seethed with venomous hatred. The nerve of someone she was giving, all total, $40,000 to keep his mouth shut, to mention her baby girl. She abruptly said, "My daughter is none of your business. I've got some trash in the trunk of my car. Can you throw it in the dumpster for me?"

She got out of the car and walked back to the trunk which had to be opened with a key.

When she turned to go to the back of her car, John thought he recognized Pauline's mother. He had seen her a few times at Facility Management.

Greta was so nervous she could not think. She wanted to be done with it all. None of this was in the plan. She was suppose to give Clarence Farmer $15,000 and be on her way home. Instead she was walking a man to the dumpster while clutching her revolver tightly. She realized she had the envelope that Clarence had given her, and did not want it.

"Here Clarence, might as well throw this in there too," Greta said nervously.

When Clarence got to the dumpster, he pulled the bolt back to open the wood door. There was a metal box to the right of the dumpster with red and black buttons.

Greta remembered from visiting her daughter at work that the dumpster made a loud noise when used. She asked Clarence, "Which one of these buttons starts the compacting? I want to be the one to press the remaining evidence of Otis Wooten into oblivion."

Clarence told her the red button. When he turned back to the dumpster, Greta hit the button quickly, pulled her .38 and fired three rounds into the back of Clarence Farmer.

Clarence never knew what hit him, never getting a chance to put the trash and envelope containing the evidence in the dumpster. Greta looked around, there was no one. Her mind was working fast. She thought, *The cops may search the dumpster.* She grabbed the bags of trash and hurried to her car and threw the bags onto the back seat. She rushed back and grabbed the envelope and Clarence's shoulder bag which had her money.

John stood frozen, hyperventilating. He had to get her license tag number to make sure it was who he thought she was. By the time she backed out and was putting her Honda in drive, John had run down the steps, and pulled the hood on his company sweater over his head and acted as if he was going to cross the street.

Greta was looking behind her, when she turned to speed off; there was a man who appeared out of nowhere. *What the hell, where the... oh he look like a homeless person.* She pressed hard on the gas. She could still hear the noise of the dumpster when she made a right onto Lane Street.

John looked toward the dumpster where Clarence lay dying or dead. Blood began seeping under the wood fence onto the concrete. The wood door was opened and John approached the scene slowly. He looked down at Clarence and saw what looked like a photo near his right arm. He was scared as hell, but something told him to take the photo. He did not look at it right away; he had to call the police. He still had the weed on him and rushed into the building and put the picture and weed into a barrel and threw rags on top of it.

He dialed 911 and told the operator who he was and his location. He had to repeat several times that he was taking trash to the dumpster and found a dead man who looked like he had been shot. The police department was around the corner on McDowell Street and John knew the place would soon be crawling with cops when he went back outside.

The lights were out at the loading dock so John went to the first floor and cut them on. The buzz of police activity came to a halt as they all looked to see the dark area around the Dobbs loading dock disappear. John took a deep breath and walked outside.

Two policemen hurried towards him. One asked, "Are you the one who called this in?"

John said yes.

The other one seemed suspicious. "Kinda late for you to be taking trash to the dumpster ain't it?"

John stayed pleasant. "No sir, it ain't. I'm in the building late many nights after my employees are gone."

Two detectives arrived. One of them was Harold Posey. The two detectives talked to a few cops, and then came over to John.

Posey said, "Hey John, wha's up. They said you called this in."

John told him what happened; that he loaded some equipment onto his truck at the New Education Building starting about eight o'clock; that he came to the Dobbs and was going through a storage room in preparation for his exit from all state buildings; that he finished around ten o'clock and saw a bag of trash someone forgot to put in the dumpster; so he did it and found a dead man.

"Do you know who it is?" Posey asked.

"No, I don't. All I could see was his back." John knew it was Clarence and hated lying; he even wondered why he was lying. He could not think.

Posey told John to wait, and came back in seconds. "His name is Clarence Farmer."

"Oh shit!" John tried to be surprised. "Yeah, I know him. He worked for me in this building."

"You don't have any idea what he's doing here?"

"He quit on me a couple of weeks ago with no notice. The only reason I could see for Clarence to be near the Dobbs this time of night is to steal something. He did not have an entry badge, so I don't know."

Posey, like all the other policemen had no clue. A man found dead with three bullet holes in him; nobody saw or heard anything.

John wanted to get the hell away from it all to think about the tragic event he had just witnessed. Moreover, he wanted to be gone before the news media arrived. He said to Posey. "Harold, can I take off? You know where I am if you guys need to talk to me further."

"Yeah, go ahead, you look a little shaken. Kiss Ashley and Sonja for me."

"I will."

John walked through the loading dock door and took the elevator to the second floor. He grabbed the weed and photo; put it under his sweater and kept moving to the south end exit. The gravity of the night's events weighed heavy on his mind. A woman murdered his former employee. The woman more than likely was Pauline's mother. He lied to police, and withheld evidence. It was too surreal. He could not wait to get home to talk to Ashley. He had called her earlier and told her to wait up for him.

Ashley was in the kitchen making coffee. Her man could be so mysterious sometimes. She knew something was wrong by the sound of his voice, but he said he could not tell her over the phone. The eleven o'clock news had ended and one of those celebrity shows was on.

Beyoncé and her husband had spent $1.5 million in preparation for their baby. It really pissed Ashley off how wealthy people wasted their money on things just because they could. She thought, *How many hungry mouths in Africa could that money feed? How many homeless people in Chicago could have been housed and fed?*

She heard John at the door.

John walked into the kitchen and dropped his bag near a chair. "Honey, I witnessed a murder tonight. I saw it with my own eyes."

"Who, where..."

"It happened at the dumpster for the Dobbs Building. You know that black guy on the third floor you said looked sneaky? His name is Clarence Farmer. I saw him get shot in the back and you will not believe who did it."

"John Colby, who was it?"

"Pauline Wooten's mother!"

Ashley was speechless. John told her everything; how he got her license tag to make sure it was her and that he called police afterwards and told them he took some trash to the dumpster and found a dead man. He told her that Posey was on the scene.

Ashley was thunderstruck by the stunning news.

"Crap, I forgot the photo."

"What photo?"

"After Pauline's mother sped away I walked over to the dumpster and looked down at Clarence and there was this worn looking picture near his right arm. Somn' told me to take it and I did. I was so scared, I haven't looked at it."

"Honey, that's tampering with a crime scene. Did you touch anything?"

"No, I've watched enough murder stories on television to know not to touch anything."

John brought his bag to the table and sat down. The Polaroid picture in color was worn, but the picture was in fair condition. "Oh my goodness, look at this."

"Good grief, that's awful, put it back in your bag," Ashley said with a grimace. "What are you going to do? Why didn't you tell the police everything? They can get you for withholding evidence."

John did not know what to do. He was so scared he could hardly think. All he had to do was recount the whole story to police, and if his hunch was right about the woman who shot Clarence, that she was Pauline's mother, it would be an open-and-shut case. Pauline's mother would be arrested for murder.

John answered Ashley's question. "My initial instinct was that Clarence must have something on Greta Wooten for her to be meeting him under the cover of darkness. And after she shot him in cold blood, I figure if I told the police they would just go arrest Pauline's mother and that would be the end of it. All my contracts would still be canceled.

"As bad as I wanted to tell Posey the truth, something just wouldn't let me. Something kept saying all this is happening for a reason. Now, I believe this might be what I need to win Pauline Wooten's help to make Revolutionary Cleaning Project a reality."

Ashley look worried. "I don't know honey. You could get in a lot of trouble; we could get in a lot of trouble.

"I know," John replied wearily.

CHAPTER 19

Greta Wooten had pulled her car into the garage and closed the gate. Before getting out she took the money out of Clarence's shoulder bag and tossed the bag onto the back seat with the rest of the trash. She would come back later and properly dispose of it.

All the evidence that Clarence had was in the envelope. She did not want to see Otis's face again, so she walked to the fireplace and put a match to it. She would have to dispose of the gun later. Greta was too nervous to think of where to dispose of things that would lead the cops to her.

She was still shaking, cursing Clarence over and over. All he had to do was take the money; but he had to be a smart mouth about the money Pauline made. It set Greta off; he would probably try to put the squeeze on his baby girl one day for something she did. She decided then to kill him. She was not sorry he was dead. She prayed she would not get caught. It was after eleven o'clock, so she took a powerful sleeping pill, rinsed off in the shower and lay down.

John and Ashley finally went to bed at 2:00 am. Before John fell asleep he thought deeply how to use what he had witnessed to break Pauline Wooten's anger and resistance against him and become the person to promote his Revolutionary Cleaning Project. If Standoff could be convinced the plan was worthy of consideration, he would know the politicians at the legislative building to get it passed. Standoff was a Republican as was Ronald Height.

Republicans ruled the Senate, and they were all about cutting the budget. John figured they would love the savings rendered through a new way to clean state buildings.

What kept him awake was whether to go after Pauline right away or wait until Monday while he formulated an attack. He fell asleep after deciding to get a little rest and go for the kill while the crime was still hot.

When their house phone rang at 8:00 am, Ashley was about to go out the door to take Sonja to her last summer school class. She answered the phone. "Hello."

"Good morning girlfriend, know you done heard the news."

Ashley thought. *You don't know half the story.* "Hey Cynthia, yeah we know. I was just on my way to take Sonja to school. Call John on his cell, it's time for him to get up anyway. I'll call ya later."

"Later baby." Cynthia dialed John's cell.

"Hello."

"Hey boss, why you go and let Clarence get himself killed?"

"Ain't that something. I'm the one who called it in."

"Say what? The report said a janitor found the body."

John laughed. "I am a janitor, who left before the media arrived. The police will probably contact you and Lenny for what you might know about Clarence. Tell them you know next to nothing."

Cynthia thought for a moment. "You know when me and Lenny saw Clarence in Bojangles he was acting all big-time. When I asked him why he quit, said he had an investment that was about to pay off; even told Lenny where to mail his last check. Then a few days later he calls Lenny all anxious about his check and said he would pick it up. Told Lenny his investment was a little late. Guess his investment killed him."

That's too much information to give a smart cop like Posey, John thought. "Like I said, don't tell the cops any of that, just tell them you only saw Clarence when you came to work."

"No problem. You coming downtown tonight?"

"Naw, you and Lenny handle it. I got some important business to tend to. See ya."

State employees who worked in the Archdale and Dobbs Buildings arrived for work Friday morning to a crime scene. The trash dumpster was roped off in yellow crime tape that extended a few feet out from the wooded fence surrounding the dumpster to where the trail of blood stopped. Most of them already knew what had happened. The report of a murdered man on government property broke onto the Internet and News 14 Carolina around midnight. It was the lead story on all the local news channels that air starting at 5:00 am.

Pauline Wooten's telephone rang repeatedly. People wanted to know what she knew, which was zilch. She told them that the dead man worked for a contractor who was losing all his contracts for getting caught with marijuana and speeding to avoid arrest. She chuckled, knowing it was wrong to make John Colby look suspicious, or somehow connected to the grisly murder. She didn't care. The receptionist buzzed her and told her that Detective Harold Posey was there to see her.

Pauline stood up to shake Posey's hand. When Posey saw her, he agreed with what John had said, that she had it all in the right places. He flashed his badge and they sat down.

"Miss Wooten, I know you are aware of the murder that took place across the street. Do you have any idea who the man was?"

Pauline responded calmly. "No, I don't know him; only that he worked for the contractor who cleans the Dobbs Building."

"You mean Colby Cleaning Service?"

"Yes. The contractor's name is John Colby. He's losing all his contracts for being caught with drugs and speeding to avoid police."

"Do you think Mr. Colby might have something to do with the shooting?"

"I don't know, you'll have to ask him that. What I do know is that everyone was surprised to see that side of him."

"What do you mean?"

"Well, he's the best company we have. He always seemed so upstanding and professional, not someone likely to be involved in drugs."

Posey saw what John meant about Pauline Wooten being out to get him, that she jumped at every opportunity to be a thorn in his side. He saw no need to tell her that John and Ashley had become good friends of his.

"How's your mother?" he asked.

The question caught Pauline off guard. She forgot he was the one to deliver the news to her mother that Otis's bones had been found. "Oh, she's fine. Why do you ask?"

Posey got up to leave. "We have not been back to talk to her about your father be…"

"Stepfather," Pauline hissed.

Posey could understand why she did not like the man. He tried to rape her, then knocked her out. "I was going to say we have not been back to see her because there are no leads. Tell her we're working on it." He handed her his card. "If you think of anything that might be helpful, don't hesitate to call me."

Pauline stood again and they shook hands.

Not long after Posey left, John Colby walked into Facility Management. He could not go back to sleep after talking to Cynthia so he went to the person that dominated his thoughts.

The receptionist started to buzz Pauline. John had known her for years, and gave her a *no need to buzz* signal. He walked into Pauline's office and closed the door behind him.

Pauline's eyes narrowed to a scowl. "I don't recall us having an appointment."

John remained standing and wasted no time getting to the point. He kept his heavy voice low so no one would hear him. "I saw your mother kill Clarence Farmer last night. I witnessed the whole thing and have proof."

He came closer to her desk, pulling the worn picture from his shirt pocket. He held the photo in front of her, close enough for her to get a good look. "If you don't know who this person is, I'll bet your mother does."

Pauline gasped. *Oh my god, it's Otis.* Her gaze was transfixed on the open eyes of her dead stepfather. She stared at the ghastly sight for a long time.

John could see that she knew who he was. He pulled the picture away and put it back in his shirt pocket. Pauline was unable to speak. John felt sorry for her, but kept his eye on the goal.

He said, "You know what I think. Your mother paid Clarence Farmer to kill the man in this picture. Evidently Clarence was putting the squeeze on her for more money to keep silent. I watched them get out of the car to get what looked like full trash bags from the trunk of her car, and go to the dumpster. That's when she shot him."

Pauline recalled the sleazy-looking man reminding her mother that he was a relative of Otis' and that he use to cut the grass. She remembered her mother was visibly shaken. The man said he would be in touch. Pauline did not know what to say or do. Her mother could be a murderer, and the man in front of her could send her to jail, if he was telling the truth. He did have a picture of a knife in Otis's chest.

Her demeanor softened. "Why haven't you told the police? The report said you found the body. And how do you know it was my mother? People do have look-alikes."

"I've seen your mother before, but to be sure, I got her license plate number and had a friend at DMV run a check.

"There is one more thing, Miss Wooten. My girlfriend hired a massage therapist who works nights at the Candlewood Suites. There was an old newspaper on the desk about Ronald Height's death. The two of them got to talking and she said she was on duty the few times he met a black woman there.

"Ashley, that's my girlfriend's name, gets the paper delivered to her office every day, and dug up the issue with you in the news being named as his replacement. This person looked at the picture and said it was you. You don't want me to start telling you what I think on this one."

The only visible sign of life in Pauline was the rising and falling of her breasts. John saw that his first goal was accomplished: paralyze her.

He continued. "I did not go to the police because there is something that I want, but this is not the place to discuss it. Ashley is the only other person that knows what I just told you. We want to meet with you and your mother. Call me at this number." He gave her Ashley's office number. "Ashley's office is in Cameron Village, so we'll be close to your mother's house when you call."

John looked into her eyes. The scowl he saw on her face when he entered her office was replaced with trepidation and defeat. "We expect you to call us soon."

Pauline Wooten was flummoxed by the news her mother might be responsible for two deaths. How strange it was that just a few minutes earlier she was happy to say she knew nothing about the murder across the street. Now, there was someone who said he saw her mother do it.

She had said to herself how cold it was of someone to shoot the poor man in the back. She wasted little time dialing her mother's number.

The telephone rang longer than usual. Her mother's groggy voice came on the line. "Hello."

"Mom, are you still sleeping? It'll be noon soon."

"Hey baby girl, had no idea it was that late." Greta Wooten was exhausted when she got home. She would still be out had the phone not rang.

Pauline tested her mother. "Then I guess you have not heard the breaking news about a murder at the Dobbs Building dumpster?"

Greta feigned surprise. "My goodness no. What happened?"

"A man named Clarence Farmer was gunned down at the dumpster. They say he was shot three times. Mom, he's that same sneaky-looking man that came to the car that day and was telling you he was some kin to Otis, and that he would be in touch."

"Well, you just never know these days. I hadn't seen him in years and now he's dead."

Pauline could feel her mother was lying. "Mom, I'm coming home, we need to talk."

"What's the…" Pauline had hung up. Greta became worried and wondered if she had been discovered.

Pauline made a few more calls and took the rest of the day off. Everything was going terribly wrong. She could not get the picture out of her mind; her dead stepfather with a butcher knife in his chest. It was the harrowing look in his eyes that made Pauline want to puke.

She wondered what Colby wanted. She figured it must be his accounts. He wanted them back. If it would keep her mother out of jail she would find a way to do it. After the way Pauline treated him, she was glad that he was not mad enough to just go to the police.

She was so anxious to talk to her mother she found herself exiting Wade Avenue to Cameron Village in record time. Five minutes later she let herself in the house where Otis had tried to rape her all those years ago.

"Is that you, baby?" her mother hollered from the bathroom.

"Yeah mom, I'll be in the dining room." Pauline poured a straight shot of Jack Daniel's, green label.

It was hard for mother and daughter to look each other in the eye. Both had secrets but Pauline needed to know the truth. She had taken one shot of the whiskey and was pouring another.

Greta spoke first. "Oh crap, it must be bad news if you're drinking this early."

Pauline threw her head back and downed the whiskey. She shook her head. The alcohol set her stomach on fire and settled her nerves…a little.

"Sit down, Mama." Pauline remained standing. She blurted out the question fearing the answer. "Did you kill that man, that man named Clarence Farmer in the news, the one that said he was a relative of Otis', did you, Mom?"

Greta's heart dropped, her mouth opened, but no words came forth..

Pauline felt dizzy and sat down. Her mother's face said yes. "Mom, John Colby, the man I finally succeeded in getting rid of, came to my office and said he saw you gun the man down." She began to cry.

Greta made one final attempt at covering up. "Baby, you can't believe a charge like that from a man who hates your guts."

"If he hated my guts you'd be in jail now. He…he had an old worn photo but you could see it was Otis." Pauline almost screamed. "Mom, it was Otis with a knife in his chest!"

Shit, I didn't even check the envelope; the picture must have slid out. Greta did not know what to say.

"Tell me the truth! John Colby did not make this all up. What did you do?"

Greta fell from the chair onto her knees. "Oh, God have mercy on me. Yes, I killed him, I killed him! And you might as well say I'm the one who drove the knife into Otis's chest, because I paid Clarence to do it."

Greta sobbed uncontrollably, pleading with God to have mercy on her soul. Pauline let her mother cry. She went to the kitchen to get a bottle of ginger ale and ice. When she came back to the dining room, she made two drinks. Her mother stopped crying and sat back down. Pauline said, "You tell me the whole story, starting with Otis Wooten."

Greta took a sip of the whiskey and stood up. "It's a horrible story, baby. I let hate drive me to kill two people. After Otis tried to rape you and then knocked you out, I vowed in my soul to kill him, or make him wish he were dead. And baby let me tell you whenever you hate someone to the point of violence, the Devil will always supply a way for you to carry it out. Enter Clarence Farmer."

Greta recounted the entire episode: how the police gave up looking for Otis but Clarence knew where he was. She would pause only to sip her drink, then resume pacing the blue carpeted floor. She ended the gory tale by saying she went to meet Clarence to give him the $15,000 he demanded for keeping his mouth shut.

She said, "At first I started not to pay him any mind. I said to myself why would he go to the police and admit he killed someone just to take me down. His answer was that his life was so bad, prison would be a step up. I believed him. He gave me the evidence he threatened to give the police in exchange for the money. Then he started talking about all the money you'd be making in your new position as director." Tears fell from Greta's eyes.

"That's when hatred…seems like it just took over my being. All I could see was this sleazy leech hitting you up for money, for something I had done. I was sure there was no one around and I shot him, Pauline. I wanted to be rid of him so badly."

Greta took a deep breath and sat down. Pauline finished her drink. In her mind she thanked Jack Daniel's for settling her nerves. She already knew her mother was a murderer. Colby would never risk his reputation on some made-up story, plus he had that picture.

Her mother looked pitiful. A helpless, aging woman with a deadly disease who might spend the rest of her days behind bars. Regardless of what she did, Pauline would do anything to keep her mother from going to jail.

It was Pauline's turn to stand. She said matter-of-factly. "Mom, I'm director of Facility Management because I was having an affair with Ronald Height."

Her mother lifted her head. Her expression said *What?*

"You heard right. I was giving the boss some tail. That's the main reason he recommended me for the position. I was with him on the night he had the heart attack."

"Sweetheart, why are you telling me this?"

Pauline came near her mother and looked her in the eye. "I don't want any more secrets."

"Oh baby, please forgive me," Greta said.

Pauline summoned her mother to stand with her outstretched hands. They hugged each other and Greta began crying again. She let her body go limp in her daughter's arms. Pauline held her mother and silently prayed *God help us, please!*

When her mother recovered, Pauline lowered her in the chair. "Mom, I don't know how he could be so damn lucky, but Colby and his girlfriend know the woman at the hotel who saw me and Ron together on more than one occasion."

Pauline told her how the affair started after a bitter argument with Tony Bizaro. When she finished her mother said, "I wish an affair was all I had to worry about." Desperately, she asked Pauline what they were going to do.

"I have to call him back to see what he wants. He wants to meet with both of us. I'm going to take a quick shower and make the call…leave Mr. Daniel's on the table; I'm not through with him."

⋏

John was sitting in Ashley's office waiting for the call he knew would come. The new therapist that Ashley hired was working on a client and would handle the office for the rest of the day.

Ashley said to him, "Suppose she does not call?"

John replied with complete confidence, "There is no need to suppose something that will not happen. She will call."

Ashley sighed. "Well, let me ask you this, Mr. Know-it-All. Do you think you can bury the hatchet and get along with Pauline?"

"Yeah I do. She's the one who started this bad blood. To tell you the truth I get along better with female professionals. I prefer female a doctor or female lawyer…"

The telephone rang. John gave Ashley a *That's her* look.

Ashley answered the phone, then passed it to John.

John talked to Pauline for a minute and told her he knew where her mother lived. She asked how. John reminded her of the license tag off her mother's car, and said they would be there in ten minutes. He hung up and said to Ashley, "It's time to negotiate. My daddy always said when you dealing with a woman, you have to use charm."

"Charm? You know this is all wrong. Two men have died. You saw one of them killed. You removed evidence from the scene of the murder, and you did not tell the police the whole story. Now that you've told me and I'm going along with all this, they could arrest me for aiding and abetting you."

John kissed her soft lips and tasted the inside of her mouth. "Well baby, just aid and abet me a little while longer."

ᐱ

Pauline ushered John and Ashley into the dining room. There was much tension in the air. They all knew they could go to jail. Moreover, Pauline had done everything she could to get rid of Colby Cleaning Service, which made it hard for her to look at Ashley. When they were seated, Pauline managed to say to Ashley, "You must hate me for trying to get rid of John."

Ashley was too nervous to feel hatred. She wished John had gone to the police so that none of this would have to be taking place. She replied, "No, I don't hate you. Hate is one of the worse emotions you can have and the only place it will get you is in trouble."

"Amen!" Greta said.

John asked, "Mrs. Wooten do you remember a man hunched over with a hood on? This man appeared right after you backed out from the dumpster."

"My goodness, that was you?"

John nodded yes. "I watched it all from the walkway bridge and the area near the second floor, over the cardboard dumpster."

John pulled from his brief case a neatly prepared, purple folder. The title was in gold letters: *Revolutionary Cleaning Project.* He saw Pauline's bewilderment.

Ashley saw it also. She said to Greta, "Maybe we should go out and let these two talk."

"You're right," Greta nervously agreed. "Let's go to the kitchen."

Ashley smiled at Greta. She thought, *Damn! It's hard to believe this sweet lady is a cold blooded killer...Poor thing...I think.*

"Pauline," John began. "I'm sorry for what I said...about somebody jumping on you, and well, you know." John was embarrassed to say the rest about jumping on her big ass and riding the evil out of her.

She nodded yes.

"Well," John continued. You took it the wrong way. I meant any man that looks at you can see how fine you are."

Pauline blushed. *It must be the Jack Daniel's* she thought. She wondered was she going have to give John Colby some pussy too, but then threw the thought out of her mind.

Before she could speak John said, "Let's bury the hatchet. Let's stop fighting. That's what's wrong with too many of us black folk. We're always fighting each other. The playing field has never been equal between white folk and black folk. White people will always spend more dollars in white neighborhoods, especially on their schools. The education for their children will always be better than the education for a black kid, because more tax dollars will be allotted for their kids' schools. Thus, you have an endless scenario of black people always at the bottom in academic achievement, but always on the top when it comes to kids dropping out of school, or crime statistics, or prison population statistics.

"So when black people in business like you and me get a chance to level the playing field a little we ought to take it. You getting my drift?"

She thought of her relationship with Chuck Davis. "Yes, I agree with you."

John brought his plea for unity to an end. "So what do you say, Miss Wooten? We will never tell anyone what happened, if you'll be willing to change course and help me with this endeavor laid out in this folder."

Pauline did not need to think long. His argument made a lot of sense. Besides she could not say no or her mother would die in prison. She looked at John with tears in her eyes. "My mother is all I got. Promise me again you two will never tell anyone what my mother did."

John held out his hand and pulled her to stand up. They hugged and John held her tightly. Pauline almost collapsed in his arms. Neither one could believe what was taking place. They were forgiving each other...bonding.

He whispered in her ear. "I give you my word. It will just be a secret between four people."

Pauline could not help but feel John's manhood as tightly as he was holding her. She said to herself, *No wonder Ashley looks so happy and content.*

John released her. The first hurdle was over.

Pauline said, "Can we drink to a new beginning?"

"I would love to," he said." He turned his head to the kitchen. "You guys can come back in. We're finished."

Ashley came into the dining room and could see from Pauline's smile and watery eyes that John had worked his charm on her. Greta's eyes pleaded with Pauline for a sign they had made a deal. Pauline raised her glass. "Thanks to John Colby, we have buried our differences." She looked at him for confirmation to which he nodded yes. "I'm going to look at his project and use all my influence to get the right people behind it. So let's drink to our friendship and trust."

They all raised their glasses. Ashley and Greta drank soda. John said, "Here, here."

Ashley asked, "Pauline, what about John's contracts? It will take a while for the project to work its way through the system. It will help us a lot if he can stay in those buildings."

"Oh shit, that's right. Max Cleland has already been notified that he was to start the Monday after John's last day." She paused to think.

Everyone looked at her. "All right, I'll do something. There's still time to rescind that notice."

"God works in mysterious ways," Ashley said. Everyone now looked at her for further insight. "He does," Ashley continued, "He can turn enemies into friends."

"That's what Mom said," John remembered.

They all agreed. Ashley changed the subject. "Honey, Posey will wonder why you and Pauline have suddenly become friends."

Pauline and her mother quivered. Pauline asked them, "Posey, you mean Detective Posey? He's working on both cases, the discovery of Otis's bones and the…" She looked at her mother who dropped her head in shame, "and you know what happened last night."

"He's my mother's boyfriend." Ashley saw how nervous mother and daughter became. "Don't worry, detective Posey is so in love he's retiring soon. He won't be too interested in solving cases…and we'll stay close to what, if anything he may find out."

John said to Greta, "When you and Clarence talked, it was probably on his cell phone. The cops would have seen your number…"

"Maybe not," Pauline interjected. "Mom has a private number so the number on Clarence's cell would register private…but then again maybe they can find that out, too."

John was concerned. "Mrs. Wooten, what did you do with Clarence's shoulder bag after you pulled into the driveway?"

"I was so nervous I left the two bags of trash in the car, took the money out of the shoulder bag and tossed it on the back seat with the rest of the trash. I was coming back later to dispose of it."

"Damn, Mom…I… I'll get the bag."

Minutes later Pauline returned, looking relieved. "I found it. The cell was in a little zipped up compartment." She flipped it open and scrolled through the numbers. "Mom, did you talk to Clarence a few days ago?"

"Yes. I was letting him know I had the money."

Pauline said to John, "Mom's number is listed as private, but we still need to get rid of it." She put a match to the fire starter log and put the phone on top of it. They watched in silence as the cell melted and popped into a blue flame. Their silence engulfed the room. They were all breaking the law and could serve time in jail. Greta would go to prison for life, or if her attorney might enter an insanity plea, she would die in a mental hospital. John and Pauline would get time for covering up a crime, and aiding and abetting a killer. Ashley was pregnant. The court would have pity on her and conclude she was negatively influenced by unscrupulous blacks. They would let her go free.

Still, they were willing to take the risk. Pauline and Greta had no choice.

John and Ashley were preparing to leave. Pauline hugged Ashley and said, "I'm sorry for everything."

Ashley told her it was great that they were parting as friends. "I just pray God will forgive us and we won't get caught in this unclean money escapade. Take a look at the Revolutionary Cleaning Project. John is really good at what he does."

Pauline agreed. "I know; he's the best company we have. I just didn't want to say it."

They laughed. Pauline promised to get deep into what John had prepared and give him a call once she had an opinion. Greta told them she would never forget what they were doing for her.

John left Wade Avenue, taking the sharp curve to Capital Boulevard where he would take 440 East back to Wendell. Ashley rested her head on his shoulder and said quietly, "David cried unto the Lord, and how did the Lord answer him, John Colby?"

John said joyfully, "And the Lord delivered him out of all of his fears!"

Chapter 20

Pauline realized how advanced John's cleaning was in comparison to the methods used by other janitorial companies, and the housekeepers who work for the state. For the third time, she watched a video of John Colby cleaning a restroom.

The video opened with him looking into the camera and saying: "You are about to witness that a clean-looking restroom might be crawling with viral pathogens."

He explained how the test was done to show the level of contamination in a restroom. The camera faded and John appeared again with an ATP meter in his hand. The device was used to measure Adenosine Triphosphate, the universal energy molecule found in all animal, plant, bacterial, yeast and mold cells. Once a housekeeper cleans a restroom, all sources of ATP should be considerably lower. He explained the test and then set out to swab different areas of the clean-looking restroom. He then dipped the swab in a special chemical and put it into the meter. "My goodness," he said into the camera, "This restroom looks clean but the reading for staphylococcus bacteria is everywhere, especially in and around the commodes and under the toilet seats."

John came to the big yellow machine. Before flicking the switch on, he said, "Once this restroom is hygienically cleaned our way, we will retest for the level of contamination and there you will see the benefit of this scientific method of removing germs and dirt."

Pauline chuckled to herself. *That's a smooth, confident brother.*

After John sprayed all the surfaces with a bacteria-removing agent he adjusted the nozzle and began power-rinsing everything.

Pauline watched in disbelief as hair, bits of paper and other gook suddenly washed to the floor. A lot of the germy debris came from under the commodes and sinks. After rinsing all the surfaces, John hooked another long, black hose to the machine and it became a power blower. He blew dry all the surfaces to a bright clean shine; and then sucked up everything on the floor with the vacuum attachment. He retested the restroom for its level of contamination, and the readings were significantly lower.

He did the same thing in the men's restroom; this time pointing out how green the water was when it hit the floor after he washed and rinsed the areas around the urinals. Pauline watched green water filled with hair and gook pop out from around the pipes on the urinals.

She was particularly interested in the savings that could be realized, if the state went to the trash collection system in RCP. John's figures revealed that the savings could be in the millions, but he was only talking about the money the Department of Administration would save in Raleigh. She asked herself what if they instituted RCP all across major cities in North Carolina; she surmised it could save billions in the long run. It would indeed be a revolution and she would get the credit for introducing the project to the governor and staff.

She leaned back from the computer, and pursed her ambitious lips. Pauline Wooten, responsible for saving the state of North Carolina millions of dollars. She is expected to be the next secretary of state. The thought made her giggle.

She would get John to do a video of an ATP test and power-wash cleaning on the first floor of the Administration Building. It was the one floor in the building that was cleaned by state housekeepers. The contractor who cleaned the building never went on the first floor where Deputy Standoff and other high-ranking government officials worked. She would show him that he was sitting his proud ass on a pile of germs. If they could convince him, he would make the right moves and work his contacts at the Legislative Building. She loved the Revolutionary Cleaning Project and called John to get the ball rolling immediately, and asked him to stop by her office Monday morning.

After John and Ashley had left Pauline and Greta around 3:30 Friday afternoon, Pauline made sure she had a letter in Max Cleland's box rescinding the award of the New Education and Dobbs Building contracts. Max read the letter on Monday morning. Not only was the award rescinded, Colby Cleaning Service was the low bid on the Albemarle and would be awarded that contract in accordance with state laws to take the lowest price from the best company.

Max was livid. He was depending on those awards. He went to his bank the day he got the award letter, showed it to the bank that he had been doing business with for years and they gave him a $50,000 line of credit. Max had already spent $25,000 making repairs on his beach house and boat.

He barreled into Pauline's office, his face a red scowl. "What the hell is this? You can't award somebody a contract and then rescind it."

Pauline responded indifferently. "Says who? The letter clearly states an error was made in awarding those two contracts. We apologize for any inconvenience."

Max Cleland burned with anger. "I don't know what has happened here, but I'm going to sue the state and heads will roll. And you will be the first one to go. I don't know how you got this job…"

"Get the fuck out of my office!"

Max was shocked. "What did you say?"

Pauline raised her voice. "I said get the fuck out of my office right now, or I'm calling Capitol Police."

Max stormed out of the building, almost knocking over Chuck Davis.

Chuck tapped on Pauline's door and peeped in. "You all right?"

"Come on in and shut the door, Chuck. I had to throw that arrogant ass cracker out of here with his innuendoes. Mad as hell I rescinded the award of John's buildings. He's the only one mad. I made a lot of people happy by rescinding that award. Purchasing was happy, they did not have to issue a new purchase order number; and the people in his buildings were happy. They loved John's cleaning."

"I hated to see John go, too. Got to tell you though, boss, I was shocked when I read your letter to Max. What changed your mind about John?"

Pauline was pleased to hear Chuck call her *boss*. Maybe he had accepted her. She knew he would ask her this question, and told him how John apologized and said it was time black people worked together and stopped stabbing each other in the back.

After telling Chuck what happened she told him she would need his support and that she saw a time in the future when he could become assistant director of Facility Management.

"John shared with me this new way to clean state buildings. The plan is titled the Revolutionary Cleaning Project, or RCP for short. Chuck, you got to examine this project. I'm going to present it to Deputy Secretary Standoff and see if he will take it to the politicians in the Legislative Building. I made a copy of everything for you to check out."

Chuck took the folder and got up to leave. "John knows his stuff, I'll go check it out now and get back to you."

"Okay, thanks, Chuck."

⋏

John and Ashley spent Sunday morning at Lenny and Cynthia's church, thanking God for all that had happened. They also sought forgiveness for the cover-up. After church they ate dinner together and John told them the good news that it was not official, but he was sure they would not be losing their contracts. John promoted Cynthia to supervisor of the Dobbs and asked Lenny to manage the Dobbs and New Education Buildings. They were all excited at not having to find new income elsewhere.

When Monday morning arrived John parked at the Dobbs and went across the street to Facility Management. He went to check his box. There was a letter saying that Colby Cleaning Service was to stay in the buildings and use the same purchase order number for all invoices. When he read he would also be awarded the Albemarle contract, he almost exploded with joy. He had forgotten about it and Pauline did not mention it.

The letter was welcomed news. He wondered how Max Cleland felt now.

Chuck's door was open. John stood in the doorway, but Chuck did not look up. John said, "Hey Chuck, must be a naked woman on that screen."

Chuck looked up and smiled. "Oh John, welcome back. I'm deep into RCP. This is an eye-opening package you gave Pauline, make us look like we don't know shit."

They both laughed. John said with enthusiasm, "Chuck, this project will make you and Pauline look super. You will have saved the state millions, and all your facilities will be hygienically cleaned. You will be promoted to director of Facility Management, and Pauline will take Standoff's job and go on to become Secretary of State."

"That's what I'm talking about. Really though, I'm behind RCP. This is good stuff."

"Thanks, Chuck, I'm on my way to see Pauline now."

Chuck gave John a suspicious look. "Level with me, John. How did you two become so friendly practically overnight? I mean, I was at the meeting when the three of us were deciding the fate of Colby Cleaning Service. She was salivating to make an example of you. She succeeds in getting rid of you; then *bam*, she makes a complete u-turn and not only gets your accounts back, but starts touting your project."

Chuck was enjoying himself. John stood in the doorway smiling.

Chuck continued, "At first I thought boss lady was giving Ron some tail, but now maybe it's you, or maybe it was Ron, and now you… Hell, when do I get my turn?"

John laughed at Chuck's analogy. "No, no, you are fantasizing too much. I'm a one-woman man. I apologized for anything I had said or done to upset her. She accepted my apology and realized the initial action taken against me was too severe. After we buried the hatchet, I asked her to take a look at RCP."

Chuck considered what John said. "Well, you guys got similar stories that I don't believe, but I'll leave it alone. Tell Pauline I'm in on RCP."

"Thanks, Chuck. Later."

John had his accounts returned and he was on his way to chat with Pauline, instead of getting into a name-calling match.

When he walked into Pauline's office she was talking to Tony Bizaro. She said into the phone. "Got to go, babe. Love ya too." She grinned at John.

John said, with a smile on his face, "You're prettier than ever, your face lights up when you grin."

Pauline blushed. "Hush John. You mean to tell me I could have had you flattering me all these years?"

He laughed. "It's never too late. Sounds like you and Tony are in love."

"We are. I hope the four of us can really get to know each other. We're going to need Tony too, since he works in purchasing."

"Chuck said he was in, so we need to prepare to meet Standoff."

Pauline told him that was why she wanted him to stop by. She gave him all the details of what she wanted done on the restrooms of the first floor in the Administration Building. Since contractors were not allowed on the first floor, Pauline said she would go with him, so there would be no problems.

She concluded, "We have to show our dear Deputy Standoff that every time he uses the toilet he's sitting his proud ass on a pile of viral pathogens."

They laughed and John realized Pauline had a great sense of humor.

"It's Monday, when do you want to do this?" John asked.

"ASAP. How 'bout tomorrow night? I'll call him now and make an appointment for me, you and Chuck to go present RCP to him on Thursday at 10:00 am. I'll have the courier take him an RCP package now."

"Sounds good. I'll meet you at the Administration Building tomorrow night around seven o'clock."

They looked each other in the eye, smiled and shook their heads. They had the same thought. *Not able to believe they were actually working together and loving it.*

John said, "Pauline, I can't thank you enough for the award of the Albemarle. I was so happy that you were going to pull some strings for me to get my two buildings back. I completely forgot I was the low bid on the Albemarle."

Pauline said in a low voice, "That's the least I could do after you saved my mother."

John's employees were glad they hadn't abandoned ship and taken jobs elsewhere. There were contractors who had a reputation for paying late, and in some cases their payroll checks bounced. In twenty years John had missed payroll only once, and then it was not his fault. A while back the state did not pay him for December's work until the end of January; so he missed the last payroll before the check came. He remembered his black employees bad-mouthed him to people in the building and accused him of being like the other crooked companies, who incidentally were black. His Hispanic employees said they understood and waited for their checks.

ⵣ

Thursday morning arrived. John Colby, Pauline Wooten and Chuck Davis sat across the cherry-red, mahogany table from Deputy Secretary Herbert Standoff. The room was used for conferences, video presentations, and a host of other things. He had examined the material in Revolutionary Cleaning Project, and was immediately impressed with the savings projected. Everyone he showed it to was impressed with the savings. They were alarmed at how unsanitary the buildings were. Something had to be done.

Standoff let the three know that he was excited about the project. He said, "I have really been engrossed in RCP since you sent it to me. Pauline, you have another short clip you want to show me?"

"Yes sir." She smiled at John and Chuck and gave him the DVD.

He watched it twice, and then with a grin on his face, "So I'm sitting my ass on a pile of germs."

John looked at Pauline and they could not hold it. They laughed longer than the Secretary thought was necessary. He said to them, "That got you going, huh?"

Pauline regained composure. "Excuse us sir, but that is the conclusion we hoped you would come to; that the toilet seat might look clean, when actually it's crawling with germs."

Standoff became serious and said, "The problem is the law, it will have to be changed to give the us freedom to choose what is the best system and what is cost effective."

Chuck broke in. "That's it, sir. Cost effective, focus on savings and healthier cleaner facilities for our employees, which in turn will boost production."

"I see your point," Standoff said. "What about the backlash and possible law suits from disgruntled contractors?"

Pauline responded. "What can they do if the law is changed? There will be losers if RCP is implemented. But the advantages far outweigh the negatives."

Standoff was quiet. No one said anything while he flipped through a few pages. He looked up and said, "This is a damn good project. How soon can you begin?"

The three of them were stupefied. Pauline managed to speak first. "Sir, we were all under the impression it would take a few months to get the laws changed."

Standoff looked disappointed. "Are you saying you would need a few months? What if we authorized a $1 million budget for you to begin? We are already furnishing supplies and chemicals to contractors; John, you and Chuck can work together on equipment chemicals and supplies. Write in the contract with Colby Cleaning Service that all equipment purchased by us under this project will become state property if the contract or arrangement is canceled."

They were dumbfounded and still at a loss for words. They were not prepared for Standoff to say they could start right away. Nevertheless, John was ready for the challenge. This was the opportunity of a lifetime. His project would change the way the State of North Carolina cleaned its facilities. He had a thought. Since Standoff was in a mood to get going, he said, "Sir, RCP is projected to save the State $5 million the first year. Surely the state could afford to start this project with $2.5 million."

Standoff thought. "If I say yes, can you start in thirty days?"

John said yes, loud and clear.

Standoff said, "Folks, our government is more broke than the public would ever know or need to know. The deficit will go over $4 billion for this fiscal year. The governor is pressing us hard to find ways to cut the budget of every department."

Standoff looked at John. "When I saw the savings in RCP I said if this new cleaning system can be carried out and the projected savings realized we need to do what's necessary to implement it."

Chuck Davis scratched his balding head. "How will we start RCP if it will take time to get the general statues governing bids changed?"

Pauline answered Chuck. "We'll have to exercise the termination clause in the contract. We have the right to terminate any contract with a thirty-day notice; right, sir?"

"That's it Pauline, use the termination clause." Standoff made motions to indicate the meeting was coming to a close. He turned off the DVD player and began gathering papers. "Look, you guys came to me with a great idea, and I'm all in. Getting the laws changed won't be hard if we can get these savings.

"What if we began RCP in other state-owned facilities in Charlotte, Winston-Salem, Greensboro and all across our great state? Hell, the savings could be in the billions." He paused and gave them a devious look. "I'd say if that happened we'd have to put a few of them dollars in our pockets, now wouldn't we?" He stood up with a laugh.

The three of them stood and heartily agreed. They could not believe what just took place.

Standoff told them he would have the money in place within thirty days. "Once RCP is in force, John's company will submit an invoice for service, just as you do now to Facility Management, who will approve and send it to purchasing for payment."

They shook hands. Chuck said, "One final question, sir. "What reason do we give to the contractors for terminating their contracts?"

"That's an easy one, Chuck," Standoff said. "Dire financial straits."

The Contractor, Director of Facility Management and the Building Manager walked out the back exit door of the Administration Building into the parking lot. They were excited as could be about introducing a revolution in the way the Department of Administration would begin to clean its facilities.

Pauline and Chuck would walk the short distance to Facility Management, while John would drive to Wendell and celebrate with Ashley. Before parting they promised to put their heads together first thing in the morning to put RCP into action.

Pauline threw her arms around John Colby's neck and hugged him with all her strength. "Thank you, John. Never have I been so wrong about a person." She kissed him on his cheek and smiled. "I'll see you tomorrow."

Chuck made a wry face. "Y'all two sho' did forgive each other huh? Maybe after RCP y'all can co-author a book on how to settle differences in the work place."

John and Pauline laughed. Pauline said, "Let's go Chuck, we got work to do."

⋏

Passing by Wake Medical Hospital, John took a deep breath to calm his mind. He would be out of debt by the end of the year. His company would be responsible for cleaning all of Facility Management's properties.

Ashley coined the dark side of their endeavor "unclean money escapade." He understood why. Two people had been murdered and they withheld evidence from the police. He was sorry that something so cruel had happened to the victims. Yet he did not feel guilty for how it resulted in his project being accepted. He had worked harder, longer, and did a much better job than all the other contractors doing business with the state of North Carolina, and could never get pas banks denying his loan request year after year. And now he would not need their high interest money. He preferred to call the outcome of their endeavor "unclean payback." Once his Revolutionary Cleaning Project was in force his salary for the first year would be close to a million dollars.

He said, *Thank you, Jesus* as loud as he could. He would call his Mom and tell her that what she predicted in her prayer came true. She told him that God could bless him when all odds were against him, and that He can make your enemies become your friends.

Wow this is sooo sweet! For the rest of the ride to Wendell, John Colby could not stop smiling.

EPILOGUE

ontractors were up in arms that their contracts were canceled, but there was nothing they could do.

Max Cleland had a debilitating stroke the day after he learned John Colby would be making $1.5 million and that he was the one who brought the Revolutionary Cleaning Project to Pauline Wooten.

John contacted his buddy and fellow contractor, Earl Horn, to help him as planned. They contacted some of the employees who had worked for the other contractors and hired them. During the month of December these potential employees were trained how cleaning would be done under RCP.

Revolutionary Cleaning Project was launched on January 3rd of the new year. After a month of operation Facility Management was flooded with calls. Employees were so appreciative that the State had finally contracted someone who knew how to clean. They were extremely happy with the cleanliness of the restrooms.

Lenny retired from his job at the university, and he and Cynthia became full time employees helping John manage the business. They got married in February.

Tony Bizaro proposed to Pauline and they planned for a marriage in the summer.

Greta Wooten had the double mastectomy, and recovered well. She started going to Ashley's Body Needs Therapy for regular massage.

Deputy Secretary Herbert Standoff took the credit for changing the way the State of North Carolina cleaned its facilities. More than a few people lost their jobs, but it was mainly the contractors and their employees, so he did not care.

Chuck Davis was happy he and Pauline decided to work together and cover each other's backs. They looked forward to the day Chuck would take her place as Director of Facility Management, and she would run for Secretary of State.

Sam Boswell kept his nose up Pauline's ass.

Frederick Parsons's furniture business was hit by the bad economy and he lost a string of furniture stores. He remarried but never had any more children. When Sonja came and hugged him that day in court, he decided he would leave his estate to her.

Harold Posey retired from the police force to spend time with Clara Whitfield, Ashley's mother.

John went to a doctor and learned his memory and attention problems were due to his many years of multi-tasking his way through stressful years of running a business. The doctor told him that straining the attention system drains memory. After the state accepted his Revolutionary Cleaning Project, he never had that problem again. He and Ashley were married in November, and in late April, Ashley gave birth to an eight-pound baby boy, making John Colby the happiest man on the planet. Sonja was the happiest eleven-year-old girl on the same planet. She had a brother to play with and take care of.

The murders of Otis Wooten and Clarence Farmer were never solved.

ACKNOWLEDGMENTS

To Palmer Writers School who got me going in the right direction;
To the North Carolina Writers Network for putting me in touch with my editor, Amy Rogers, who showed me how much I didn't know, and who helped bringing this project to fruition;

And most importantly to Jesus, the Son of God, who instilled in me the art of fantasy.

About the author

Jerry Hayes based his novel, *UNCLEAN PAYBACK*, on his professional expertise and on events he observed in his career as a successful janitorial contractor.

Although the book is fictional, Hayes was inspired by the racism he experienced. It fueled his anger against a system that was slow to implement reforms that would allow participation by minority-owned businesses.

He spent one year as human interest writer/reporter for a bi-weekly newspaper, and continues to study writing on his own.

He is a Vietnam War veteran and lives with his family near Raleigh, North Carolina.